C2000004649504

BIRMINGHAM LIBRARY SERVICES
DISCARD

KT-445-633

STRANGERS IN PARADISE

STRANGERS
IN PARADISE

Heather Graham

This first hardcover edition published 2012
in Great Britain and in the USA by
SEVERN HOUSE PUBLISHERS LTD of
9–15 High Street, Sutton, Surrey, England, SM1 1DF,
by arrangement with Harlequin Books.
First published 1988 in the USA in mass market format only.

Copyright © 1988 by Heather Graham Pozzessere.

All rights reserved.
The moral right of the author has been asserted.

British Library Cataloguing in Publication Data

Graham, Heather.
  Strangers in paradise.
  1. Love stories.
  I. Title
  813.6-dc23

  ISBN-13: 978-0-7278-8125-0 (cased)

Except where actual historical events and characters are being
described for the storyline of this novel, all situations in this
publication are fictitious and any resemblance to living persons
is purely coincidental.

All Severn House titles are printed on acid-free paper.

Severn House Publishers support The Forest Stewardship Council [FSC],
the leading international forest certification organisation. All our titles that
are printed on Greenpeace-approved FSC-certified paper carry the FSC logo.

Typeset by Palimpsest Book Production Ltd.,
Falkirk, Stirlingshire, Scotland.
Printed and bound in Great Britain by
MPG Books Ltd., Bodmin, Cornwall.

STRANGERS IN PARADISE

Prologue

June 2, 1863
Fernandina Beach, Florida

"Miz Eugenia! Miz Eugenia! Look!"

Eugenia straightened, easing the pain in her back, and stared out through the long trail of pines to the distant beach, where Mary's call directed her. Her sewing fell unheeded to her feet; she rose, her heart pounding, her soul soaring, dizzy with incredulity and relief.

A man was alighting from a small skiff. The waves on the beach pounded against his high black cavalry boots as he splashed through the water. From a distance, he was beautiful and perfect.

"Pierre!" Upon the porch of the old house, Eugenia whispered his name, afraid to voice it too loudly lest he disappear. She wanted so badly for him to be real and not a fantasy created by the summer's heat, by the shimmering waves of sun pounding against the scrub and sand.

"Pierre!"

He was real. Tall and regal in his handsome uniform of butternut and gray, with his medals reflecting the sun. He was far away, but Eugenia was certain that he saw her, certain that his blue hawk's eyes had met her own and that the love they shared sang and soared likewise in his soul.

He started to run down the sand path, which was carpeted in pine needles and shaded by branches. Sun and shadow, shadow and sun—she could no longer see his face clearly, but she gave a glad cry and leaped down the steps, clutching her heavy spill of skirts in her hand so that she could run, too—run to meet her beautiful man in his butternut and gray and hurl herself into his arms.

Sunlight continued to glitter through the trees, golden as it fell upon her love. She felt the carpet of sand and pine under her feet, and the great rush of her breath. She could see the fine planes and lines of his features, the intelligence and tenderness in his eyes. She could see the strain in his face as he, too, ran, and she could see the love he bore for her, the need to touch.

"Pierre..."

"Eugenia!" He nearly wept her name. She flew the last few steps, those steps that brought her into his arms. He lifted her high and swirled her beneath the sun. He stared into her face, trembling, cherishing the mere fact that he could look upon her, and she was beautiful.

Eugenia saw that in truth he was not perfect. His butternut and gray were tattered and worn, there were slashes in his handsome boots, and his medals were rusted and dark.

"Oh, Pierre!" Eugenia cried, not so much from his uniform as from the strain that lined his handsome face. "Tell me! What has happened? Pierre, why are you here? Is something wrong?"

"Are you not glad to see your husband?" he charged her.

"Ever so glad! But—"

"No, Eugenia! No buts, no words. Just hold me. And I'll hold you, tenderly, this night. Tenderly, with all my love."

He carried her back along that path of softest pine and gentle sand. His eyes held hers, drinking in the sight of her so desperately. And she, in turn, could not take her gaze from him, her cavalier. Pierre, handsome, magnificent, tender Pierre, with his fine eyes and clear-cut features and beautiful golden hair. Pierre, scarred and hard and wounded and sometimes bitter, but ever gentle to her, his bride. They reached the house. Mary mumbled something in welcome, and Pierre gave her a dazzling smile. He paused to give her a hug, to ask after his infant son, who was asleep in Mary's old, gnarled arms. Tears came to Mary's eyes, but she winked back as Pierre winked at her and asked if they might have dinner a wee bit late that night.

Eugenia was still in his arms as he kicked open the screen door with his foot. He knew the house by heart, for it was his house; he had built it. He did not need to look for the stairs; he walked to them easily, his eyes, with all their adoration, still boring into those of his wife. He climbed the stairs and took her to their room, and although they were the only ones on the barren peninsula, he locked the door.

And then he made love to her.

Desperately, Eugenia thought. So hungry, so hard, so fevered. She could not hold him tightly enough, she could not give enough, she could not sate him. He was a soldier, she reminded herself. A soldier, long gone from home, barely back from battle. But he touched her again and again, and he kissed her with a fascinated hunger, as if he had never known the taste of her lips before. He entwined his limbs with hers and held her, as if he could not bear to part.

"My love, my love," she whispered to him. She adored him in turn; sensed his needs, and she gave in to them, all. Stars lit the heavens again and again for her, and when he whispered apologies, thinking himself too rough, she hushed him and whispered in turn that he was the only lover she could ever want.

Dinner was very late. Pierre dandled his son on his knee while Mary served, and Mary and Eugenia did their best to speak lightly, to laugh, to entertain their soldier home from the war. Dinner was wonderful—broiled grouper in Mary's old Louisiana creole sauce, but Pierre had noted that fish was the diet because the domestic fowl were gone, and when Mary took their little boy up to bed, Eugenia was forced to admit that, yes, the Yankees had come again, and they had taken the chickens and the pigs and even old Gretchen, the mule. Pierre swore in fury, and then he stared at Eugenia with panic and accusation. She went to him, swearing that the Yanks had been gentlemen plunderers—none had shown her anything but respect.

She hesitated. "They'll not come here again. Even as they waltz in and out of Jacksonville. They won't come because—"

"Because of your father," Pierre supplied bitterly, referring to Eugenia's father, General George Drew of Baltimore. His home was being spared by the Yanks because his wife was one.

"Dammit," Pierre said simply. He sank back into his chair. With a cry of distress, Eugenia came to him, knelt at his feet and gripped his hands.

"I love you, Pierre. I love you so much!"

"You should go back to him."

"I will never leave you."

He lifted her onto his lap and cradled her there, holding her tight against the pulse of his heart. "I have to leave," he said softly. "The Old Man—General Lee—is determined to make a thrust northward. I have to be back in Richmond in forty-eight hours."

"Pierre, no! You've just—"

"I have to go back."

"You sound so...strange, Pierre." She tightened her arms around him.

"I'm frightened, my Genie, and I can't even describe why," he told her. "Not frightened of battle anymore, for

I've been there too many times. I'm frightened . . . for the future."

"We shall win!"

He smiled, for his Northern-born belle had one loyalty: to his cause, whatever it should be.

An ocean breeze swept by him, drawing goose pimples to his flesh, and he knew. They would not win.

He buried his face against his wife's slender throat, inhaling her scent, feeling already the pain of parting. He held her fiercely. "You need not fear, Eugenia. I will provide for you—always. I've been careful. The money is in the house." He whispered to her, though they were alone.

"Yes, yes, I will be fine—but I will not need anything. When this is over, we will be together, love."

"Yes, together, my love."

Eugenia loved him too well to tell him that she knew the South was dead. She did not tell him that the money he had hidden in the house, his Confederate currency, was as useless as the paper it had been printed on. He was her man, her provider. She would not tell him that he had provided her with ashes.

And he did not tell her that he felt a cold breeze, a cold, icy wind that whistled plaintively, like a ghost moaning and crying. Warning, foreboding. Whispering that death was ever near.

He took her in his arms and carried her up the stairs once again. Their eyes met.

They smiled, so tenderly, so lovingly.

"We're having another baby, Pierre."

"What?"

His arms tightened. She smiled sweetly, happy, pleased, smug.

"A baby, Pierre."

"My love!"

He kissed her reverently.

All through the night, he loved her reverently.

Pierre woke before Eugenia. Restless, he wrapped a sheet around himself and checked his hiding place, pulling the brick from the wall in silence.

A beautiful glitter greeted him. He inhaled and exhaled. He had to go back to the war. He wanted to take his pregnant wife and his young son and disappear forever. But he was a soldier; he could not forsake his duty. He could assure himself, though, that whatever came, Eugenia would not want for anything.

He replaced the brick.

No, Eugenia would not want for anything.

1

The fear she felt was terrible. It tore into her heart and her mind, and even into her soul. It paralyzed and mesmerized. With swift and stunning ease, it stole Alexi's breath, and as in a nightmare, she could not scream, for the sound would not come. She knew only that something touched her. Something had her.

And that it was flesh.

Flesh touched her, warm and vibrant. Flesh...that seemed to cover steel. Fingers that were long and compelled by some superhuman strength.

Flesh...

For what seemed like aeons, Alexi could do nothing but let the fact that she had been accosted sweep into her consciousness. It was so dark—she had never known a darkness so total as this night. No stars, no moon, no streetlights—she might have fallen off into a deep pit of eternal space, rather than onto the dusty floorboards of the decaying, historic house. She might be encountering anyone or anything, and all she recognized was...

Flesh. Searing and warm and frightfully powerful against her own. It had come so quickly. She had crawled through the window and the arms had swept around her, and she had been down and breathless and now, as fear curled into her like an evil, living thing, she could begin to feel the body and the muscle.

And she still couldn't scream. She couldn't bear force. She had known it before, and she had come here to escape the threat of it.

She tried for sound, desperately. A gasped whimper escaped from her—she knew that she was being subdued by a man. Even in the darkness, she knew instinctively that he was lean but wiry, that he was lithe and powerful. Her position was becoming ever more precarious. Her wrist was suddenly jerked and she was rolled, and there was more warmth, warmth and power all around her as she was suddenly laid flat, her back to the floor.

A thigh straddled roughly over her; she was suffocating.

Good God, fight!

She tried to emerge from the terror that encompassed her. Again she could feel heat and strength and tremendous, taut vitality. In the darkness she felt it—the fingers groping to find her other hand, to secure it so she would be powerless in the horrible darkness.

At last the paralysis broke. Sound burst from her, and she screamed. She could fight; she had learned to fight. Panic surged through her, and she twisted and writhed, ferocious and desperate in her attempt to escape.

She tried to kick, to wrench, to roll, to flail at the body attacking her. Her voice rose hysterically, totally incoherent. And she punched with all her strength, trying to slap, scratch, gouge—cause some injury. She caught him hard in the chin.

He swore hoarsely. Belatedly she wondered if she shouldn't have remained still. Who was he? What was he doing in the house? She hadn't heard a thing, hadn't seen a thing, and he had suddenly come down on top of her. He was a thief, a robber...or a rapist or a murderer. And screaming probably wouldn't help her; here she was, out in this godforsaken peninsula of blackness, yelling when there was no help to be had, struggling when she was bound to lose.

She screamed again anyway. And fought. He was breathing harder; she knew it despite her own ragged gulps for air. She could feel his breath against her cheek, warm and scented with mint. She could feel more of his body, hard against hers, as he silently and competently worked to subdue her.

Flesh . . .

She felt more flesh against her wrists, and then he had her again in a vise. She felt her hands dragged swiftly and relentlessly high over her head, and she knew that she was at the mercy of the dark entity in the night.

No . . .

Tears stung her eyes. She had run too far for it to come to this! With an incredible burst of energy, she wrenched one hand free and sent it flying out full force. She struck him, and she heard him grunt. And she heard his startled "Dammit!"

His arm snaked out in the blackness to catch and secure her wrist once again.

And then all she knew was the sound of breathing.

His, mildly labored, so close it touched her cheeks and her chin. Hers, maddened, ragged, racing gulps. Fear was a living thing. Parasitic, it raged inside of her, tore at her heart and her soul, and she couldn't do anything but lie there, imprisoned, thinking.

This was it. Death was near. She'd been desperate to run away, and now, for all her determination, she was going to die. She didn't know how yet. He might strangle her. Wind one hand around her throat and squeeze . . .

"Stop it! I don't want to hurt you! All right, now, don't move. Don't even think about moving. Do you understand?"

It was a husky voice. Harsh and coolly grating.

I don't want to hurt you. The words echoed in her mind, and she tried to comprehend them; she longed to trust him.

The darkness was so strange. She couldn't see, but she felt so acutely. She sensed, she felt, as he released her, as he balanced on his feet above her.

She was still shivering, still yearning to give way again to panic and strike out at him and run. She was dazed and she needed to think, desperately needed to be clever, and she could not come up with one rational thought. She could smell him so keenly in the black void of this world of fear, and that made her panic further, for his scent was pleasant, subtle, clean, like the salt breeze that came in from the ocean. She was so well-known for her reserve, for her cool thinking under pressure, and here she was, in stark, painful panic, when she most desperately needed a calculating mind. But how could she have imagined this situation? So close to that which she had run from, taking her so swiftly by surprise, stripping away all veneers and making her pathetically vulnerable.

Fight! she warned herself. Don't give up....

"Please..." She could barely form the whisper.

But then, quite suddenly, there was light. Brilliant and blinding and flooding over her features. She blinked against it, trying to see. She raised her arm to shield her eyes from the brutal radiance.

"Who are you?" the voice demanded.

Dear God, she wasn't *just* being attacked; she was being attacked by a thief or a murderer who asked questions. One of them was mad. She had every right to be! She was going to be living here. He had been prowling around in the darkness. He must have waited while she had fumbled with the door; he had stalked her in silence, watching while she came to the window and broke it to tumble inside—and into his ruthless hold.

She couldn't speak; she started to tremble.

"Who are you?" he raged again.

Harsh, stark, male, deliberate, demanding. She lost all sense of reason. Her arms were free. He had even moved back a little; his weight rested on his haunches rather than full against her hips.

"Arrgh!" Another sound escaped her, shrill with effort. He swore, but did not lose his balance. Alexi managed to do more than twist her skirt higher upon her hips and bring him harder against her as he struggled to maintain his new hold on both her wrists with one hand and keep the flashlight harsh against her face with the other.

She wanted to think; she kept shaking, and her words tore from her in gasping spurts. "Don't kill me. Please don't kill me."

"Kill you?"

"I'm worth money. Alive, I mean. Not dead. I'm really not worth a single red cent dead. My insurance isn't paid up. But I swear, if you'll just leave me—alive—I can make it worth your while. I—"

"Dammit, I'm not going to kill you. I'm trying very hard not to hurt you!"

She didn't dare feel relief. Still, sweeping sensations that left her weak coursed through her, and to her amazement, she heard her own voice again. "Who are you?"

"I asked first. And..." She could have sworn there was a touch of amusement in his voice. "And *you're* the one asking the favors."

She swallowed, stretching out her fingers. If he'd only move that horrible flashlight! Then she could think, could muster up a semblance of dignity and courage.

"Who the hell are you? I want an answer now," he demanded.

His fingers were so tight in their grip around her wrists. She clenched her teeth in sudden pain, aware of the fearsome power that held her.

"Alexi Jordan."

"You're not."

He had stated it so flatly that for a moment she herself wondered who else she might be.

"I am!"

He moved. The heat, the tight, vibrantly muscled hold he had on her body was gone; he was on his feet and was dragging her along with him.

"Ms. Jordan isn't due until tomorrow. Who are you? Speak up, now, or I'll call the police."

"The police?"

"Of course. You're trespassing."

"*You're* trespassing!"

"Let's call the police and find out."

"Yes! Let's do that!"

He was walking next, pulling her along. Alexi was blinded all over again when the light left her face to flash over the floor. She tried to wrench her hand away as the light played eerily over the spiderweb-dusted living room, with its shrouded sofa and chairs.

He wrenched her hand and she choked, then spewed forth a long series of oaths. She was close to sobs, ready to laugh and to cry. She should have been handling it all so much better.

"You'll go to jail for this!" she threatened.

"Really? Weren't you just asking me nicely not to kill you?"

She fell silent, jerked back against him, this unknown man, this stranger in the darkness. Her heart was pounding at a rapid, fluttering speed; she could feel its fevered pulse against the slower throb of his own, so close had he brought her to himself.

And she still didn't know his face—whether he was young or old, whether his eyes were blue or gray. She would never forget his voice or mistake it for another, she knew. The low, husky quality to the sure baritone. Cool and quiet and commanding...

And he had just said "kill." She was at his mercy and she had forgotten and lashed out in fury and now...

"What do you want?" she whispered, licking her lips.

She gasped as he lifted her; she landed upon the dusty sofa before she could protest again. He fell into the chair opposite her; she heard the movement, heard the old chair creak. The small splay of illumination from the flashlight fell upon her purse, which was in the hands that had so easily subdued her. She thought about bolting—but she could never make an escape. She could see the outline of his body. He was casually sprawled in the chair as he delved into her bag. She was still certain that he could move like the wind if she made any attempt to rise.

Alexi cleared her throat. It was only her purse, not her body. Despite that, despite her fear, she felt violated. "You don't—you can't..."

Her voice faded away, she could feel his eyes on her. She couldn't see him, but she could feel his eyes—compelling, scornful...amused?

"Five lipsticks? Brush, comb, pencil, pad, more lipstick, compact, keys, more lipstick, tissue, more lipstick—aha! At last, a wallet. And you are *really*...Alexi Jordan."

The light zoomed back to her face. Alexi bit her lip, reddening, and she didn't know why. If he was going to kill her, she didn't need to blush for her own murderer. But he had said something about calling the police. He had said that he didn't want to hurt her.

"Please..." she said.

He was silent. The light continued to play mercilessly over her features.

She was something out of a fairy tale, Rex decided, staring at her in the flood of light. Surely she was legendary. He barely noted that her eyes were still filled with terror; they

were so incredibly green and wide. Tendrils of hair were escaping from a once-neat knot—hair caught by the light, hair
that burned within that light like true spun gold. It wasn't
pale, and it wasn't tawny; it was gold. It framed a face with
the most perfect classical features he had ever seen. High,
elegant cheekbones; small, straight nose; fine, determined
chin; arching, honeyed brows. Even in total dishevelment,
she was stunning. Her beauty was breathtaking. Stealing the
heart, the senses, the mind...

He realized he was still standing there, thoughtlessly lev-
eling the light into her eyes. At last he saw how badly she
was shaking.

She was Alexi Jordan. Gene's granddaughter. Hell, he'd
supposedly been guarding the place. He'd attacked her. He
hadn't wanted her here—he hadn't wanted anyone here. But
he sure as hell hadn't meant to battle it out with her. He
opened his mouth to say something. Then he knew that it
wouldn't be enough. He had to go to her, touch her. She was
still so afraid.

Alexi gasped as fear again curled through her. The man
was coming toward her. She cringed; he leaned over her,
touched her cheek, then took her hand.

"My God, you're shaking like a leaf!"

"You, you—"

"I'm not going to hurt you!"

"You attacked me!"

"I had to know who you were. I thought you were a thief,
coming in that window the way that you did. You're all right
now."

No, she wasn't. She was sitting in complete darkness with
a man who had attacked her, and she couldn't stop trembling. He sat beside her, and she wasn't sure what he was
saying, only that his words were soft and reassuring. Then,
to her horror, she was half sobbing and half laughing and
he was sitting beside her, and in that awful darkness she was

in his arms as he stroked her hair—and she still didn't have any idea who he was or even what he looked like.

"Shush, it's all right now. It's all right." The same hands that had held her with such cold, brutal strength were capable of an uncanny tenderness. He held her as if she were a frightened child, easing his fingertips under her chin to lift her face. "It's all right. My God, I'm sorry. I didn't know."

She knew his voice, knew his scent. She knew the harshness and the tenderness of his arms, but she didn't know his name or the color of his eyes. She stiffened, her tremors beginning to fade at last with the reassurance of his words and the new security of his form.

"I'm, uh, sorry." She pushed away from him, feeling a furious rush of embarrassment. She was apologizing, and he was in *her* house. Gene's house. A total stranger. "Who are you?"

He stood. She instantly felt the distance between them. It was over—whatever it had been. The violence, and the tenderness.

"Rex Morrow."

Rex Morrow. Her mind moved quickly now. Rex Morrow. He wasn't going to kill her. Rex murdered people—yes, by the dozens—but only in print. Alexi had decided long before this miserable meeting between them that his work was the result of a dark and macabre mind.

She sprang to her feet, desperate for light. Rex Morrow. Gene had warned her. He had told her that he shared the peninsula with only one other man: the writer Rex Morrow. And that Rex was keeping an eye on the place.

He had promised that the electricity was on, too. She fumbled her way toward what she hoped was a wall, anxious to find a switch. She bit her lip, fighting emotion. Emotion was dangerous. Maybe she was better off with the lights off. She'd panicked at his assault; she'd fallen hysterically into his arms with relief. She'd screamed, she'd cried—

she, who prided herself on having learned to be calm and reserved, if nothing else, in life.

The flashlight arced and flared abruptly, its glare of light showing her plainly where the switch was. She came to it and quickly hit it, swiveling abruptly to lean against the wall and stare at the man who already knew her weaknesses too well. Perhaps light would wash away the absurd intimacy; perhaps it could even give her back some sense of dignity.

He was dark, and disturbingly young. For some reason she'd been convinced that he had to have lived through World War II to have written some of the books he had on espionage during the period. He couldn't have been older than thirty-five. Equally disturbing, he was attractive. His jeans were worn, and his shirt was a black knit that seemed almost a match for the ebony of his hair. His eyes, too, were dark, the deepest brown she had ever seen. He was tanned and handsome, with high, rugged cheekbones, a long, straight nose—somewhat prominent, she determined—and a full mouth that was both sensual and cynical. He didn't seem to resent her full, appraising stare, but then he was returning it, and she was alarmed to discover herself wondering what he was seeing in her.

Dishevelment, she decided wearily. It would be difficult for anyone to break into a house through a window and be attacked and wrestled down and still appear well-groomed.

"Alexi Jordan—in the flesh," he murmured. His tone was cool, as if everything that had happened in the darkness was an embarrassment to him, too. He shook his head as if to clear it, strode toward Alexi and then right past her in the archway by the light switch, apparently very familiar with the house. She watched him, frowning, then followed him.

He went through the big, once-beautiful hallway and disappeared through a swinging door.

The door nearly caught her in the face, fueling her anger and irritation—residues of drastic fear. She was the one with the right to be here—and he had assaulted her and mauled her, and had not even offered an apology.

Light—blessed light! She felt so much more competent and able now, more like the woman she had carefully and painstakingly developed. She paused, reddening at the thought of how she had whimpered in fear, reddening further when she recalled how easily she had cried in his arms when he had simply told her that he wasn't going to kill her. She should call the police. She had every right to be furious.

She slammed against the door to open it and entered the kitchen.

He'd helped himself to a beer. The rest of the house might be a decaying, musty, dusty mess, but someone had kept up the kitchen—and had apparently seen fit to stock the refrigerator with beer.

"Have a beer," Alexi invited him caustically.

He raised the one he had already taken and threw his head back to take a long swallow. He lowered the bottle and pulled out one of the heavy oak chairs at the the butcher-block table.

"Alexi Jordan in the flesh."

What had he heard about her? she wondered. It didn't matter. She had come here to be alone—not to form friendships. She smiled without emotion and replied in kind. "The one and only Rex Morrow."

He arched a dark brow. "I take it your grandfather told you that I lived out here."

"Great-grandfather," Alexi corrected him. "Yes, of course. How else would I know you?" She should have known right away. Gene had told her that Rex Morrow was the only inhabitant of the peninsula. She had just been too immersed in her own thoughts at the time to pay proper at-

tention. Thinking back, she should also have known that
Gene might have him watching the place. She'd heard that
Morrow had tried to buy the house so that he could own the
entire strip of land. But, though Gene seemed fond of his
neighbor, he would never sell the Brandywine house.

"My picture is on my book jackets," Rex told her.

"I certainly wouldn't buy your books in hardcover, Mr.
Morrow."

He smiled. "You don't care for my writing, I take it?"

"Product of a dark mind," she said. Actually, she admired him. She couldn't read his books easily, though. They
were frightening and very realistic—and tore into the hu-
man psyche. They could make her afraid of the dark—and
afraid to live alone. She didn't need to be afraid of imagi-
nary things.

And his characters stayed with the reader long after the
story had been read, long after it should have been forgotten.

Besides she felt defensive. She'd known him a few minutes; because of the circumstances, he had seen far too
deeply into her fears and emotions. And he'd attacked her.
He still hadn't apologized. In fact, it seemed as if he was
annoyed with her.

"Would you like a beer, Ms. Jordan?"

"No. I'd like you out of my house. I'd like you to apologize for accosting me on my own property."

He gazed down, then looked up again with a smile, but
there was a good deal of hostility in that smile.

"Ms. Jordan, it isn't your house. It's Gene's house. And
I don't owe you any apology. I promised Gene I'd watch out
for the place. You weren't due until tomorrow—and who the
hell would have expected you out here, alone, in the pitch
darkness, breaking into the house through a window?"

"I wasn't expecting anyone to be inside."

"I wasn't expecting anyone to break in. We're even."

"Far from even."

As he watched her, she had no idea of what he was thinking; she felt that his assessment found her wanting.

"You won't be staying," he said at last with a shrug and a smile.

"Won't I?"

She liked his smile even less when it deepened and his gaze scanned her from head to toe once again.

"No. You won't be here long." He stood again and walked toward her. His strides were slow, and didn't come all the way to her. Just close enough to look down. She estimated that he was six-three or six-four, and she was barely five-six. She silently gritted her teeth. She wasn't going to let him intimidate her now. He had already done so, and quite well. There was light now, and he wasn't touching her. She could bring back the reserve that had stood her so well against so much.

"This is a quiet place, Ms. Jordan. Very quiet. The biggest excitement in these parts is when Joe Lacey pinches the waitresses in the downtown café. There are only two houses out here on the peninsula—Gene's here, and mine. I get the impression that you need a certain amount of society. But you've only got one neighbor, lady, and that neighbor is me. And I'm not the sociable type."

"How interesting." Alexi crossed her arms over her chest and leaned back against the wall. "Well, then, why don't you take your beer out of my refrigerator and then get your gruesome soul out of my house, Mr. Morrow?"

He took a long moment to answer; his expression in that time gave away nothing of his emotions.

"You can keep the beer. You're going to need it."

"Why is that?"

"This place is falling apart."

"Yes, it is, isn't it?" she returned pleasantly.

"And you're going to handle it all?"

"Yes, I am. Now, if you'll please—"

"I don't want company, Ms. Jordan."

"You keep saying that—and you're standing in my house!"

He hesitated, taking a long, deep breath, as if he were very carefully going to try to explain something to a child.

"Let me be blunt, Ms. Jordan—"

"You haven't been so yet? Please, don't be at all polite or courteous on my account," she told him with caustic sweetness.

"I don't want you here. I value my privacy."

"I'm really sorry, Mr. Morrow. I think I did read somewhere that you were a total eccentric, moody and miserable, but there are property laws in the good ol' U.S. of A. And this is not your property. You do not own the whole peninsula! Now, this house has been in my family for over a hundred years—"

"It's supposed to be haunted, you know," he interrupted her, as if it might have been a sudden inspiration, an if-you-can't-bully-her-out-scare-her-out technique.

She smiled.

"As long as the ghosts will leave me alone, I'll be just fine with them," she told him.

He threw up his hands. "You can't possibly mean to stay out here by yourself."

"But I do."

"Ah...you're running away."

She was—exactly. And the old Brandywine house had seemed like the ideal place. Gene had been pleading with someone in the family to come home. To this home. Admittedly, she'd humored him at first, as had her cousins. But then the disaster with John had occurred, and...yes, she was running away.

"Let me be blunt, Mr. Morrow," Alexi said. "I'm staying."

He stared at her steadily a long while. Then he took in her stature from head to toe once again and started to laugh.

"I'll lay odds you don't make a week," he said.

"I'll last."

He made a sound that was like a derisive snort and walked past her again. "We'll see, won't we?"

"Is that some kind of a threat?" Alexi followed him down the beautiful old hallway toward the front door. The light was low once again, filtering into the hallway from the living room and the kitchen. His dark good looks were a bit sinister in that shadowed realm. He really was striking, she thought. His features were both beautifully chiseled and masculine, and his eyes were so very dark.

Mesmerizing, one might have said.

"I wouldn't dream of threatening you," he told her after perusing her once again. "I'd thought you would be even taller," he said abruptly.

It had taken him a long, long time to realize that he had seen her before this night. That he should have known Alexi Jordan for being more than Gene Brandywine's expected relation. He had seen her in a different way, of course. In a classic, flowing Grecian gown. With the wind in her hair. He had seen her on the silver screen, seen her in fantasy.

Her classical features had been put to good use.

Despite herself, Alexi flushed. "You recognized me."

"'The Face That Launched a Thousand Ships,'" he quoted from her last ad campaign for Helen of Troy products.

"Well, you son of a—!" she said suddenly, her temper soaring. "You kept denying that I was Alexi Jordan when you must have known—"

"No, I didn't know then. I didn't really recognize you from the ad until we were in the kitchen." He was irritated;

she really irritated him. She made him feel defensive. She made it sound as if he had enjoyed scaring her.

And, somewhere deep inside, she scared him in return. Why? he wondered, puzzled. And then, of course, he knew. Maybe part of it had been the way that they had met. Part of it had been the terror in her eyes, the fear he had so desperately needed to assuage.

And part of it was simply that she was so achingly beautiful. So gloriously feminine. She made him wish that he had known her forever and forever, that he could reach out and pull her into his arms. To know her—as a lover.

He didn't mind wanting a woman. He just feared needing her. And she was the type of lover a man could come to need.

"You don't resemble the glamorous Helen in the least at the moment, you know," he told her bluntly. It was a lie. Her face could have launched a thousand ships had it been covered in mud.

"And whose fault is that?"

He shrugged. Despite herself, Alexi tried to repin some of the hair that was falling in tangles from her once neat and elegant knot.

He laughed. "I should have known from all the lipstick."

"Go home, Mr. Morrow, please. I'm looking for privacy, too."

His laughter faded. He studied her once again, and again, despite herself, she felt as if she was growing warm. As if there was something special about his eyes, about the way they fell over her and entered into her.

"Go—" She broke off, startled, as a shrill sound erupted in the night. She was so surprised that she nearly screamed. Then she was heartily glad that she had not, for it was only the phone.

"Oh," she murmured. Then she sighed with resignation, looking at him. "All right, where is it?"

"Parlor."

"Living room?"

"That living room is called a parlor."

She stiffened her shoulders and started for the parlor. She caught the phone on the fifth ring. It was Gene. Her great-grandfather had turned ninety-five last Christmas and could have passed for sixty. Alexi was ridiculously proud of him, but then she felt that she had a right to be. He was lean, but as straight as an arrow and as determined and sly as an old fox. He seldom ailed, and Alexi thought that she knew his secret. He'd never—through a long life of trials and tribulations—taken the time to feel sorry for himself, he had never ceased to love life, and he had never apologized for an absolute fascination with people. Everything and everyone interested Gene.

But he was too old, he had assured Alexi, to start the massive project of refurbishing his historical inheritance, the Brandywine house outside Fernandina Beach.

He had known she needed a place. A place to hide, to nurse her wounds. She had never explained everything to him; the bitter truth had been too hurtful and humiliating to admit, even to Gene.

Gene's voice came to her gruffly. "Thank God you're there. I tried the hotel in town, and the receptionist told me you had never checked in."

"Gene! Yes, I—"

"Young woman, where is your sense?"

At that moment, Alexi wanted to rap her beloved relative on the knuckles. His voice was so clear that she was sure Rex Morrow, who had followed her back into the parlor, was hearing every word.

"Gene, I really didn't want to stay in town. I made it into the city by six—"

"It's pitch-dark out there!"

"Well, yes—"

"Alexi, there are dangerous people in this world, even in a small place—maybe especially in a small place. You could have been attacked or assaulted or—"

There *are* dangerous people out here, and I *was* assaulted! Alexi almost snapped. Rex Morrow was watching her, smiling. He could hear every word.

He took the phone out of her hand.

"What are you—"

"Shh," he told her, sitting on the back of the Victorian sofa and casually dangling a leg. He smiled with a great deal of warmth when he spoke to Gene.

"Gene, Rex here."

"Rex, thank God. I'm glad I asked you to watch the place!"

"Gene, there's really not much going on out here, you know. No real danger, though Alexi might tell you differently. We had a bit of a run-in. Why didn't you give her the key?"

Alexi snatched the phone from him, reddening again. "He did give me the key."

"What? What?" They could both hear Gene's voice. "Key? I did give Alexi the key."

Rex arched a brow. "Why didn't you...use it?" he asked her slowly, once again as if he were speaking with a child who had proved to have little adult comprehension. "Or do you prefer breaking in the window over walking through the front door?"

"You broke a window?" Gene was shouting. For such an incredibly old man, he could shout incredibly loudly, Alexi thought.

"The key doesn't work!" Alexi shouted back.

There was a long sigh on the other end. "The key works, Alexi. You have to twist it in the lock. It's old. Old things have to be worked as carefully as old people. They're temperamental.''

Rex Morrow stretched out a hand to her, palm up. "Give me the key."

"You go find it!" she hissed. "It's in my purse that you were tearing up!"

"Now what's going on?" Gene asked.

"Your wonder boy is going to go check it," Alexi said sweetly.

"Well, it works—you'll see," Gene said, mollified. "Now, you get someone in there right away to fix that window. You hear me?"

"First thing tomorrow, Gene," Alexi promised. "Hey!" she protested. Rex had dumped the contents of her purse onto the sofa to find the single key.

"Found it," he assured her.

"Oh, Lord," she groaned.

"What's wrong now?" Gene demanded.

"Nothing. Everything is wonderful. Just super," she muttered.

Rex Morrow was on his way back to the hallway and the front door. "Really, Gene. I'm here and I'm fine, and you just take care of yourself, okay?"

"Maybe you should get a dog, Alexi. A great big German shepherd or a Doberman. I'd feel better—"

"Gene, why ever would I need a dog when you left me a prowling cat?" she asked innocently.

Her great-grandfather started to say something, but he paused instead. She could see him in her mind's eye, scratching his white head in consternation.

"I'll keep in touch," Alexi promised hastily. "I'm excited to be here; it's a wonderful old place. I promise I'll fix it up with lots of love and tenderness. Love you. Bye!"

She hung up before he could say anything else. Then she stared at the phone for a moment, a nostalgic smile on her

lips. She adored him. She was very lucky to have him, she
knew. In the midst of pain, chaos and loneliness, he had always been there for her.

"The key works fine," Rex announced.

He was back in the room, extending the key to her. She
took it in silence, compressing her lips as he stared at her.

"You have to pull the door while you turn it," he said.
"Want to try it while I'm still here?"

"No. Oh, all right—yes. Thank you."

Stiffly she preceded him down the hallway to the door.
She thought that maybe she'd rather lock herself out and use
the window again than falter in front of him, but really, why
should she care?

She opened the door and threw the bolt from the inside.
She slid the key in and twisted it, and it worked like a dream.
Disgusted, Alexi thought it was a sad day when one couldn't
even trust a piece of metal.

"I guess I've got it," she murmured.

Arms crossed over his chest, he shook his head. "Step
outside and lock the door and try it. That's when you have
the problem."

She stepped outside, but before she closed the door she
asked him, "How did you get in?"

"I have my own key." He closed the door for her.

Alexi slipped her key into the lock. With the door closed,
it was frightfully dark again. She could barely find the hole,
and then she couldn't begin to get the damn thing to twist.

"Pull! Pull on the knob!"

She did. After a few more fumbles she got the key to
twist, and the door opened.

She walked in, a smile of satisfaction brightening her eyes.

"Got it." She gritted her teeth. "Thank you."

"I wouldn't be quite so pleased. It took you long
enough." Arms still casually crossed, he stared down at her,

shaking his head. "And you're going to take on the task of reconstruction?"

"I'm a whiz at electricity."

"Are you?"

"Will you please go home?"

He smiled at her. "Your face is smudged."

"Is it?" She smiled serenely. She was sure it was. Her stockings were torn, her skirt was probably beyond repair, and she undoubtedly resembled a used mop.

He came a step nearer to her, raising a hand to her cheek. She remembered the tenderness with which he had held her when she was trembling and shaking in fear. When she had been vulnerable and weak.

She felt that same tenderness come from him now and the sensual draw of the rueful curl of his mouth. She should have stepped back. She didn't. She felt the brush of his thumb against her flesh and caught her breath. He didn't want her there; he had said so. And she wanted to be alone.

She didn't move, however. Except for the trembling that started up, inside of her this time. She just felt that touch.

"Good night, Ms. Jordan," he said softly.

He was out the door, warning her to bolt it, before she thought to reply.

2

Alexi rinsed her face at the sink and dried it with paper towels. She had showered in the powder room beneath the stairs, but that was as far as she had ventured in her new realm—which wasn't really new at all. Twenty years before, she had spent a summer here with Gene. But twenty years was a long time, and the house was truly a disaster since Gene had left it so many months ago.

She sat at the butcher-block table to do her makeup, thinking that she didn't look much better than she had the night before. She had slept poorly. Sleeping on the kitchen floor hadn't helped, but strangely, once Rex Morrow had left, she had been really uneasy—too frightened to explore any further. But when she had slept, nightmares had awakened her again and again. Nightmares of John combining with the horrid fear that had assailed her with Rex's first touch last night. Naturally, perhaps. She'd been attacked. But then her dreams had become even more disconcerting. She'd dreamed of Rex Morrow in a far gentler way, of his eyes on her, of his touch, of his smile. Dreamed of the assurance in his voice. All night the visions had filtered through her mind. Violence, tenderness—both had stolen from her any hope of a good night's sleep.

She felt better once her makeup was on. Even before she had left home on her own—before John—she had learned that with makeup she could pretend that she was wearing a mask and that she could hide all expression and emotion behind it. That wasn't true, of course. But as she had aged, she had learned to create masks with her features, and the more years slipped by her, the greater comfort she took in concealing her feelings.

Rex Morrow had seen her feelings, she reminded herself. But it had proved as uncomfortable for him as it had for her. He wanted her gone, right? He valued his privacy; he wanted the land all to himself.

"Sorry, Mr. Morrow," she murmured out loud. "I'm not quite as pathetic as I appeared last night. And I'm staying."

She took a sip of coffee, then bit her lower lip. She wished she could forget how his eyes had moved over her, how his thumb had felt when he'd smoothed away the smudge on her cheek.

And she wished that she would get up and start cleaning. But she decided that she wasn't going to plunge right in. Chicken? she challenged herself. Maybe. After last night, she deserved to take her time. She'd explore later. She was simply feeling lethargic. Today she'd go into town and find a rental car. Today, she reminded herself, was half over. It had been almost twelve when she had risen, because it had been at least six when she had finally slept.

It was three in the afternoon when she requested a taxi at last. She'd called Gene to assure him that her first night had gone well and that she was happy at the house. She told him the truth about what had happened with Rex when she had arrived, but she didn't tell him how frightened she had been or how she had collapsed in tears into a total stranger's arms. She laughed, making light of the incident. Anyone would have been terrified, she assured herself. But Gene was astute. She was afraid he might have learned more about her past from the incident than she wanted.

By four-thirty she had rented a little Datsun. She had made friends with the taxi driver and the rental car clerk—

everyone knew Gene, it seemed. They were glad to meet his great-granddaughter and fascinated to discover that she was the Helen of Troy lady. Alexi was a bit uneasy to find that she was so recognizable—she would have preferred anonymity. She convinced herself that it would be okay, then decided that she was going to like small-town living. The people were warm—if just a little bit nosy.

"You just be careful out there," the old gentleman at the agency warned her. "That peninsula can be a mighty scary place."

"Why?" Alexi asked. But he had already turned to help the businessman in line behind her. She shrugged and left for her car. Once inside, she tapped idly against the steering wheel. She should get going on her shopping. There was nothing in the house. And whether she had a professional cleaner or not, she needed all kinds of detergents. And bug sprays. She was sure that except for the kitchen the place was crawling.

But she wasn't really ready for work yet. And she decided she would drive back to the peninsula. It would be dark before long, and she wanted to see the little spit of land in its entirety.

Alexi started the car, then froze. She stared at the blond head and broad shoulders of a man slipping into a rented Mustang next to her car. For a moment, her stomach and heart careened; panic set in. Then he turned. It wasn't John. She exhaled, shaking.

He couldn't have followed her here, she promised herself. She had finished up with the Helen of Troy campaign—and then she had run. He couldn't know where. And no one would tell him.

She took several deep breaths and eased out of the parking lot. She got lost only once, and then she was on the one road that led to Gene's house. It was a horrible road, she quickly discovered. The town didn't own it, Gene had told her once; he and Rex Morrow owned it jointly. And apparently, Alexi thought with a smile, neither of them had been very interested in keeping it up. There were potholes everywhere.

She slowed to accommodate the bumps and juts, but apparently she did so just a moment too late. The car suddenly sputtered and died, spewing up a froth of steam from the front. Alexi stared at it in disbelief for a moment, then swore at herself and crawled out of the driver's seat.

For fifteen minutes she tried to figure out how to open the hood; once it was open, she wondered why she had bothered. Steam was still spewing out, and she didn't have the faintest idea of what to do. She looked around, wondering how long a walk it was to the house. The peninsula was only about four miles long and one across, but both houses were at the far end of it.

Alexi swore and kicked a tire. She decided that people lied when they said that doing such things couldn't help—she felt ten times better for having kicked the car. She was annoyed that she didn't know what to do, but then she had never kept a car. She just hadn't needed one in New York.

It was getting dark, she perceived suddenly. And if she hadn't been stuck here, she would have thought that it was beautiful. The sky was burnt orange and pink, a lovely background for the pines and shrubs that littered the sandy ground. She had no idea how quickly the darkness fell there.

Alexi gave the car a withering stare, then decided she had best start walking toward the house. She could phone the rental agency, and they could call a mechanic and get the car out to the house for her.

Swinging her bag over her shoulder, Alexi started to walk. It really was beautiful, she assured herself. The sandy road at sunset, everything around it silent, the smell of the ocean heavy on the air. A breeze lifted her hair and touched her cheeks. She could imagine having a horse out here; it would be a beautiful place to ride. All the wonderful pines and palms and the endless sand, and beyond the trees, the endless ocean.

The sunset coloring around her slipped; the sky became gray. Alexi was glad that the house was on a peninsula; she knew she was walking in the right direction. There were no lights out here; she remembered the horrid blackness of the night before.

Suddenly she became aware of a sound behind her, following her. She stopped; the sound stopped. It was her imagination, she told herself. Darkness and solitude could do things like that. Who was she kidding? She was frightened. And she had a right to be. After last night...

Last night, Rex had pounced upon her right away. She had crawled through the window, and he had quickly grabbed her. This sound behind her was...stealthy. She was being stalked.

No. Her fears were getting out of hand. Rex had had an explanation. He'd thought that she was breaking into the house. But John couldn't have followed her—and John was a memory of misery, not terror. And this...this was a feeling that something evil was breathing down her spine. That some real injury was intended for her.

She inhaled—and then she started to run. Maybe her parents, in their distant wisdom, had been right. Maybe she shouldn't have come here, where there was no help, where there was nothing but darkness and the whisper of the breeze and if she screamed forever, no one would hear her.

She was breathless; she was certain that she heard soft footfalls on the sand behind her. She turned around to look and then screamed with total abandon as she ran smack into something hard.

She swung around again, looking up in amazement. She was about to fall when arms steadied her.

"Rex!"

"What in God's name are you doing, running like that?"

"Someone was following me."

She saw the doubt in his eyes and turned around again. Naturally, no one was there. Rex's hands were still on her arms. She looked up at him again, cleared her throat and stepped back. "I'm telling you the truth."

He walked around her and picked up her purse, which she hadn't realized she had dropped. He handed it to her. "We're the only inhabitants out here," he said lightly. She could still see doubt in his eyes.

"I didn't imagine you last night," she said angrily. His eyes seemed to darken as he studied her more intently, and for some reason she flushed uneasily. "I don't imagine things."

"I'm sure you don't."

He didn't believe her; she could hear it in his tone.

"I'm telling you—"

"What are you doing walking out here, anyway?"

"I was driving. The stupid rental car blew."

"Blew what?"

"Something."

He nodded. "Come on. We'll go back for it."

They didn't speak during the walk; he strode quickly and Alexi had enough to do to keep up. She was panting when they reached the car.

The steam had stopped. Rex took a look under the hood, then walked around to the driver's seat, arching a brow at Alexi as he took the keys from the ignition. He opened the trunk, found a container of water and filled something in the front. He slid into the driver's seat, turned the motor over—and it caught. He opened the passenger door.

"You blew a hose, that's all. I can pick one up for you in the morning. Come on, get in. I'll get you home. It'll go that far."

Alexi crawled in beside him and leaned against the seat.

"Thank you." She didn't look at him; she could feel his gaze slide her way as he drove. She wondered uneasily what he was thinking.

Rex drove the car up to the house. When they got out, he tossed her the keys, pointing to the house. "Glad you left a night-light on."

"I didn't know I had," she murmured.

"What?"

"Nothing, nothing," she said quickly. But she'd be damned if she could remember leaving lights on. She hadn't even explored the house yet—all she had really seen was the kitchen.

Rex automatically walked with her up the path to the front door. He frowned, when he saw the window that she had broken.

"You didn't get that fixed today. You should have."

"I will." She wondered why she had said it so quickly, so defensively. She didn't owe him any explanations.

She managed to open the door on the first try, and that was a nice boost to her ego. She turned and smiled at Rex, laughing. "I did it."

"Yes, you did."

She hesitated, wondering if she should invite him in. But then, he didn't want her anywhere near him, and she'd had a miserable night on his account. Still . . .

She trembled suddenly, looking down. He was a very attractive man. Tall, dark and—masculine. They were far from friends, yet in their first meeting they had taken a forbidden step toward intimacy. She had taken a step. . . and she wanted to retreat from it. He was rugged and blunt—a loner. They both wanted privacy.

"Thank you," she murmured.

"You're welcome," he said, staring at her as she went into the house. "I'll pick up that hose for you tomorrow."

"I should make the rental agency do it."

"It's no big thing."

She nodded, then realized that she was returning his stare. His eyes were so dark in the night. He was wearing jeans again, and a navy polo shirt. His arms, which were mostly bare, were tanned and nicely muscled.

She wanted to ask him in. Of all the things that had happened the night before, she remembered the tenderness in his voice and the feeling of his arms as he'd held her. Something warm inside her stirred, something she quickly fought.

She wasn't ready for a relationship. She might never be ready again in her life.

She knew he didn't want her here on the peninsula. He had warned her to go—he had even laid odds against her staying. Still, she wanted to see him smile, to hear him laugh. She wanted to know what lay in his past that he would crave this solitude, that could have made him so ruthless when he had first touched her, so gentle when he had realized how terrified she had been.

"Good night, then. Sleep well, Alexi."

"Good night, and thanks again."

Alexi stepped into the house, frowning as she looked around the lighted hallway.

But then, even as she stared, she heard a little noise—and the house was plunged into total darkness.

She didn't scream at first. Her heart shuddered instinctively, but she wasn't really afraid. The Brandywine house had been built in 1859, there could easily be problems with such things as electricity.

But then she heard the footsteps, loud and clear. They came crashing down the stairway. She could feel the wind.... The stairway was at the other end of the hall, and she was very aware that someone was close—very close—to her.

And it certainly wasn't Rex Morrow—not tonight. He had just gone out the front door.

She did scream then, just like a banshee. Someone had been upstairs. In the house.

"Alexi!"

There was a fierce pounding on the front door, and she knew the voice shouting her name belonged to Rex.

She turned around, groping madly in the darkness and found the lock. The stubborn thing refused to give at first. Where was the person who had made the sound of footsteps? Her scream had cut off all other sound, and now she didn't know if someone was still coming for her in the darkness or if that same someone had bolted on past.

"Please, please...!" she whispered to the ancient lock, and then, as if it were a cantankerous old man who needed to be politely placated, it groaned and gave.

She threw the door open. In the darkness she could just barely make out Rex Morrow's starkly handsome features. She nearly pitched herself against him, but then she remembered that the man was basically a hostile stranger, even though she knew Gene held him in the highest regard—and even though she had already clung to him once before.

She stepped back.

"Why did you scream?"

"The lights went out and—"

"I thought you were a whiz with electricity."

"I lied—but that's not why I screamed. Someone came running down the stairway."

"What?"

He looked at her so sharply that even in the darkness she felt his probing stare. Did he think that she was lying—or did he believe her all too easily?

"I told you—"

"Come on."

He took her hand, his fingers twining tightly around hers, and, with the ease of a cat in the dark, strode toward the parlor. He found the flashlight and cast its beam around. No intruder was there.

"Where did the...footsteps go?" he whispered huskily.

"I—I don't know. I screamed and...I don't know."

He brought her back into the hallway and stopped dead. Alexi crashed into his back, banging her nose. She rubbed it, thinking that the man had a nice scent. She remembered it; she would have known him anywhere by it. It was not so much that of an after-shave as that of the simple cleanliness of soap and the sea and the air. He might be hostile, but at least he was clean.

There was only so much one could expect from neighbors, she decided nervously.

He walked through the hall to the stairway, paused, then went into the kitchen. The rear door was still tightly locked.

"Well, your intruder didn't leave that way, and he didn't exit by the front door," Rex said. His tone was bland, but she could read his thoughts. He had decided that she was a neurotic who imagined things.

"I tell you—" she began irately.

"Right. You heard footsteps. We'll check the house."

"You think he's still in the house?"

"No, but we'll check."

Alexi knew he didn't believe anyone had been there to begin with. "Rex—"

"All right, all right. I said we'll search. If anyone is here, we'll find him. Or her. Or it."

He released her hand. Alexi didn't know how nervous she was until she realized that her fingers were still clinging to his. She flushed and turned away from him.

"Why did the lights go, then?" she demanded.

"Probably a fuse. Here, hold the flashlight and hang on a second."

She turned back around to take the flashlight from him. He went straight to the small drawer by the refrigerator, then went toward the pantry.

"I need more light."

Alexi followed him and let the beam play on the fuse box. A moment later, the kitchen light came on.

He looked at her. "Stay here. I'll check out the library and the ballroom and upstairs."

"Wait a minute!" Alexi protested, shivering.

"What?"

Impatiently he stopped at the kitchen door, his hand resting casually against the frame.

She swallowed and straightened with dignity and tried to walk slowly over to join him.

"I do read your books," she admitted. "And it's always the hapless idiot left alone while the other goes off to search who winds up...winds up with her throat slit!"

"Alexi..." he murmured slowly.

"Don't patronize me!" she commanded him.

He sighed, looked at her for a moment with a certain incredulity and then started to laugh.

"Okay. We'll search together. And I'm sorry. I'm not patronizing you. It's just usually so quiet out here that it's hard to imagine..." His voice trailed away, and he shrugged again. "Come on, then."

Smiling, he offered her his hand. She hesitated, then took it.

They returned to the hallway. Alexi nervously played the flashlight beam up the stairway. Rex grinned again and went to the wall, flicking a switch that lit the entire stairway.

"Gene did have a few things done," he told her.

There were only two other rooms on the ground floor—except for the little powder room beneath the stairway, which proved to be empty. To the right, behind the parlor, was the library, filled with ancient volumes and wall shelves and even an old running oak ladder reaching to the top shelves. Upon a dais with a wonderful old Persian carpet was a massive desk with a few overstuffed Eastleg chairs around it. Apart from that, the room was empty.

They crossed behind the stairway to the last room—the "ballroom," as Rex called it. It was big, with a dining set at one end with beautiful old hutches flanking it, and a baby grand across the room, toward the rear wall. Two huge paintings hung above the fireplace, one of a handsome blond man in full Confederate dress uniform, the other of a lovely woman in radiant white antebellum costume.

Forgetting the intruder for a moment, Alexi dropped Rex's hand and walked toward the paintings for a better look.

"Lieutenant General P. T. Brandywine and Eugenia," Rex said quietly.

"Yes, I know," Alexi murmured. She felt a bit awed; she hadn't been in the house since she'd been a small child, but she remembered the paintings, and she felt again the little thrill of looking at people from another day who were her direct antecedents.

"They say that he's the one who buried the Confederate treasure."

"What?" Alexi, forgetting her distant relatives, turned around and frowned at Rex.

He laughed. "You mean you never heard the story?"

She shook her head. "No. I mean, I've heard of Pierre and Eugenia. Pierre built the house. But I never heard anything about his treasure."

He smiled, locking his hands behind his back and casually sauntering into the room to look at the paintings.

"This area went back and forth during the Civil War like a Ping-Pong ball. The rebels held it one month; the Yankees took it the next. Pierre was one hell of a rebel—but it seems the last time he came home, he knew he wasn't going to make it back again. Somewhere in the house he buried a treasure. He was killed at Gettysburg in '63, and Eugenia never did return here. She went back to her father's house in Baltimore, and her children didn't come back here until the 1880s. Local legend has it that Pierre haunts the place to guard his stash, and the locals on the mainland all swear that it does exist.''

"Why didn't Eugenia come back?"

Rex shrugged. "He was a rebel. At the end of the war, Confederate currency wasn't worth the paper it had been printed on. There was no real treasure. Maybe that's the reason that Pierre had to come back to haunt the place."

Alexi stared at him for a long moment. There seemed to be a glitter of mischief in his eyes. A slow, simmering anger burned inside her, along with a sudden suspicion. "Sure. Those footsteps belonged to my great-great-great-grand-father. You will not scare me out of this house!"

"What—?" He broke off with a furious scowl. "You foolish little brat. I'm not trying to scare you."

"The hell you're not! You want me out of here—God knows why. You don't have to see me, you know."

His eyes narrowed. "Maybe I should leave now."

She lifted her chin. She wanted him to stay. She wasn't afraid of ghosts, but someone alive had been in the house. Someone who had come here in stealth. Even if Rex didn't believe her.

She swung around. "This is ridiculous! I came to my old family home on what is supposed to be a deserted, desolate peninsula, and it's more like Grand Central Station!"

"Alexi—"

"Just go, if you want to!"

Rex watched her, his mouth tight and grim, then swung around. "I'll check the upstairs. If someone tries to slit your throat, just scream."

He was gone. Alexi stared after him, shivering, hating herself for being afraid. She hadn't been afraid to come—she'd been eager. She'd desperately wanted to be alone. Where there were no crowds, where people didn't recognize her. But she'd just barely gotten there, and already the darkness and the isolation were proving threatening.

Nothing was going to happen, she assured herself. But she wrapped her arms nervously about herself and returned to stare up at the paintings. Perhaps some kids believed in the legend about the gold. High school kids. They didn't want to harm her; they just wanted to find a treasure—a treasure that didn't really exist.

She smiled slowly. They were really marvelous-looking people; Pierre was striking, and his Eugenia was beautiful.

"Even if you could come back as a ghost," she said to Pierre's likeness with a wry grin, "you certainly wouldn't haunt me—I'm your own flesh and blood."

"Do you often talk to paintings?"

Startled, she swung around. Rex Morrow was leaning casually against the doorframe, watching her.

"Only now and then."

"Oh." He waited a moment. "Upstairs is clear. If anyone was in the house, he or she is definitely gone now."

"Good."

"Want me to call the police?"

"Think I should?" She realized that he still didn't believe her. Or maybe he didn't think she was lying—just that she was neurotic. Paranoid. And maybe he even felt a little guilty about her state of mind, since he had attacked her last night.

He paused, then shrugged at last. "Whoever it was is gone. Probably some kid from the town looking for Pierre's treasure. He probably left by that broken window. You *must* get it fixed."

"I will—tomorrow. First thing. And maybe it was some-one looking for Pierre's treasure. Numismatically or his-torically, maybe those Confederate bills are worth something."

"Maybe."

"They could be collectible!"

"Sure. Confederate money is collectible. It's just not usually worth..."

"Worth what?"

"Only rare bills from certain banks are worth much. But who knows?" he offered.

They stood there for several moments, looking at each other across the ballroom.

"Well," he murmured.

"Well..." she echoed. Her gaze fell from his, and once again she wasn't at all sure what she wanted. He'd checked the place for her; she was sure now that it was empty.

He didn't want her on the peninsula. He had said so himself. It was certainly time that he left—and she should be happy for that, since he was such a doubting Thomas. But she couldn't help feeling uneasy. She didn't want him to go.

Fool! she told herself. Tell him "Thank you very much," then let him go. A curious warmth was spreading through her. If he left now, they could remain casual acquain-tances. But if she encouraged him to stay...

It was more than fear, more than uneasiness. She wanted him to stay. She wanted to know more about him. She wanted to watch him smile.

A slight tremor shook her; the warmth flooding her in-creased. She had the feeling that if she had him stay now, she would never be able to turn her back on him again. She was still staring at him and he was still watching her and no words were being spoken, but tension, real and tangible, seemed to be filling the air. Alexi inhaled deeply; she cleared her throat.

"I think I'll have one of your beers," she said. "Since they *are* in my refrigerator."

"Help yourself."

She hesitated. Then she spoke. "Want one?"

He, too, hesitated. It was as if he, too, sensed some form of commitment in the moment. Then he shrugged, and a slow smile that was rueful and sexy and insinuating curled the corners of his lip.

"Sure," he told her. "Sure. Why not?"

3

Alexi passed him quickly and hurried on into the kitchen. She dug into the refrigerator for two beers.

"Are you the one who has kept the kitchen clean?" she asked casually. It was spotless; Alexi imagined that one could have eaten off the floor and not have worried about dirt or germs. The rest of the place was a dust bowl.

"In a manner of speaking. A woman comes out twice a week to do my place. She spends an hour or so here."

Alexi nodded and handed him a beer. She walked past him, somehow determined to sit in the parlor, even though the kitchen was by far the cleaner place.

Maybe it was the only way she could get herself to go back into the room.

She knew he was behind her. Once she reached the parlor she sank heavily into the Victorian sofa, discovering that she was exhausted. Rex Morrow sat across from her, straddling a straight-backed chair. Cool Hand Luke in a contemporary dark knit.

He smiled again, and she realized he knew she was staring at him and wondering about him. And of course, at the same time, she realized that he was watching her speculatively.

"You're staring," he said.

"So are you."

He shrugged. "I'm curious."

"About what?"

He laughed, and it was an easy sound, surprisingly pleasant. "Well, you are Alexi Jordan."

She lifted her hands, eyeing him warily in return. "And you are Rex Morrow."

"Hardly worthy of the gossip columns."

"That's because writers get to keep their privacy."

"Only if they hole out in places like this."

She didn't say anything; she took a long sip of her beer, wrinkling her nose. She really didn't like the brand; its taste was too bitter for her.

It was better than nothing.

"Well?" he said insinuatingly, arching a dark brow.

"Well, what?"

"Want to tell me about it?"

"About what?"

"The rich, lusty scandal involving the one and only Alexi Jordan."

Only a writer could make it all sound so sordid, Alexi decided. But she couldn't deny the scandal. "Why on earth should I?" she countered smoothly.

He lifted his hands, grinning. "Well, because I'm curious, I suppose."

"Wonderful," she said, nodding gravely. "I should spill my guts to a novelist. Great idea."

He laughed. "I write horror and suspense, not soap operas. You're safe with me."

"Haven't you read all about it in the rags?"

"I only read the front pages of those things when I'm waiting in line at the grocery store. One of them said you left him for another man. Another said John Vinto left you for another woman. Some say you hate each other. That there are deep, dark secrets hidden away in it all. Some claim that the world-famous photographer and his world-famous wife are still on good terms. The best of friends. So, what's the real story?"

Alexi leaned back on the couch, closing her eyes. She was so tired of the whole thing, of being pursued. She still felt some of the pain—it was like being punch-drunk. The divorce had actually gone through almost a year ago.

"Who knows what is truth?" she said, not opening her eyes. She didn't know why she should tell Rex Morrow—of all people—anything. But an intimacy had formed between them. Strange. They were both hostile; neither of them seemed to be overladen with trust for the opposite sex. Still, though he was blunt about wanting the peninsula to himself, she felt that she could trust him. With things that were personal—with things she might not say to anyone else.

"We're definitely not friends," she blurted out.

"Hurt to talk?" he asked quietly. She felt his voice, felt it wash over her, and she was surprised at the sensitivity in his tone.

She opened her eyes. A wary smile came to her lips. "I can't tell you about it."

"No?"

"No." She kicked off her shoes and curled her stockinged toes under her, taking another long sip of the beer. She hadn't eaten all day, and the few sips of the alcohol she had taken warmed her and eased her humor. "Suffice it to say that it was all over a long time ago. It wasn't one woman— it was many. And it was more than that. John never felt that he had taken a wife; he considered himself to have acquired property. It doesn't matter at all anymore."

"You're afraid of him." It was a statement, not a question.

"No! No! How did—?" She stopped herself. She didn't want to admit anything about her relationship with John.

"You are," he said softly. "And I've hit a sore spot. I'm sorry."

"Don't be. I'm not. Really."

"You're a liar, but we'll let it go at that for the time being."

"I'm not—"

"You are. Something happened that was a rough deal."

"Ahh . . ." she murmured uneasily. "The plot thickens."

He smiled at her. She felt the cadence of his voice wash over her, and it didn't seem so terrible that he knew that much.

"You don't need to be afraid now," he said softly.

"Oh?"

She liked his smile. She like the confidence in it. She even liked his macho masculine arrogance as he stated, "I'm very particular about the peninsula. You don't want him around, he won't be."

Alexi laughed, honestly at first, then with a trace of unease. John could be dangerous when he chose.

"So that's it!" Rex said suddenly.

"What?"

He watched her, nodding like a sage with a new piece of wisdom that helped explain the world. "Someone running after you on the sand, footsteps on the stairway, your blind panic last night. You think your ex is after you."

"No! I really heard footsteps!"

"All right. You heard them."

"You still don't believe me!"

He sighed, and she realized that she was never going to convince him that the footsteps had been real. "You seem to have had it rough," he said simply.

She wasn't going to win an argument. And at the moment she was feeling a bit too languorous to care.

"Talk about rough!" Alexi laughed. She glanced at her beer bottle. "This thing is empty. Feel like getting me another? For a person who doesn't like people, you certainly are curious—and good at making those people you don't like talk."

He stood up and took the bottle. "I never said that I don't like people."

She closed her eyes again and leaned back as he left her. She had to be insane. She was sitting here drinking beer and enjoying his company and nearly spilling out far too much truth about herself. Or was she spilling it out? He sensed too much. After one bottle of beer, she was smiling too easily. Trusting too quickly. If he did delve into all her secrets, it would serve her right if he displayed them to the world in print. He would change the names of the innocent or the not-so-innocent.

But, of course, everyone always knew who the real culprit was.

Something cold touched her hand. He was standing over her with another beer. She smiled. She was tired and lethargic enough to do so.

"My turn," she murmured huskily.

"Uh-uh. We're not finished with you."

He didn't move, though. He was staring down at her head. If she'd had any energy left, she would have flinched when he touched her hair. "That's the closest shade I've seen to real gold. How on earth do you do it?"

She knew she should be offended, but she laughed. "I grow it, idiot!"

"Oh, yeah?"

"Oh, yeah. How do you get that color? Shoe polish?"

"No, idiot," he said in turn, grinning. "I grow it."

He returned to his chair and cast his leg easily over it to straddle it once again. "So let's go on here. Why are you so afraid of John Vinto? What happened?"

"Nothing happened. We hit the finale. That was it."

"That wasn't it at all. You married him...what? About four years ago or so?"

"Yes."

"You've been divorced almost a year?"

"Yes," Alexi said warily. "He, uh, was the photographer on some of the Helen of Troy stills," she said after a moment. She shrugged. "The campaign ended—publicity about the breakup would have created havoc on the set."

"You worked with him after."

"Yes."

"And you spent that year working—and being afraid of him."

She lowered her head quickly. She hadn't been afraid of him when there had been plenty of other people around. She'd taken great pains never to be alone with him after he...

She sighed softly. "No more, Mr. Morrow. Not tonight. Your turn." She took a sip of her new beer. The second didn't taste half as bitter as the first, and it was ice-cold and delicious. She mused that it was the first time she had let down her guard in—

Since John. She shivered at the thought and then opened her eyes wide, aware that Rex had seen her shiver. Something warned her that he missed little.

"You shouldn't have to fear anyone, Alexi," he told her softly.

"Really..." She suddenly sat bolt upright. "Rex, I don't talk about this—no one knows anything at all."

"I don't really know anything," he reminded her with a smile. There was a rueful, sensual curve to the corner of his lip that touched her heart and stirred some physical response in the pit of her abdomen.

"No one will ever know what I do know now," he said. "On my honor, Ms. Jordan."

"Thanks," she murmured uneasily. "If we're playing *This Is Your Life*, then you've got to give something."

He shrugged, lifting his hands. "I married the girl next door. I tried to write at night while I edited the obituaries during the day for a small paper. You know the story—trial and error and rejections, and the girl next door left me. She didn't sue for divorce, though—she waited until some of the money came in, created one of the finest performances I have ever seen in court and walked away with most of it. She was only allowed to live off me for seven years. I bought an old house in Temple Terrace that used to belong to a famous stripper. I raised horses and planted orange groves— and then went nuts because my address got out and every weirdo in the country would come by to look me up. They stole all the oranges—and one jerk even shot a horse for a souvenir. That's when I moved out here. The sheriff up on the mainland is great, and it's like a wonderful little conspiracy—the townspeople keep me safe, and I contribute heavily to all the community committees. Gene—when he was still here—was a neighbor I could abide. Then he decided he needed to be in a retirement cooperative. I tried to buy the house from him; he wasn't ready to let go.'' He stopped speaking, frowning as he looked at her.

"Have you eaten anything?"

"What? Uh, no. How—why did you ask that?"

He chuckled softly. "Because your eyes are rimmed with red, and it makes you look tired and hungry.

"Want me to call for a pizza?"

"You must be kidding. You can get a pizza all the way out here?"

"I have connections," he promised her gravely. "What do you want on it?"

"Anything."

Alexi leaned her head against the sofa again. She heard him stand and walk around to the phone and order a large pizza with peppers, onions, mushrooms and pepperoni from a man named Joe, with whom he chatted casually, saying that he was over at the Brandywine house and, yes, Gene's great-granddaughter was in and, yes, she was fine—just hungry.

He hung up at last.

"So Joe will send a pizza?"

"Yep."

"That's wonderful."

"Hmm."

She sat up, curling her toes beneath her again and smoothing her skirt.

"Hold still," he commanded her suddenly.

Startled, she looked at him, amazed at the tension in his features. He moved toward her, and she almost jumped, but he spoke again, quietly but with an authority that made her catch her breath.

"Hold still!"

A second later he swept something off her shoulder, dashed it to the ground and stomped upon it.

Alexi felt a bit ill. She jumped to her feet, shaking out her hair. "What was it?"

"A brown widow."

"A what?"

"A brown widow. A spider. It wouldn't have killed you, but they hurt like hell and can make you sick."

"Oh, God!"

"Hey—there are spiderwebs all over this place. You know that."

Alexi stood still and swallowed. She lifted her hands calmly. "I can—I can handle spiders."

"You can."

"Certainly. Spiders and bugs and—even mice. And rats! I can handle it, really I can. Just so long as—"

"So long as what?"

She lowered her head and shook it, concealing her eyes from him. "Nothing." Snakes. She hated snakes. She simply wasn't about to tell him. "I'll be okay."

"Then why don't you sit again?"

"Because the pizza is coming. And because we really should eat in the kitchen. Don't you think?"

He grinned, his head slightly cocked, as he studied her. "Sure."

They moved back to the kitchen. The light there seemed very bright and cheerful, and Alexi had the wonderful feeling that no spider or other creature would dare show its face in this scrubbed and scoured spot.

"Why didn't you have the rest of the place kept up?" Alexi complained, sliding into a chair at the butcher-block table.

He sat across from her, arching a brow. "Excuse me. I kept just the kitchen up because Gene asked me to keep an eye on the place—and I'm not fond of sitting around with crawling creatures. If I'd known that the delicate face that launched ships would be appearing, I would have given more thought to the niceties."

"Very funny. I am tough, you know," she said indignantly.

"Sure."

"Oh, lock yourself in a closet."

"Such vile language!"

He was laughing at her, she knew. Tired as she was, Alexi was back on her feet, totally aggravated. "Trust me, Mr. Morrow—I can get to it! And I will do it. I'll make it here. You can warn me and threaten me, but I'm not leaving."

He lowered his head and idly rubbed his temple with his fingertips. She realized that he was laughing at her again. "I will, and you'll see."

"Listen, the closest you've probably been to a spider before is watching Spiderman on the Saturday-morning cartoons. You grew up with maids and gardeners and—"

"I see. You toiled and starved all those years to make your own money, so you know all about being rough and tough and surviving. You couldn't have starved too damn long.

You're what—? All of thirty-five now? They made a movie out of *Cat in the Night* ten years ago, so you weren't eating rice and potatoes all that long! And for your information, having money does not equate to sloth or stupidity or—"

"I never implied that you were stupid—"

"Or incapable or inept! I've damn well seen spiders before, and roaches and rats and—"

"Hey!" He came to his feet before her. A pity, she thought—it had been easier to rant and rave righteously when he had been sitting and she had been able to look down her nose at him. But now his hands were on her shoulders and he was smiling as he stared down at her and she knew that he was silently laughing again.

"No one likes things crawling on her—or him. And let's face it—you can't be accustomed to such shabby conditions," he said.

His smile faded suddenly.

"Or," he added softly, "a different kind of creepy-crawly. Intruders in the place."

"Oh!" She had forgotten all about the footsteps. Forgotten that someone had been in the house. That he or she or they had escaped when the lights had gone out and blackness had descended.

She backed away from Rex. "What...what do you think was...going on?"

Rex shrugged and grimaced. "Alexi, if—and I'm sorry, I do mean if—someone was in the house, I don't know. A tramp, a derelict, a burglar—"

"All the way out here?"

"Hey, they deliver pizza, don't they?"

"Do they? The pizza hasn't even gotten here yet!"

"Well, I'm sorry! It is a drive for the delivery man, you know. He isn't a block away on Madison Avenue."

"Oh, would you please stop it? We are not in the Amazon wilds."

"No, but close enough," Rex promised her good-naturedly. She stared at him with a good dose of malice. Then she nearly jumped, and she did let out a gasp, because the night was suddenly filled with an obnoxious sound, loud and blaring.

"Joe's boy's horn." Rex lifted his hands palm up. "It plays Dixie."

It did, indeed. Loudly.

"I'll get the pizza," he told her.

Still smiling—with his annoying superiority—Rex went out. Alexi followed him.

Joe's boy drove a large pickup. He was a cute, long-haired kid, tall and lanky. By the time Alexi came down the walkway, Rex was already holding the pizza and involved in a casual conversation.

"Oh, here she is."

"Wow!" the boy said. He straightened, pushed back his long blond hair and put out his hand to shake her hand soundly. "The Helen of Troy lady! Boy, oh, boy, ma'am, when I see that ad with your hair all wild and your eyes all sexy and your arms going out while you're smiling that smile, I just get...well, I get—"

"Um, thanks," Alexi said dryly. She felt Rex staring at her. Maybe he had expected her to be like the woman in the ad. He was probably disappointed to discover she was quite ordinary. "The magic of cameras," she murmured.

"Oh, no, ma'am, you're better in the flesh!" He blushed furiously. "Well, I didn't mean flesh—" he stammered.

"I don't think she took any offense, Dusty," Rex drawled. "Well, thanks again for coming out. Oh, Alexi, Dusty wants your autograph."

"Mine?"

He lifted his hands innocently. "He already has mine."

She gave Dusty a brilliant smile—with only a hint of malice toward Rex.

"Dusty, if you don't mind waiting a day or two, I'll get my agent to send down some pictures and I'll autograph one to you."

"Would you? Wow. Oh, wow. Could you write something... kind of personal on it? The guys would sure be impressed!"

"With pleasure," she promised sweetly.

"Wow. Oh, wow."

Dusty kept repeating those words as he climbed into the cab of his truck. Alexi cheerfully waved until the truck disappeared into the night. She felt Rex staring at her again, and she turned to him, a cool question in her eyes.

"Well," he said smoothly, "you've certainly wired up that poor boy's libido."

"Have I? Shall I take the pizza?"

"No, my dear little heartbreaker. I can handle it."

He started back toward the house. Alexi followed him. To her surprise, she discovered herself suddenly enjoying the night. She felt revived and ready for battle.

But there was to be no battle—not that night.

Rex went through the hall to the kitchen and put the pizza box on the table. "There's a bolt on the wood door to the parlor. If you just slide it, you can be sure that no one will come in by way of the window you broke. It was probably just some tramp who thought the house was unoccupied, but I'd bolt that door anyway. You can get the window fixed in the morning. You should have done it today."

"You're leaving?"

He nodded and walked to where she stood by the door, pausing just short of touching her. He placed a hand against the doorframe and leaned toward her, a wry grin set in the full, sensual contours of his mouth.

"You're playing a bit of havoc with my libido, too." He pushed away from the wall. "If you should need me, the number is in the book by the phone. Good night."

For some reason, she couldn't respond. She felt as if he had touched her . . . as if some intimacy had passed between them.

Nothing had happened at all.

By the time she could move, he was gone. She heard the front door quietly closing.

She hurried to it, biting her lower lip as she prepared to lock the door for the night. She was still so uneasy. Rex's being there had given her a certain courage. She knew that someone had been in the house. Had he really left? Was there, perhaps, some nook or cranny where the intruder could be hiding?

She gasped. There was another tapping at the door. Her fingers froze; she couldn't bring herself to answer it.

"Alexi?"

It was Rex. She threw the door open and prayed that he wouldn't hear the pounding of her heart.

"Rex," she murmured. She lowered her face quickly, trying to hide her relief, trying not to show the sheer joy she felt at seeing him again. "Um, did you forget something?"

"Yes."

He leaned against the doorframe, his hands in the pockets of his jeans. He studied her for the longest time, and then he sighed.

"You're making me absolutely insane, you know."

"I beg your pardon," she murmured.

He shook his head ruefully, then straightened. He placed his hands on her shoulders and pushed her into the hallway to allow himself room to enter. Wide-eyed, Alexi stared up at him.

"I'm staying!" he seemed to growl.

"You're what?" she whispered.

"I'll stay."

"You—you don't need to."

He shook his head impatiently. "I'll curl up in the parlor. Since you haven't gotten the guest rooms prepared yet," he added dryly.

"Rex . . . you don't have to."

"Yes, I have to." He started for the parlor.

"You should at least have some pizza!"

"No. No, thanks. I should lie down and go to sleep as quickly as possible."

"Rex—"

"Alexi—dammit! I—" He cut himself off, his jaw twisting into a rigid line. He shook his head again and walked into the parlor. She heard the door slam. Hard.

Alexi retreated to the kitchen. She leaned against the door and breathed deeply. He was going to sleep in her house. She shouldn't make him do it. She shouldn't allow him to do it.

She trembled. She couldn't help it. She was very, very glad that he was just a few feet away.

4

Even though she knew Rex was in the house—or perhaps because she knew Rex was in the house—Alexi spent a miserable night.

The kitchen floor was still a horrible bed; she swore to herself that she would get going on the house. When she first dozed off she nearly screamed herself awake, dreaming of a giant brown widow. She hadn't even known that "widows" came in "brown"—but she didn't want to meet another one.

Having woken herself up, she ate some of the pizza. Rex, bleary-eyed and rumpled, stumbled in, and at last they shared some of the pizza. When he returned to the parlor, she determined to settle down to sleep again. More dreams and nightmares plagued her. Disconcerting, disconnected nightmares in which men and women in antebellum dress swirled through the ballroom, laughing, chatting, talking. Beautiful people in silks and satins and velvets—but the dancers were transparent and the ballroom retained its dust and webbed decay. The only man with substance in her dreams was Rex Morrow—darkly handsome and somewhat diabolical, but totally compelling as he grinned wickedly and pointed in silence to the portraits of Pierre and Eugenia on the wall. She kept trying to reach him through the translucent dancers. She didn't know why, only that she needed to, and the more time that passed, the more desperate she became. Then, at the end, a giant brown spider with

John's face pounced down between them and Alexi gasped and sprang up—and came awake, swearing softly as she realized a warm sun was spilling brilliantly through the windows.

She put coffee on and went in search of Rex, only to find the sofa empty, with a note where his body should have lain.

Gone home to bathe, shave and work. Checked on you—you were sleeping like a little lamb. Well, a sexy little lamb. Libido, you know. It's light and all seems well. Fix the window today, dammit! If you need anything, give me a ring. I'll be here.

So he was gone. Funny... she had been looking forward to seeing him. To sharing coffee. To laughing at her fears by the morning's light. She smiled, remembering how they had shared cold pizza. Neither of them had really been awake. She could barely remember anything they had said. She'd liked his cheeks looking a little scruffy; she'd liked all that dark hair of his in a mess over his forehead.

Well, Rex probably wouldn't be the same by daylight, either. He'd be hostile, annoyed, superior, doing that eccentric artist bit all over again. She swore that the next time she saw him she'd be in control. Competent, able—fearless.

Oh, yeah! But she had to get started.

Definitely. She had to do something here, she warned herself. When her dreams began to include shades of *The Fly*, she was falling into the realm of serious trouble.

By morning's light she was able to roam around the lower level of the house. The place appeared even shabbier.

"Steam cleaners will make a world of difference," she promised herself out loud.

Still hesitant of the creepy-crawly possibilities, she kept her suitcase in the kitchen. When the coffee had perked, she poured herself a cup and sipped it while she opened her suitcase. It tasted good. Delicious. But not even the dose of caffeine really helped her mood. Her extended-wear contact lenses weren't "extending" very well—her vision was all blurry, and she swore softly again, wishing she could wear them with comfort and ease. She peered at her watch. It was only eight. She'd take a long shower, then remove her contacts, clean them and put them back in.

Alexi found her white terry robe, finished her coffee and considered exploring the upstairs for a bedroom and bath. Then, deciding that she would tackle the upstairs after she was dressed, she called and asked the steam cleaners in town to come out. Once they were finished, she would start vacuuming and sweeping and choose a room for herself. She really wasn't afraid of a few spiders and bugs—she just wanted to be a bit more fortified to deal with them.

So, determined, she grabbed her robe and headed for the little powder room beneath the stairs. She had noticed the night before that it did have a small shower stall. In fact, the little bathroom was really quite nice—tiled in soft mauve, with a darker purple-and-gold-lined wallpaper. Gene must have had it updated fairly recently.

Alexi turned on the light and grimaced at her reflection in the mirror over the sink. There were purple shadows beneath her red-rimmed eyes. She certainly didn't look one bit like the Helen of Troy lady. She was pale and drawn and resembled a wide-eyed, frightened child. She pinched her cheeks, then laughed, because she hadn't given them any color at all. She reflected a bit wryly that the only real beauty to her face lay in its shape; it was what was called a classical oval, with nice high cheekbones. John had told her once that a myriad of sins could be forgiven if one's cheekbones were good.

She laughed suddenly; she looked like hell, cheekbones or no.

"Tonight," she promised her reflection out loud, "I am going to sleep!"

Sobering, she turned away from her image and stripped off her clothing; there were a million things she wanted to do that day. Clean, clean, clean. And Rex was supposed to be bringing a new hose for the car. She also wanted a stereo system and a television—modern amenities that had never interested Gene.

Alexi stepped into the little shower stall, surprised and pleased to see the modern shower-massage fixtures. She fiddled with the faucets, gasped as the water streamed out stone-cold, swore softly—then breathed a sigh of relief as heat came into the water. For several long, delighted moments she just stood there, feeling the delicious little needles of wet heat sear her skin. Steam rose all around her, and she closed her eyes, enjoying it. The shower felt so good, in fact, that everything began to look better. The Brandywine house was beautiful. A little elbow grease and she could make it into a showplace again. Gene had really done quite a bit already; the kitchen was warm and nice, and this little bathroom was just fine. Of course, she could see all sorts of possibilities. The kitchen could use a window seat, a big one, with plump, comfortable cushions. Some copper implements, some plants. It was a huge room and could be made into an exquisite family center.

Alexi reached for the shampoo, scrubbed it into her hair and rinsed it. She paused then, reflecting that she really did mean to get things together.

She really couldn't wait to ask Rex in for a drink or a cup of coffee once she had things straightened out. I wonder why, she thought as the water beat against her face. Because, she reasoned, everything had gone wrong every time she'd seen him. She just wanted something to go right.

As she stood there, a little curl, warm and shimmering, began to wind in her stomach. She inhaled and exhaled quickly, alarmed at the realization that she wanted to see him again . . . just because she wanted to see him again. She was eager to hear the tone of his voice; she felt secure and comfortable when he was near.

It was a foolish feeling. She didn't want any entanglements; she didn't think she was really even *capable* of an entanglement. But the feeling was there, an ache, a nostalgia, poignant and sweet. She wanted to see him. No . . . he didn't even want her in the house. He wanted the land all to himself. He saw her as an intrusion on his privacy. But she couldn't help it; she found herself wondering about his relationships with other women. He had been blunt about his divorce, more cold than bitter. Yet she knew that his marriage had left a taste of ash in his mouth. Still, having met him . . . having experienced that strange feeling of intimacy on the first night, she started to shiver again.

She couldn't imagine him being alone, either. He was a man who liked women, who would attract them easily—with or without fame and fortune. But once burned . . . She knew the feeling well. He was quiet in his way; he spoke plainly but gave away very little emotion.

Maybe it wasn't there to give.

But she had been determined to come into the shower and scrub her hair and herself and be as . . . perfect as she could be. For when she saw him again. She didn't want to be breaking in; she didn't want to be running because she'd blown a hose in the car. She wanted to be composed and poised. Perhaps even cool . . . cool enough to regain the control that seemed to be slipping from her.

Alexi sighed and turned off the shower. She had steamed herself until the water had gone cold as she'd thought about Rex Morrow. If she could put that much concentration into the house, she'd have it a showplace in no time.

Alexi opened the shower door and groped for her towel. She found it and patted her face, blinking to clear her eyes.

The mist from the shower should have cleaned her lenses somewhat, but they felt grittier than ever. It must have been all the dust from last night, she reasoned.

She started to step out of the stall, then noticed a curious dark line on the floor. A wire? She blinked, wishing again that she had better luck with her lenses. There shouldn't be a wire on the floor.

Nor did wires move by themselves.

Alexi gasped, hypnotized at first. There was something on the floor about a foot long and as thick as a telephone wire. Except that the top of this wire was rising and moving, and it had a little red ribbon of color right under the . . .

The head!

"Oh, my God!" she breathed aloud.

It was a snake—a small one, but a snake nonetheless, slithering, slinking across the bathroom floor.

Her throat constricted; she didn't move. She didn't know whether the snake was poisonous or not, and at that point it didn't really matter. She hated snakes; they scared her to death.

The creature paused, raised its head again, then started slithering toward the toilet bowl.

She swallowed. She had to move.

Trembling, Alexi reached out for her robe. Soaking wet, she slipped into it and belted it, still standing in the shower stall—and barely blinking as she kept her eyes trained on the snake. In desperation she looked around the little bathroom. A little tile side pocket in the wall held a magazine. Alexi grabbed it and rolled it up.

Panicked thoughts whirled through her mind. If she didn't kill it on the first swipe, would it bite her? She could just run. . . .

No. Because if it slithered out of sight, she would never, never be able to sleep in the house again.

She stepped from the shower stall with her rolled-up weapon. She inhaled sharply, then smacked the snake. She jumped back, screaming. The blow hadn't stopped the creature in the least. It was just writhing and slinking more wildly now.

She attacked again—and again. Somewhere in her mind she realized that paper would not kill the serpent. It might not be big, but it had a tough hide.

Finally, though, the thing stopped. Or almost stopped. She had most of the body smashed against the base of the toilet. Only the head wavered a bit.

She swallowed sickly. What was the damn thing doing in her house? She felt like a torturer—but she was terrified.

Alexi dropped the paper. She had to get something. A spade—something with which she could scoop the creature up and out.

And kill it. It wasn't dead—and even though it was a snake, she hated to think of herself torturing the thing.

She backed away, then ran—into the kitchen and into the pantry. She wasn't sure what lay in the bottom shelves, but she had seen a number of tools there.

She found a heavy spade. Armed with it, Alexi made her way back to the bathroom, where she stopped dead still. The snake had disappeared.

"It couldn't have, it couldn't have," she whispered aloud, leaning against the wall. But it had.

She searched the bathroom, the floor, the shower stall. But there was no snake. She began to wonder if she had imagined the creature. Had the night been so bad that she had gone a little crazy? She didn't like spiders and bugs, but she could tolerate them. She was terrified of snakes, though. She had almost told Rex Morrow so last night after he had killed the spider.

Calm yourself, calm yourself. She tried to think rationally. She had seen the creature. And now it was gone. She drew in a deep breath. Had it been poisonous? What had it looked like? She was going to have to find out. She'd have to ask. She'd have to...

"Argh!" A gasping, desperate sound escaped her as she felt something slither over her foot. She looked down in terror. It was the snake.

She had her spade. She screamed, jumped—and slammed it down.

She dropped the spade, leaving the snake pinned beneath it, and backed away. Nearing the kitchen door, she turned.

Only to see another of the foot-long blackish creatures.

Sweat broke out all over her. Shaking, Alexi wrenched open the kitchen door and ran to the pantry again. She found a pipe wrench and raced back into the hallway. She swung the wrench down with force, careless of what she might do to the fine wooden floor.

She wasn't about to pick up the spade or the pipe wrench. She burst into the parlor instead. With trembling fingers she found Rex Morrow's phone number and dialed it.

"C'mon, c'mon, c'mon, c'mon...!" she muttered as the phone rang. When she heard Rex's voice on the other end, she started to speak, then realized it was an answering machine. He didn't identify himself by name; in a deep, pleasant voice said merely, "I can't get to the phone right now, but if you'll leave your name and number at the sound of the beep, I'll get back to you as soon as possible."

Alexi waited for the beep. "Rex, it's Alexi. Rex—" Her eyes widened, and she broke off with a long scream. There was another one! Another one, coming into the parlor!

She dropped the phone and raced to the fireplace. Grabbing the poker, she went for the snake.

She got it. Or at least got it pinned beneath the poker.

She had to get out. Just for a minute; just to breathe. Her hair was soaking wet, she was barefoot, and her robe was hardly even belted, but she had to get out.

Tears stinging her eyes, she raced for the front door. By the time she got the stubborn bolt to work, she was crying in great, gulping sobs.

She flung the door open and went running out and down the path, right into a pair of strong arms.

"Alexi!"

She screamed in panic at the feel of the strong fingers tight around her shoulders. Everything that touched her had become a snake, and she couldn't see anything, as her face was crunched to his chest.

"Alexi! What is it? Oh, my God, what happened? Is someone in there? Did someone hurt you? Alexi!"

Somehow the fact that it was Rex filtered into her mind.

"Oh, Rex!" She grabbed his shirt, her fingers like talons as they dug in. She moved even closer to him, trembling.

He shook her gently.

"Dammit, Alexi, what the hell happened? Did someone attack you?"

She shook her head, unable to talk.

"Alexi!"

He caught her hands and gently unwound her fingers from their death clutch upon him. He held them between his own, then slipped his hand beneath her chin to raise her eyes to his. She saw the concern in them, the raw anxiety in the hardened twist of his jaw.

"I tried to call you—" she gasped out.

"I know, dammit, I know! I was there! I heard you scream, and I ran here as fast as I could. Alexi, what—"

"Oh, it was horrible, Rex!"

"What, Alexi, for God's sake! What?"

Her eyes were glazed, her lips were trembling, her whole body was shaking. She was deathly pale, terrified.

And she was beautiful. Not even his confusion and fear for her could block that fact. She was scrubbed and damp, and her hair was soaked, but she was beautiful. Her eyes were huge and as green as emeralds with their glazing of moisture. She was pure and glorious beneath the sun. Her scent was soft and dazzling, as soft as the pressure of her body against his. She was a barefoot waif in a white robe, and he was painfully aware that she wore nothing beneath it.

And she called on everything primitive within him. He wanted to go out and do battle for her. He wanted to sweep her into his arms, hold her to his heart and swear that things would be okay. And he wanted, with a throbbing intensity, to take her away with him, away from any horror, and make love to her. To tear away that slim barrier of terry and drown in the soft, feminine scent of her.

"Alexi!"

He shook himself, mentally, physically. There could be some horrible, stark danger at hand, and he was nearly as mesmerized as she, shuddering with the hot pulse that rent a savage path throughout his body.

"Rex! Rex! They—they..."

"They—who?" he shouted.

"Sna—" She had to pause to wet her lips. "Snakes!"

"Snakes?" he queried skeptically, looking at her as if she had lost her mind.

His tone returned some of her sanity to her. "Snakes!" she yelled back. "Slithery, slimy, creeping creatures! Snakes."

"Where?"

"In the house!"

She was still trembling, but much less. He himself was shaking now, with emotion and with a growing anger. He'd half killed himself to reach her, terrified that a murder was afoot, and she was babbling along about snakes.

The glaze was gone from her eyes. They were still a deep emerald green, but she was angry, too. He set her from himself and strode quickly up the path to the house.

Well, Rex quickly discovered, she hadn't been lying. The house looked like a scene from a macabre murder mystery. Pipe wrench, spade, fire poker. A smile curving his lips, Rex walked up to the first of the victims in the hallway.

It was just a little ringneck, not even a foot long. It was still wobbling pathetically. Rex picked it up carefully and decided the creature still had a chance. He returned to the doorway and tossed the snake into a row of crotons that rimmed the front porch. Alexi, standing further down the path, stared at him incredulously.

"Alexi, it's just a ringneck."

"It's a snake!"

Rex frowned. "You shouldn't have tried to kill it; you should have just swept it out."

"It! There's a litter in there!"

He laughed. "Them."

"Don't you dare make fun of me! They could have been poisonous, and I wouldn't have known one way or the other. You do have poisonous snakes in the state, I take it?"

"Yes, we do have poisonous snakes. And I'm sorry. You're right; you wouldn't know. But these guys are harmless. They're actually good. They eat bugs. They till the soil. You should have just swept them all out."

"Fine!" she retorted. "They're welcome to be in the soil! But not in the house!" She was still shaking, he noted. "I'm not going back in! There are more, Rex! I have to get an exterminator. Today!"

He couldn't help it; he started laughing. She drew herself very, very straight and stared at him coldly. He raised his hands in the air.

"All right, all right. I'll see if I can rescue any of your other victims, then we'll go over to my house. It might be a good idea to get an exterminator."

Rex went back into the house, shaking his head at each "scene of the crime." The snakes were still alive—they were tough little creatures. He collected them in the spade and dropped them into the bushes. Alexi was still standing on the path. His brow arched, he waved to her, then went back inside and searched. He couldn't find any more of the ringnecks.

After putting her murder weapons away in the pantry, he paused, noting that her suitcase was on the kitchen table. He probably should take it for her, he thought.

He smiled slowly thinking, Uh-uh. After all, she had probably taken ten years off his life when she had screamed like that over the phone and then dropped the damn thing! He'd had horrible visions of a man's hands around her throat—and it had all been over a few harmless garden snakes!

Uh-uh. She was coming to his house now—because she was scared. With a streak of mischief, Rex determined that this was going to be a come-as-you-are party.

Still smiling, he closed the kitchen door. He had his own key to lock up the front.

He walked down the path, not sure if he wanted to strangle her himself... or take the chance of touching her again. He did neither; he walked past her a few feet, realized that she wasn't following him and turned back impatiently.

"Are you coming?"

She looked from him to the house. It irritated him a bit that she made it seem like a choice between two terrible evils. But then, he'd been irritated since he had met her. He'd thought that she was a sneak thief at first. Then she'd been so indignant. Aloof, remote—and condemning. Then she'd turned on the charm for the poor kid with the pizza, and he'd felt the allure of it sweep over him, a draw like a potent elixir. And then he'd felt such acute terror...

Then such acute desire. Feeling her nearly naked, crawling against him, almost a part of him. He wondered vaguely if she had any idea just what she had done to him. She was

so sensual, his reaction was instant. And he didn't like it.
Dammit, he was a cynic. He deserved to be. His marriage
had taught him a good lesson.

Especially when the female in question was Alexi Jordan. "Alexi," he began crossly, wishing Gene's great-
granddaughter could have been someone else. "You can always just go back in and—"

"No!" Ashen, she ran to catch up with him. Gasping a
little, she tugged at her loosening belt. Rex turned forward,
a slightly malicious grin tugging at the corners of his mouth.
But it was also a wry smile. He wasn't sure whom he was
tormenting in his subtle way: her—or himself. He should
have been cool; he shouldn't have cared. Life ought to have
taught him a few good lessons. But she got to him. She had
crawled instantly into his system and more slowly into his
soul, and he felt damned already.

"Where is your house?" she asked him.

"Just ahead," he replied curtly. He realized that she was
panting in her effort to keep up with him, but he didn't slow
down. "This isn't a big spit of land. Your house... Gene's
house," he said, correcting himself, "is first. Mine is just
past the bend."

Alexi looked around. By daylight, it seemed very wild and
primitive to her, barren in its way. Right around the house,
plants grew beautifully. There were tall oaks and pines, the
colorful crotons and a spray of begonias. Out on the road,
though, the terrain became sandy; there was scrub grass and
an occasional pine. In the distance, toward the water, sea
grapes covered the horizon.

They made a left turn. There was only one other man-
made structure on the peninsula. Rex's house. Like hers, it
was Victorian. The porch that ran around the upper level
was decorated with gingerbread. The house was freshly
painted in a muted peach shade and seemed a serene part of
the landscape. Also like her house, it seemed to sit up a bit

from the low, sandy turf that surrounded it. Right beyond it, she knew, was the Atlantic. She could hear the surf even as they approached it. There was a draw, warm and inviting, to the sound of the waves, she mused. Alexi bit her lip, thinking that she was crazy, that she wanted to be anywhere but here. But then again, there was no way she was going to go back into a house with snakes.

A sudden stab of sharp pain seared into her foot. She swore and stopped. Trying to balance on her right foot to see the left one, she started to keel over.

Rex caught her arm, steadying her. "What did you do?" he asked.

"I don't know..." she began, but then she saw the trail of blood streaming from her sole.

"Must have been a broken shell," he said, in a voice that seemed just a bit apologetic. As if he had just realized that he had been moving as if in a marathon race while she had been barefoot, Alexi thought.

"It's all right," she murmured. "I can manage."

"Don't be absurd," he said impatiently. "You get too much sand in it and you'll have a real infection."

Before she could protest, he swept her into his arms. Out of a will to survive the rest of his breakneck-speed walk, she slipped her arms around his neck, flushing. "Really, I..."

"Oh, for Pete's sake."

Alexi fell silent. Maybe she would have been better off with the snakes after all. The sun was beating down on them both, but she wasn't at all convinced it was the sun that was warming her. He was hot, like molten steel. His chest was hard and fascinating; the feel of his arms about her was electric. She could feel his breathing, as well as each little ripple and nuance of his muscles, hard and trim, but living and mobile, too. She swallowed, because the temptation to touch was great. It was pure instinct, and she fought it. In fact, she hated instinct. He was probably annoyed that she

might be thinking that being in his arms was more than it
was....

And she couldn't quite fight that damned instinct, that
feeling that he was everything wonderful and good about the
male of the species, that the sun was warm, the surf inviting. That she wanted to touch all that taut muscle and flesh
and that it might well be the most natural thing in the world
to lie with him in the sand.

So much for being perfect! So much for being cool and
aloof and completely in control! She thought of when she
had been in the shower, where she'd dreamed of her next
meeting with him. And here she was—cool, remote and
dignified. Hah! She looked like hell again. Barefoot, with
not a shred of makeup, her hair soaking wet, and dressed in
nothing but a robe. And it wasn't just the miserable indig-
nity of how she looked. She'd been hysterical at first, and
she wasn't doing much better now. No wonder he wanted
her out; she was nothing but trouble to him. Of course, he
had been there when she'd needed him. And sometimes,
when he looked at her, he was so very masculine and sexual
that she was certain she must appeal to him in some sense.
He was rude, but he could also be kind.

He had been very frank in saying that he wanted the
house, that he wanted her out—but he had still helped her.
Of course, he had tried to scare her last night, too. All that
ridiculous bit about ghosts.

She paled in his arms, feeling ill. He'd brushed the spider
off her and killed it. And she had almost told him how
frightened she was of snakes. She had almost said the word.
He had pressed her.

He had known. Known that she didn't like the bugs, but
that she could bear them. He was intuitive; he was quick. He
wanted her out...

She gasped suddenly, released her hold about his neck and
slammed a tight fist against his chest.

"Hey—" Startled and furious, he stared down at her.

"You bastard!"

"What?"

"You did it! You knew I was terrified of snakes! You put them in there. Here I thought that you were being decent. You did it! You put me down, you—"

She didn't go any further, because he did put her down. In fact, he almost dropped her, then stood above her with a dark scowl knit into his features, his hands locked aggressively on his hips.

"I did no such damn thing!"

"You knew—"

"I didn't know anything, Ms. Jordan. And trust me, lady, I don't have the time to go digging up a pack of harmless little ringnecks just to get to you. You don't need help to blow it—I'm sure you'll manage on your own."

"Oh! You stupid—" She had tried to rise, but the weight on her foot was an agonizing pain. She broke off, gasping against the pain, teetering dangerously. He stretched an arm out; she tried to push him away, but as she started to fall she grabbed at him desperately.

Rex, unprepared, lost his balance, too. They crashed down into the sand together.

In a most compromising position. He was nearly stretched on top of her. And her robe...

Was nearly pushed to her waist.

And they were both aware of the position. Very painfully aware. Alexi couldn't think of a word to say; she couldn't move. She could only stare, stunned and miserable, into the hard, dark eyes above her. It seemed like an eternity in which she felt her naked body pressed to him, an eternity in which she felt all his muscles contract and harden.

An eternity...while she wished that she could be swallowed up by the sand.

Abruptly he pushed himself away from her. With supple agility, he landed on the balls of his feet. Blushing furiously, Alexi pushed her robe down.

"Damn you!" he said angrily. "Now, this time you just keep quiet! Throw out your accusations once we're there."

His arms streaked out for her so fast that she almost shrieked, afraid for a second that he meant violence. He picked her up again, his arms as rigid as pokers, shaking with anger. He started off again, his pace faster than ever.

He walked her up the steps to the porch, threw open the screen door and carried her inside. He turned almost instantly to the left, to the parlor. Seconds later she was deposited roughly upon a couch that was covered in soft beige leather. She scrambled to right herself, to pull her robe down around her knees.

"Don't move!" he warned her sharply. She tried miserably to relax. She made herself breathe slowly in and out as she looked at her surroundings. It was a nice room. Contemporary. The soft leather sofa sat across the width of a llama-skin rug from two armchairs, all on warm earthen tile. A deer head sat over the mantel, and a wall of arched windows looked out on the sea below. Her house and his were similar in construction, but here two rooms had been combined to make one huge one. To the rear, bookshelves lined the walls, and there were two long oak desks angled together with a computer-and-printer setup. She imagined that Rex must like his view of the sea very much. He could work, then stop and walk to the windows to watch the endless surf and the way the sun played over the water.

She tried not to imagine Rex at all.

And then he was back.

He had a bowl of water and a little box, and he sat by her on the sofa without a word, pulling her foot up onto his lap. His dark hair fell over his forehead; she couldn't see his eyes.

He moved quickly and competently, not apologizing or saying a word when she winced as he washed off her foot.

"Shell . . . it was still there," he said at last. She didn't reply, but bit her lip. He wasn't big on TLC, she mused wryly.

He opened the little box and sprayed something on her foot, then wrapped it in a gauze bandage. He moved back, dumping her foot less than graciously on the sofa. He stood, picked up the bowl and the box and disappeared again. The pain, which had been sharp, began to fade, and she wondered distractedly what he had sprayed on it. She felt like a fool. She realized that he most probably had not dug around in the ground to find a pack of snakes to set loose in her bathroom. Snakes. It was just the damn snakes. Anything else she could surely have dealt with. . . .

She'd been half-naked. He'd known it; she'd known it. And they'd both felt the hard, erotic flow of heat. Where was he? She had to get out of here. Her palms began to sweat. She couldn't go back if there were more snakes. But she couldn't stay away forever. She couldn't stay on his couch, barely dressed. . . .

Then he was back. He set a steaming mug on a small side table beside her, then walked across to sit in one of the chairs, staring at her. With hostility, she was certain. He had his own mug of steaming liquid, and sipped it broodingly.

Alexi tried to sit properly. She had to moisten her lips to speak. "Rex, I'm sorry. Perhaps—"

"Drink the coffee. It's spiked. It will help."

"I doubt it—"

"It's sure as hell helping me."

She didn't know why; she picked up the coffee cup. She didn't know what it was laced with, but it was good, and it was strong. It warmed her hands and her throat, and it did help.

"I—" she began.

"The exterminators don't really do snakes," he told her dryly, "but they're coming out. I talked to a guy who said that they were probably just washed up by the rain and came through the broken window. When they finish, you won't have anything else. No spiders, no bugs. And a friend of mine from Ace GlassWorks will be out this afternoon to fix that window. His sister manages a cleaning outfit, and they'll be out, too. They do the works—sweep, wash and steam-clean. You should be in business then."

"Rex, thank you, but really—"

"You've got objections?"

"No, dammit, but really, it's my responsibility—" She broke off, frowning. She could hear the front door opening. Rex heard it, too. His brow knit, and he started to rise. Then he sat back.

"Who is that?" Alexi asked.

But by that time the woman was already in. "Rex?" She came into the parlor, carrying a bag of groceries. Trim and pretty, she looked to Alexi to be approximately fifty. There was an immense German shepherd at her heels; the dog instantly rushed to Rex, barking, greeting him.

The woman stared uncomfortably at Alexi, who sat there in a robe and nothing else, curled on the couch, the coffee cup in her hands.

The woman blushed.

Rex smiled. "Emily, hi. I forgot you were coming this morning." He stood. The dog sat by his chair, panting, and woofing at Alexi.

"Shush, Samson. That's Alexi. She's a . . . friend. Alexi, this is Emily Rider. Emily, Alexi Jordan. Emily keeps everything in order for me."

"How do you do," Alexi said, wishing she could scratch Rex's eyes out. "I—I cut my foot."

"Oh," Emily said in disbelief. She smiled awkwardly, then gasped. "*The* Alexi Jordan?"

"There's only one," Rex said. "I hope."

"It's—it's a pleasure," Emily murmured. "I didn't mean to interrupt."

"There's nothing to interrupt!" Alexi said quickly—too quickly, she realized, for a woman who was sitting in her robe on a man's couch.

"Ah, well... have you had breakfast? I make wonderful omelets, Ms. Jordan."

"Really," Alexi protested. "Please don't go to any trouble—"

"No trouble at all!" Emily insisted. It was obvious to Alexi that the woman was dying to escape.

"Thanks, Emily," Rex called. Samson whined. Rex sat again, watching Alexi as he scratched the dog's head. "That is a most glorious shade of red," he told Alexi.

"What?"

"Your skin."

She whispered an oath to him.

He stood, still smiling. Samson trailed along with him, loyal and loving.

"Emily might need some help," he said.

Alexi rose carefully on one foot, using the couch for balance.

"Tell her the truth! She thinks that..."

"That what?"

"That I—that we—that we were sleeping together!"

"I suppose she does."

"Well, set her straight! Do you want her to think that?"

Rex chuckled softly. He cupped her cheek for an instant; the warmth of his breath feathered over her flesh. "Why not?"

"Why not?" Alexi echoed furiously.

"Doesn't every man fantasize about sleeping with the face that launched a thousand ships?" His brow was arched; he was mocking her, she was certain.

"Rex, damn you—"

"Of course, Alexi, there's much, much more to you than a beautiful face—isn't there?"

Samson barked; Rex walked out. Alexi, trembling, wanted to scream at him.

But she didn't want to scream with Emily there, so she sank weakly back to the sofa.

5

Emily was busy cracking eggs when Rex came into the kitchen. He walked over to the refrigerator and pulled out the milk for her, smiling as he set it on the counter. He had seen her watching him covertly as she pretended great interest in the eggs.

"She's cute, huh," he commented, stealing a strip of green pepper and leaning against the counter.

Emily arched a brow. "Alexi Jordan? All you have to say about her is 'cute'?"

"Real cute?"

Emily sniffed. "She's probably the most glamorous woman in the world—"

Rex broke in on her with soft laughter. "Emily! Glamorous? You just saw her with wet hair in a worn terry robe!"

"She's still glamorous."

"She's flesh and blood," Rex said irritably, wondering at the bitterness in his own tone. He wanted her to be real, an ordinary woman, he thought dismally.

"Nice flesh," Emily commented dryly, pouring the eggs into the frying pan.

"Very nice." He grinned.

"When did you meet?"

"A few nights ago."

"Oh."

Her lips were pursed in silent disapproval, and Rex couldn't help but laugh again and give her a quick hug.

"There's nothing going on, Emily. Alas, and woe is me—but that's the truth. She called over here this morning because her house was suddenly infested with snakes."

"Snakes?"

"Just some harmless ringnecks."

"How many?"

"Five."

Emily shuddered. "That poor creature! Well, you were right to bring her over here. I wonder if she should stay the night."

"I'd just love it," Rex told her wickedly.

"I'll stay, too, Casanova," Emily warned him. When she saw that he was about to take another pepper, she rapped him on the hand with her wooden spoon.

"Emily...you're showing no respect to me at all."

She sniffed again. Emily had a great talent for sniffing, he thought with a smile.

"Well, Mr. Popularity, maybe this is just what you need. The lady is far more renowned than you."

"Oh, really?"

"She's glamorous. You're merely...notorious."

Rex laughed good-naturedly.

"And you're usually rude to women," she went on.

"I am not."

"You are. You had a bad break with your wife, and you think they're all after something. So you figure you'll just use people first—and not get hurt in the end."

He was grateful that Emily didn't see that his features had gone taut; she was busy adding ingredients to her omelet. She wouldn't have cared anyway; she loved him like a son and had no qualms about treating him like one.

"Emily, Emily, you should be opening an office instead of cooking and cleaning for me," he said coolly.

"Well, it's true," Emily murmured. "I've seen you do it a million times. Some sexy thing moves in and you're all charm. Then you get what you want—and you're bored silly when the chase is over. But you always win. You've got the looks; you've got the way with women." She turned, pointing her spoon at him. "But maybe you are in trouble this time. She has tons and tons of her own money, and..." Emily paused to grin. "She's prettier than you are, too."

"Thank you, doctor!" Rex retorted. "What makes you think I'm after her?"

"You're not?"

"I'm not half as black as you paint me," Rex said flatly. "I only deal with ladies who know the game—and are willing to play. By my rules."

"The rule being fun only."

"Emily, come on! Fine, I've been around; they've been around. What's so wrong?"

"What's wrong is that you're lacking caring and commitment, growing together—love!"

"Love is a four-letter word," Rex told her flatly. Then he paused, swinging around. He could have sworn he'd heard movement by the kitchen door. He strode toward it and got there just in time to see the figure clad in white hobbling across the hall toward the parlor. He followed, angry. He didn't like being spied upon.

She had almost reached the couch. He didn't let her make it; he caught her elbow. "Can't I help you, Ms. Jordan?"

She spun to look at him, her cheeks flaming. "I—"

"You were spying on me!"

"Don't be absurd! You're not worth spying on! I was trying to see if I could do something, but I realized that I had stumbled on a personal conversation and I didn't want to hear it!" She jerked her elbow away from him, lost her balance and crashed down onto the couch.

Rex didn't know why he was so enraged at her. He didn't move to help her; he just stared at her. "The thing to do would have been to make your presence known!"

"This is ridiculous!"

Her eyes really were emerald, he mused, especially when they glittered with righteous anger.

She squared her shoulders, undaunted by his wrath or his form, which was rather solidly before her. She managed to stand, shoving by him, limping out of his way. "This whole thing is ridiculous! Thank you—I really do thank you for picking up the snakes. But I think I'll go home now. The snakes, at least, have better manners!"

She really was going to try to stumble home by herself. She was already heading toward the door.

"Alexi!"

She just kept going.

"Alexi, dammit—" He came after her, caught an arm and swung her around. He knew she would have to clutch at him to maintain her balance. She did; she curled her fingers around his arms and swore softly under her breath, tossing back her head to stare at him. Her hair was drying and it was wild, he saw, a beautiful, disheveled golden mane to frame her exquisite eyes and perfect features. He inhaled sharply, remembering what it was like to feel her body. Fool, he chided himself. He knew why he was so angry. She had heard everything that Emily had said to him. Every damning thing.

And he wanted her. Really wanted her, as he had never wanted anything in his life.

"Alexi...I'm sorry." Apologies weren't easy for him. They never had been.

"And I'm leaving," she said.

He smiled. "Back to the snakes?"

She looked down fleetingly. "There are all kinds of snakes, aren't there, Mr. Morrow?"

He laughed. She had heard everything. "Look, Ms. Jordan, I really am sorry. Be forgiving. After all, you cost me

ten years of life with that scream this morning. Stay...
please."

She lowered her head. "I feel—ridiculous. Your house-
keeper must think that I'm—that I'm worse than what the
tabloids say. And I can't wear a robe all day..."

"You can take it off," Rex said innocently, which immediately drew a scathing glance from her.

He shook his head ruefully. "No... you can't take it off.
Look, sit down with Emily and have some breakfast. I'll go
back over for your things. Maybe the exterminators will be
there by now and I can get them started."

"You don't need to—"

"I want to. Relax. Enjoy Emily's company." He stepped
away from her and whistled. "Samson!" The German
shepherd came bounding in. He was huge, and when he
swept by Alexi, she teetered dangerously, trying to catch her
balance again. "Samson!" Rex chastised him, stepping
forward quickly to catch Alexi. He smelled the soft, alluring scent of her hair as he caught her; he felt its velvet tex-
ture graze his cheek. He wanted to swear all over again.

"You'd better stay seated," he muttered, lifting her
swiftly and depositing her upon the couch. Another mistake. He felt too much of her body. Too much smoothness
beneath the terry. Smoothness that reminded him that there
was nothing beneath it.

"I'll be back with your things," he said brusquely, then
strode out, the shepherd obediently at his heels.

He was barely gone before Emily came to the doorway,
smoothing her hands over her apron. She smiled shyly at
Alexi. "I have everything ready." She frowned. "Where's
Rex?"

"He—he went back over to my house. To Gene's house,"
Alexi said apologetically. She flushed again, wondering
what the woman must think of her. Rex Morrow—he was
like a cyclone in her life. She never knew what to think. One

moment she was fascinated; the next second she wanted to carve notches in his flesh...slowly. He was dangerous to her. To any woman, she thought, flushing all over again at the pieces of conversation she had heard. Oh, she couldn't be so foolish as to imagine having an affair with him. He was striking, sensual and sexual—and she was still reeling from the impact of her marriage. If there was anything she didn't need, it was an affair with someone like him.

Emily smiled at her suddenly; the smile was warm, shy, only slightly awkward.

"You really are beet red. I apologize if I gave you the idea that I was thinking...something...that I shouldn't have been thinking," she added hastily. "Rex told me about the snakes." She shuddered. "Ugh. I *know* they're harmless snakes—and I would have been in a tizzy, too, I assure you."

"Thanks," Alexi said, a little huskily. And before she really thought she murmured, "Rex told you—the truth?"

"Oh, he can be a pill, can't he?" She shook her head, but then it was clear to Alexi that Emily's affection for him rose to the fore. "But he's really very ethical." Emily laughed. "Honestly. He can be hard—but he does play up-front, and he's a strangely principled man. For this day and age, anyway," she added with a soft sigh. "Oh, here I am, going on and on, when your food is nice and hot. I'll bring it out—"

"Oh, no, please don't bother! I can get to the kitchen with no problem, really. I have to start walking. I have a lot of things to do."

"Let me help you."

Alexi protested; Emily insisted. They walked back to the kitchen, Alexi learning to put a little more weight on her foot with each movement.

Emily sat down with her, sharing the omelet that Rex had left behind. Alexi found out that Emily was a widow with four grown children. She also learned that Emily counted

Rex as an adopted fifth child—and adored him with a fierce loyalty.

There was something about Emily, she reflected. The woman was warm and open and giving, and Alexi found herself trying to explain what she wanted to do. It began when Emily asked her why on earth she would want to leave modeling.

Alexi smiled, then laughed. "It's a miserable profession, that's why. People poke at you and prod at you for hours for a 'perfect' look. It's hour after hour under hot lights doing the same thing over and over again. But still, it isn't really that I'm trying to leave modeling." She hesitated, smiled ruefully, and stumbled into a lengthier explanation. "It's strange; I did come from money. But there's always been a golden rule in the family: everyone goes to work. Gene, my great-grandfather, owns a number of businesses, and everyone does something. We aren't expected to go into a family business, but there can be no freeloaders. My older brother is a lawyer; my cousins went into the business side of things. But then, suddenly, when I came along, no one thought that... I don't know; they didn't seem to think I was capable of anything! I went to college and studied interior design, and they all thought, Well, great, she can marry the right boy and be a perfect wife, mother and hostess. It was serious to me." She sighed. "Anyway, I walked out in a huff one night and wound up in New York City. Broke. And I wasn't about to call home. None of the design studios wanted much to do with a beginner—and I didn't have the time to wait for a job. Out of desperation I walked into one of the modeling agencies. And I was lucky. I did get work."

"But you want to be a designer?"

Alexi chewed on her omelet, thought a minute, then shrugged. "I don't know anymore. I lost a lot of confidence somewhere. But..." She paused, a grin curling her lip. "Gene is great. He has always been willing to take a chance.

He was desperate for someone to come take care of the house—he doesn't want it out of the family after all of these years. And he believes in me. So I want to do the house for him, and I want to do it right.''

Emily nodded as if she understood perfectly. "And you will do it!" she said firmly.

Alexi laughed dryly. "I'm not so sure. Last night I couldn't get the old key to work in the lock. This morning I ran in terror from garden snakes. I'm not proving very much, am I? And now Rex is out there with the exterminators and cleaners."

Emily smiled and put her hand over Alexi's. "Young lady, that doesn't mean a thing. That's one of the problems with people today—men and women! All this role business! Alexi, you'll do just fine. So what if you don't handle snakes well? That does not take anything away from your competence. We all need help now and then, and if people could just learn not only to give it but to accept it, the world would be a better place. And the divorce rate would be lower!"

"I don't know," Alexi said, chuckling. "I feel like an idiot right now. But maybe things will improve." She cut off another piece of her omelet, feeling that maybe she had blurted out too much to a stranger, no matter how nice that stranger was.

"Emily, where did Samson come from? Is he Rex's dog or yours?"

"Oh, no! That beast belongs to Rex. Body and soul." She went on to tell Alexi about Samson as a little puppy, and Alexi relaxed, feeling that the conversation had taken on a much more casual tone.

Tony Martelli, from Bugs, Incorporated, was just driving up to the Brandywine house when Rex reached it. He gave Rex a wave and hopped out of his truck, smiling. Rex waved back, smiling in turn. He liked Tony. He was a live-

and-let-live kind of a guy. The man had a tendency to chew
on a toothpick or a piece of grass and to listen much more
than he talked. He gave Rex's house monthly service and
was one of the few people Rex had invited to wander his
beach when he had the chance.

"Snakes, huh?"

Rex laughed. "And everything else under the sun."

Tony squinted beneath the glare of the sun. "Well, we'll
spray, but snakes... Well, you kind of have to find the little guys and put them out." He scratched his head. "It
rained last night, but it wasn't really a flood. Wonder how
they got in."

"There was a broken window."

"Maybe." Tony shrugged. "It wouldn't be unheard-of,
but I find it kind of strange."

Rex frowned, remembering how Alexi had accused him
of putting the snakes into the house himself to scare her out.
She was convinced that someone had been in the house last
night. Maybe that same person had come back in after he
had left early this morning.

He walked up the path with Tony and opened the door.
Tony whistled. "How long has Gene been out of here?"

"Awhile. Nine months, maybe."

"Nine months of breeding bugs. Well, I'll spray her real
good. And I'll look out for a nest of ringnecks. I just doubt
it, though, you know? If they were in the house, Miz Jordan should have noticed them when she came in, not this
morning." He laughed suddenly, "I've heard of ghosts in
this place, but not snakes."

"Yeah." Rex laughed with Tony, but he wasn't amused.
Tony went out for his equipment. Rex went on into the parlor and called the sheriff's office. A friend of his—a bud-
ding story-teller named Mark Eliot—was on the desk. Rex
listened patiently to Mark's newest plot line, then told him

that he was pretty sure someone was sneaking around the Brandywine house.

"Anything broken into?" Mark asked.

"Well...only by the rightful tenant. She couldn't get her key to work," Rex explained. Then he told Mark about Alexi's hearing footsteps racing down the stairs—and about the snakes. He was annoyed when Mark chuckled.

"Snakes? You think somebody snuck in to leave a pack of ringnecks?"

"Never mind..."

"Sorry, Rex, sorry," Mark apologized quickly. "Want me to come out?"

"No, there's nothing you can do now. Maybe someone could make an extra patrol at night and keep an eye on things."

"Sure thing, Rex. Will do."

Rex hung up, wondering why he still didn't feel right about things. He heard a whining sound and felt a cold nose against his hand. He patted the dog absently; he had forgotten that Samson was with him. "You should have been here last night, monster," he told the dog affectionately. "You might have caught whoever ran. If there was a 'whoever.' Come on, boy. Let's get Alexi's stuff, huh?"

That didn't even seem to be such a good idea. In the kitchen, Rex began to close the open suitcase on the table; he hesitated. Everything of hers had a wonderful scent. Her clothes...

He picked up the soft silk blouse on top and brought it to his face. It seemed to whisper of her essence. He dropped it back into the suitcase and slammed the suitcase.

Samson stood by him, thumping his tail against the floor. "This is getting serious, Samson. Frightening. I barely know her."

How well did someone need to know a face that could launch a thousand ships?

He groaned out loud at the thought and picked up the suitcase. He found her purse in the parlor, called out to Tony that he would be right back and left the house. Ten minutes of brisk walking brought him back to his own.

To his own amazement, he didn't go in. He set Alexi's suitcase and purse inside the screen door, called out that he was dropping them off and turned around to walk back, Samson still at his heels.

His fingers were clenched into fists, braced behind his back. He knew he wouldn't go back that night. He'd give Emily a call and tell her that he would just stay at Gene's—making sure no more snakes appeared—and that he'd be back in the morning.

He just couldn't see Alexi Jordan again right away. It was still true that he barely knew her, and it was damned true that she was having an extraordinary effect on him. Unsettling. Insane.

The exterminator was just finishing up when Rex returned, and when Tony pulled out with his van, the cleaners were pulling in with theirs. Rex let them in with all their heavy-duty equipment, then went into the kitchen and heated up the remainder of the pizza, which he found in the refrigerator. He had it with a beer, reflecting that everything had suddenly turned into a sad state of affairs. He should have been working, and instead he was over here, hiding out from a blonde.

"Well, she is damned good-looking," he told Samson, stretching his legs out under the table. "The type that can seduce a guy and steal his soul, you say, Samson, boy? I agree, a hundred percent. I should stay away, huh? Hmm. Those eyes. With my luck, I'd be dumb enough to fall in love again. And she'd stay around for a month, then take off for the big city and her glamorous career. Aha!" He was silent for a minute, staring at the bottle. "I'll go nuts if I don't give it some good, sturdy effort." He sipped his beer reflectively. "But not until tomorrow. I'm not so sure I could take seeing her again today—take it and behave civilly. Okay, Samson, so I haven't been so civil so far. I'm supposed to be a rude eccentric. I have my reputation to live up to, you know."

Just then the phone started to ring. It was Emily, worried. He assured her things were going fine. "Just tell Alexi to stay there tonight and I'll stay here. The cleaners seem to be doing just fine; Tony sprayed, and I can still smell the stuff all over. It will be much better by tomorrow.... Okay, take care."

He hung up, and walked into the hall, his hands in his pockets. The cleaning crew consisted of four men. They all knew what they were doing; they moved economically and efficiently. The house already looked better, and they hadn't even started with the steaming. He wandered back to the kitchen, restless. This was rough. He didn't know what to do. He didn't really know how to be idle.

He stared out the window over the sink for a moment, then smiled. In the drawer was a legal pad. He drew it out and sat at the table again. He could make this work.

He sketched out a rough story line about a wealthy family with a suddenly deceased patriarch. A family that began to die off rather quickly. He used Gene's house, and his victims fell as the snakes had, by the same weapons Alexi had utilized.

Within ten minutes, his fingers were flying over the page. A studious frown knitted his brow, and time became meaningless. His concentration was complete.

But then he realized that his heroine looked exactly like Alexi.

And his hero was strangely similar to himself.

He sat back, then forward again.

Well, what the hell, he thought. Who was he to argue with creative forces?

He was planning an awful lot of sex scenes for a murder mystery, though, he reflected. He paused, then laughed dryly.

What the hell...

Alexi stared up at the sun through the swaying fronds of a huge palm. She closed her eyes, the sun was so bright. But the warmth felt good against her flesh.

She rolled on her beach sheet and stared out at the water. The surf curled in softly, then ebbed in near silence. It was beautiful. Exquisitely beautiful. From here, the Atlantic seemed to stretch away forever. The sky tenderly kissed the water. It was exquisitely peaceful and private. The sand was fine and white; the palms gave lovely shade.

She lay on her stomach, her chin cupped in her hands. She could even understand why Rex had seemed so aggrieved to discover that she was taking over the house. This was a paradise. Remote and exotic. Who would want intrusion?

She stretched and rolled onto her side again, idly drawing patterns in the sand.

Then, despite herself, she began to wonder if he came here often. Of course he did. Who wouldn't? The beach belonged to him. Not to both houses—to him.

He loved it, surely. His windows looked out over it. He probably walked over the sand all the time, possibly at sunset. At sunset, it would probably be even more beautiful. So very private.

And if he had a date...

He probably took her here. At sunset. He would hold hands with her, and they would walk along the sand. And maybe they would play where the water washed over the sand in a soft gurgle. Maybe she would laugh and spray him with water, and maybe he would retaliate and they would fall to the sand. They would make love with the water sliding over them, warm and exciting. Their clothing would lie strewn on the beach, but they really wouldn't need to worry; it was so private here. What would he look like...nude? Beautiful, she decided. He was so tall, broad-shouldered, lean where he should be, bronzed and so nicely, tightly sinewed.

"Hello."

Alexi gasped and whirled around. Instantly fire-red coloring flushed her cheeks.

It was Rex. Of course it was Rex—it was his beach. But she hadn't expected him here. She hadn't seen him since he'd dropped her suitcase on his hallway floor. That was almost two days ago. She still hadn't been back into her house; she'd been in his, and he in hers. Impatience had brought her to the beach. Impatience and frustration. The cleaners had stayed so late on Monday that she hadn't gone back, and on Tuesday he had told Emily that the fumes were still too strong for Alexi to be able to do anything worthwhile.

Alexi had been determined to go back anyway. Emily had convinced her to stay, telling her that she would do much better for herself in the next few days if she allowed her foot to heal properly. And, Emily had told her with a wink, Rex was working—he was too immersed to notice the fumes.

"I said 'Hello,' not 'Take your clothes off, please.' Do you have to look so horrified to see me?"

"I'm not," she said quickly. She was. She looked down to the sand, not sure how to explain that he had interrupted her when she was imagining *him* without his clothes.

Not that he was wearing much. He was in a pair of cutoffs—and what she could see was very near what she had imagined. His flesh was very bronze, very sleek. His shoulders and chest were hard and sinewed; his legs were long and his thighs powerful. Dark hair grew on his chest in a swirl that tapered into a soft line down to the waistband of his shorts. He wore a gold St. Christopher medal and a black-banded sports watch.

He sank down beside her. She felt his gaze move over her, and it touched her with greater warmth than the sun. Actually, she wasn't exactly cocooned in clothing herself. Her bathing suit was one-piece, but it had no back, and the cut was very high on the thighs. To her horror, she felt her heartbeat quicken. Surely he could see the throb of her pulse in a dozen different places.

"Must you?" she demanded huskily.

"Must I what?"

"Come out with all those things."

"What things?"

"About clothing. Or lack of them. Or sleeping with the Helen of Troy Lady."

He was silent for a moment, looking out to sea. He shrugged, then stared at her again. It took a lot of effort, but she finally lifted her eyes to his—and watched him as coolly as she could.

He smiled slowly, the curl of his lip very deliberate and sensual. "You were blushing before I opened my mouth."

"The sun—"

"Hah!"

Alexi threw her hands up. "Mr. Morrow, meet Ms. Jordan. How do you do? How do you do? Pleasant weather, isn't it? Lovely weather, really lovely. That, Mr. Morrow, is the type of conversation that people who have just met exchange!"

He laughed, leaning back on an elbow. "You're forgetting the way that we met."

"You mauled me."

"And I loved every minute of it."

"Would you stop?"

"If you want me to stop," he said evenly, "why are you out here on my beach in that bathing suit?"

"It *is* a beach! People wear bathing suits on beaches."

"Mmm. But not people who look like you, in bathing suits like that."

"I'll wear my long johns next time."

He laughed softly, then suddenly reached out for her shoulder and toppled her down beside him. She gasped, ready to protest, but then the smile left his face and he stared down at her so intently that all words fled from her mind. There was something about him. His eyes were so sharp they were almost pained; his features were taut and haggard.

He drew a finger down her cheek very slowly, barely touching her. Then he breezed that same finger over her lower lip, very slowly, never losing the sharp, hungry tension of his gaze upon her.

For the life of her, she couldn't move. She could only imagine him as she had before: with a nameless woman on the beach—naked.

He was Rex Morrow, the famous, talented recluse, who used women—and the world couldn't possibly know that she was incredibly naive and pathetically vulnerable. Well, she had some pride, and she couldn't be used!

"Rex—"

"It's going to happen, you know."

"What?"

"Us. You and me. We're going to make love. Maybe right here, right where we are now."

"You're incredibly arrogant."

"I'm honest. Which you aren't at the moment."

"Someone should really slap you—hard," she told him disdainfully, though with some difficulty. He was still halfway over her. She could feel his body, so warm from the sun beating down upon it. So close. And both of them so...barren of substantial clothing. Her pulse was beating furiously again. And she wanted to touch him. She had never before known such temptation—a desire that defied good sense and pride and reason.

"Is that someone going to be you?" he said slyly.

"If you don't watch it," she warned.

"Can't you feel it?" he asked her lazily. "The sun-baked sand, the whisper of the waves, rising, ebbing...rising. Can't you feel the heat from the sun, from the earth, becoming a part of us?"

He touched the rampant pulse at the base of her throat.

"Can't you feel the rhythm...throbbing?"

"You're an arrogant SOB—that's what I can feel," she said coolly.

He laughed. The tension was gone; the hardened hunger of his gaze. He pushed himself up and landed on his feet with the grace of a great cat. He offered a hand to her. "Come on. I've got a present for you."

She stared warily at his hand, causing him to chuckle again.

"Nervous, Alexi? Think I'm going to toss you to the sand and maul you?" Impatiently he grabbed her hand and pulled her to her feet.

And then against his body. He arched a brow wickedly. "Don't worry. When we get to it, you'll be breathlessly eager."

Alexi coolly took a step backward, raising her chin, smiling as sweetly as she could.

"I hardly think so, Mr. Morrow."

He laughed, slipped an arm around her waist and started back toward the house. When they were nearly there, he lowered his head and murmured near her ear, "Liar."

"Ohh..." she groaned. *Really*. What incredible insolence, she thought. She stepped ahead of him again and turned around to face him challengingly. "You really like the suit, huh?"

"I like what's in it."

Alexi groaned. "Eat your heart out, then!" she teased.

Rex laughed. But when he caught up with her again and whispered what he did intend to do, it was so insinuative that the sensations that ripped through her, jagged and molten, felt dangerously as if he had followed through.

6

At the path to the house, Rex suddenly stood still, crossing his arms over his chest. He nodded toward the front door.

"You first, Ms. Jordan."

She arched a brow, then shrugged, heading down the path. At the door she paused. "I don't have a key with me."

"It isn't locked."

She raised her brow more. "I'm having problems with people and footsteps, and you left the door open?"

"Samson is inside. I assure you—no one is in there with him."

"Oh." Alexi pushed open the door. Rex had been telling the truth; Samson was sitting in the hallway, just like a sentinel. He barked and thumped his tail against the floor. He was standing behind a large wicker basket with a red-white-and-blue checked cotton cloth extended beneath the handle.

"Good boy, Samson, but what is this?" Alexi said, then turned to look at Rex again.

"It's your present," he told her.

He smiled—a little awkwardly, she thought—and she lowered her head quickly, wondering if she was blushing again. There had been a nice touch to that smile. Endearing...frightening. She barely knew him, really. One minute he was making sexual innuendos, the next he was avoiding her—and then the next he was doing wonderful things for her.

"Well, open it up," Rex urged her.

Alexi knelt down and gingerly lifted up a piece of the cotton cloth. She saw movement first, and then she gasped, reaching into the basket. There were two of them—two little balls of silver fur. The one she held mewed, sticking out a tiny paw at her.

"Oh!" It was adorable. The cutest kitten she had ever seen. It was all that soft, wonderful silver color, except for its feet and its nose, which were black. Its hair was long and fluffy—and made it look much bigger than it was.

Samson barked excitedly. Alexi reflected that the giant shepherd could consume the kitten in one mouthful, but he didn't seem the least bit interested in trying. He barked again, watching Alexi as if he had planned it himself or as if he was very aware that he and Rex were handing out a present.

"Oh!" Alexi repeated, stroking the kitten. The second ball was crawling out of the basket, and she laughed, scooping that one up, too. "You're adorable. You're the cutest little things...."

She gazed up at Rex at last, aware that she was starting to gush. But they were a wonderful present. She was also certain that they were silver Persians—and that they had cost him a fair amount of money.

"Rex—"

He stooped down beside her, idly patting the dog. "I don't want Samson here getting jealous," he said lightly. "Do you like them ... really?"

He gazed at her—somewhat anxiously, she thought—and she felt that the hall had suddenly become small. The two of them were very close and very scantily dressed, and yet it wasn't that at all, really; it was that expression in his eyes.

"They're darling. But Rex, I—I can't accept them."

"Why?"

"They're Persians, right? They must have cost a mint."

"What?" He threw back his head and laughed, relieved. "I was afraid that you were allergic to them or something. Yes, they're Persians. They're three months old, but the breeder assured me they'd be perfect."

"Perfect?"

He grinned, a little wickedly now. "Mousers—except that I don't think you have any mice. You could, though—mice are rather universal. 'Snakers,' I guess you could call them. Cats are simply great to have for anything that creeps and crawls around."

"Oh! Oh, Rex, how thoughtful! Thank you, really. But again, how can I accept them?"

He shrugged. "You did me a great favor."

Alexi laughed. "I did you a favor? I haven't done a thing for you."

He grinned. "Want to pay me in trade?"

"Ha-ha. No."

"Ah, well." He shrugged. "I didn't think so. But, honest, you did me a favor."

"What?"

"I have my best plot in ages going now—thanks to your little murder victims all over the house."

"What?"

"The snakes," he explained. "I turned them into people. All murdered. One with the spade, one with the pipe wrench, and so on. I added some family greed and passion and jealousy, etcetera. It's going great."

"Oh!"

"See what I mean? You did me the favor."

"Oh. Oh..." Alexi stood up, cradling the kittens to her. She looked down the hallway. There wasn't a speck of dust. She hurried to the parlor door and threw it open. The window she had broken on her first night had been repaired; the room had been cleaned. The whole place smelled faintly and wonderfully of fresh pine. There couldn't possibly be a living bug in it, it was so spotless.

Rex stayed in the hallway, leaning idly against the doorframe. Alexi glanced at him, then brushed past him, hurrying to inspect the rest of the house. The ballroom had been scrubbed from ceiling to floor; the library, too, was devoid of a hint of dirt. The drapes and furniture even seemed to be different colors—lighter, more beautiful.

And there wasn't a trace of a snake—or of any of the weapons she had left lying around.

Rex was by the stairway, watching her. She maintained a certain distance from him as she rubbed her cheek against the kitten's soft fur.

"It's fabulous," she murmured. "Rex, thank you."

"Want to see upstairs?"

She nodded. He didn't move; he waited for her to precede him up the stairs. Samson rushed by, though, barking, and she nearly tripped over him.

She couldn't remember climbing the stairs as a child, so she didn't really have any comparisons to make. But it was wonderful. The subtle, clean scent of pine was everywhere; the windows were all open, and sunlight was streaming in. The house, which had always been fascinating, although a bit depressing in its dirt and darkness, now seemed warm and welcoming and bright. The runners over the hard wood were cream, with flower patterns in bright shades of maroon and pink and green. The hallway draperies were a cream tapestry, and the eight-paned windows were crystal clear.

Alexi switched both protesting kittens to one arm and began to throw doors open. There were four of them, two on either side of the landing. To her left was the master bedroom, a man's room with heavy oak furniture. She found the mistress's bedroom next, all done more delicately than Pierre's. The molded plaster showed beautifully on the clean ceilings. The wood was shining; the beds were immaculate.

Alexi stopped by Rex in the hallway and shoved the kittens into his arms, startling him so that he had to straighten and abandon his lazy lean against the banister.

"It's wonderful," she said.

"Thank you. Well, I didn't do it. The company did—and they'll bill you, you know."

"Oh, I know, but..." Her voice trailed away, and she walked down the hall to the next doors.

One of the rooms was a nursery. A shiny wooden cradle rocked slightly with the breeze coming in through an open window. The closet stretched wall-to-wall, and there was an old rocking horse, a twin bed and a cane bassinet. How darling! Alexi thought, and she hurried on out, eager to finish exploring.

The last room was a guest room—a genderless room, comfortable and quaint. The headboard was elaborately carved and went on to stretch the distance of the wall on either side of the bed to create great bookcases. The opposite wall was covered with a tapestry of a biblical scene. There was a fine brocaded Victorian love seat and another rocker; both faced the window, a little whatnot table between them.

Alexi loved it. She determined right away that this would be her room. She'd fill the cases with her books and also store discs and tapes for a stereo and television system. She could modernize for convenience without really changing anything.

She started to turn, only to collide with Rex. All of him. He must have set the kittens down somewhere, because she hit solid chest. Solid, masculine, hairy chest. Coarse dark hair teased too much of her own bare skin, and she stepped back.

"It's spotless. It's wonderful. They did a great job," she told him quickly.

He nodded. "They've got a good reputation."

Alexi stepped around him. The day wasn't hot; it was perfect, with a nice cooling breeze. But she was suddenly warm. Hot flashes soared through her, and now she was very determined not to be alone with him. Her imagination had come vividly alive, all in an instant, living color. Perhaps it was more than imagination. Maybe it was the feel of the heat in the room, of the tension . . . of his nearness. She could visualize him sweeping her into his arms and falling with her upon the antique bed. They really shouldn't have been past the "How do you do, lovely weather" stage, and she wanted to reach out and stroke the planes of his cheek. Intimacy had never been that easy for her; making love had taken time, and it had come far from naturally. It was, by its nature, something that should come after knowing a man deeply and well.

But this one . . . she wanted simply by virtue of something that lived and stirred inside her, an aching, a wanting. And, though she was certain she could never instigate anything, he surely could. But to him it wouldn't mean anything; to her it would.

Alexi hurried into the hallway. Her heart was thundering; her palms were damp. She didn't want him to see her eyes, knowing they could bare her soul, tell him everything she'd been thinking. One thing she had decided about Rex Morrow—it would not pay for him to be aware of all her weaknesses.

He was following her; she could feel him. She hurried on down the stairs, talking.

"Rex, it's all wonderful. No spiderwebs, no dirt, no creeping, crawling creatures. Thank you. Thank you so much. And you went to just the right degree . . . I mean, thank you, but if you'd gone any further, it wouldn't have been good. Do you know what I mean? I'm trying to prove that I can do it. No, I don't have to prove anything. Well, that's not the truth, really. I suppose that I am trying to prove—"

"You're babbling—that's what you're doing."

She'd reached the landing; he spoke from behind her—close. A tingling crept along her spine, she was so aware of him. I'm confused! she wanted to scream. She'd never had feelings like this, and she didn't know what to do with them—but she did know that she should take things slowly and carefully.

"Am I?" she said, but she didn't turn around. She started walking again, pushing through the kitchen doorway. She let the door fall back, aware that he had plenty of time to catch it. She went straight to the refrigerator. "I'm dying of thirst. Don't you want something? The sun is murderous out on the beach. Hmm. I don't even know what's in here. I'm going to have to get out to the store today."

He curled his fingers gently around her arm and pulled her head out of the refrigerator and her body around so that she faced him. He wore a quizzical expression that was handsome against the fine, strong lines of his face. "What is wrong with you?"

"Nothing." She was breathless. "What do you want?"

He smiled slowly. "You."

"To drink."

"Are you afraid of me?" he asked.

"Not in the least."

"Good. I'll have a beer. And I'll get it myself, thanks. Want one? That is all you've got in the refrigerator."

"I shouldn't—"

"Why?"

He brought two out. Alexi nervously sat at the table. He sat across from her, and their knees brushed.

"Ah..." he murmured, and she saw that a secret smile had curved into his lips. "You *are* afraid."

"Of what? That you're going to attack me in my house? You've already done that, right? The first night."

"There's attack, and then there's attack...."

"Whatever." She waved a hand dismissively in the air. He reached across the table and opened her beer. Damn him! She took a long sip, and he was still smiling, fully aware that she was drinking the beer as if reaching for a lifeline.

He lifted his bottle to her.

"Me and thee and Eden."

"Do you try to pick up every woman over eighteen and under fifty?"

"No. Actually, I don't." He took a long swallow from his bottle, watching her. "Alexi...you have to know that you're beautiful. A woman who does Helen of Troy commercials has to be aware that she—"

He broke off abruptly. Alexi's eyes widened, wondering what he had been about to say that would have offended her.

"That she's what?" she demanded.

"Beautiful," he said with a shrug.

"That's not what you were going to say."

"All right." He sounded angry, she thought. "Sexy. Sensual, sexual. Is that what you want to hear?"

"No! No—no, it's not!"

"Well, then, why the hell push the point?"

"Could you go home, please?" She realized that she was sitting very straight, very primly, and that, in the bathing suit, she wasn't dressed for dignity. Nor did the beer bottle she was clutching do much for a feeling of aloofness, either.

"Yeah," he said thickly, rising. "Yeah, maybe I should do just that. 'Cause you know what, lady? You scare the hell out of me, too."

"What?" she demanded, startled. No one could scare him; it had to be a line. But she felt bad—no, she felt guilty as hell. He had done everything for her. And somehow he seemed to understand her. She didn't want anyone in the family to know that she was anything but entirely competent; Rex didn't think that she wasn't competent, just because the snakes had nearly paralyzed her. He'd had the cleaners in; he hadn't really changed anything. He'd known instinctively just how far to go. He'd given her his own home; he'd spent time here—and he was a busy man. He'd bought her the beautiful kittens, just so that she would feel that she had some protection against things that slithered and crawled.

Rex reached across the table and gently cupped her cheek in his hand, stroking her flesh lightly with his thumb. "I said you're kind of scary yourself, my sweet. You own and you possess and you steal into a soul...without a touch."

Into a soul... She couldn't look away from his eyes. Dark and fascinating. All of him. She remembered spilling out everything on their first meeting, remembered thinking of him on the beach, aware that he was there, strong and masculine, and wishing that she could curl against him and laugh, because he seemed to understand so easily the things she needed.

She lowered her head; his hand fell away. She wondered if it wasn't time for a little more honesty, and she was amazed that she could bluntly say what she intended. "You'd find me atrociously disappointing," she said. Her voice was low, even weary. But she looked up and met his eyes again and felt the warmth suffuse her. "Looks can be deceiving. What you see isn't the real me."

"I see fire and warmth and beauty."

"It—it isn't there."

"It needs only to be awakened."

"And you're the one to do it, I take it."

"I think I already have."

"I think you have tremendous nerve."

He laughed suddenly. "Probably. But then, like I said, you do things to the psyche and the body...." His voice trailed away, and he shrugged. He had a bunch of papers on the counter, and he turned away, shuffling them together.

"Don't forget to feed the kittens."

"You're leaving?"

"You told me to."

"Well, I didn't mean it. I'm sorry. All right, well, I meant it when I said it, but only because—"

"Because I was hitting on you?" He was amused, she thought. She cast him an acid gaze, and he laughed again. "Well, I can't promise to quit, especially when you're half-naked."

"You're more naked than I am."

He smiled. "I suppose I should be glad that you noticed. Aha! That's it."

"What's it?"

He thumped an elbow onto the table, then leaned forward. "You're more afraid of yourself than you are of me."

"Don't be absurd."

"You are. You don't want me asking, because you're willing to give."

Alexi groaned, wishing she weren't trembling inside. "You win; I give up. Go home."

"For now," he promised, straightening and going for his papers once again. "But you know how it is. A man, a woman, an island—"

"This isn't an island."

"Close enough. But for now, goodbye, my love."

Alexi stood and followed him out to the hallway. He whistled, and Samson came bounding out from the parlor. The kittens followed after him. Poor Samson had a tortured look about him. It seemed that the kittens hadn't recognized the fact that the shepherd was a hundred times their size; they had adopted him as a surrogate parent.

"Henpecked by a couple of kittens, huh, boy?" Rex said, laughing.

"His master would never be henpecked, I take it?" Alexi queried, crossing her arms over her chest.

He looked at her across their menagerie. He took a long moment to answer, and when he did, his tone was careful, measured.

"No. His master would never be henpecked. Nor would he peck in return. Any relationship only works with give-and-take."

Alexi lowered her head suddenly, feeling a little dizzy. There were things she liked about him so much. He'd been amazed that she had been somewhat insane over a nest of little snakes, but he hadn't played upon that fear. She realized suddenly that he was blunt because he was honest, but that he would never gain his own strength from the weakness of another.

He opened the door and started to leave. Alexi nearly tripped over the kittens to reach him, bracing herself against it as she called him back.

"Rex!"

"Yeah?" Shading his eyes from the sun, he turned back to her.

"Thank you. For the kittens, for the house . . . thank you very much."

"How much?"

She merely smiled at the innuendo. "Dinner? I really can cook."

"I believe you. But not tonight. Let's go out."

"Tonight?"

"Tonight." His expression turned strangely serious. "I want to ask you a few questions."

"About what?"

"We'll eat at about eight; I'll come by here by six-thirty."

"Why so early?"

"I have all your clothing, remember?"

"Oh!"

He was right; her suitcase was now at his house, and she was here.

"See you then." He turned and walked away then. Samson barked, as if saying goodbye, too.

Alexi didn't leave the doorway. She watched them walk away, the man and his massive dog. She looked at Rex's broad, bronzed shoulders and at the ripple of muscle as he moved, and she shivered. He was right; she was very afraid of herself.

At precisely six-thirty, Alexi heard him knocking at the door. She answered it in one of Gene's scruffy old velvet smoking jacket, but apart from that she was ready. She had showered for nearly an hour, washed and blow-dried her hair and carefully applied her Helen of Troy makeup. She was smiling and radiant—and the warm caress of his gaze as it swept over her was a charming appreciation of her labors. He also issued a tremendous wolf whistle.

Alexi tried to whistle in return—she wasn't very good, but he did look wonderful all dressed up. His suit was a conventional pinstripe, his shirt was tailored, his tie was a charcoal gray. Color meant nothing—it was the fit upon him that was so alluring. That and the crisp scents of his clothing and after-shave.

"You're gorgeous," she said.

"So are you."

"Thanks—but I really do have to change. Where are we going?" He had a bouquet of flowers for her in one hand and her suitcase in another. She smiled and thanked him, and he followed her into the kitchen so that she could put them in water.

"Can I help?" he offered.

"I've got a vase—"

"I meant with the changing."

"You would," Alexi retorted, but she was still smiling. It seemed fun. She felt curiously secure with him, even though she didn't doubt his intent for a moment.

And somehow it was tremendously exciting. He definitely let her know he wanted her; he also let her know that it would be at her time, when she was ready.

And that she wouldn't have to be frightened.

"You seem happy," he said.

Alexi poured water into the vase. "I am. I've been studying the original blueprints all day. I talked to Gene, and I checked on some contractors. I thought you might know something about them."

"I know a few."

"How about a glass of wine? I found a super-looking Riesling down in the cellar."

His brows flew up. "You ventured into the cellar?"

She chuckled softly. "I took the kittens with me. Your bug man did a good job—there's nothing crawling down there."

He smiled and said lightly, "A Riesling sounds great."

Alexi set the flowers in the water and made a little face at him. "Good. You open and pour. I'll run up and get dressed."

He nodded, reaching into the right drawer for the corkscrew. "Call me if you need any help," he told her.

"I'll do that," she promised sweetly.

He'd left her suitcase in the hall. Alexi grabbed it and raced up the stairs. She set it on the bed in the room she had chosen and quickly opened it. She wished she had followed him back earlier, for then her things wouldn't be so crushed.

She dumped everything, trying to decide what to wear. She settled on a cream knit, since it wouldn't need to be ironed, and then brushed aside other things to find the embossed stockings that went with it. Slipping into her underwear, she wondered if it was Rex who had repacked for her; then she knew that it must have been, because Emily had left to run errands right after breakfast this morning. She colored slightly, wondering what he must have thought. Her slips, chemises, panties and bras were all very feminine and exotic—her agent's sister owned a lingerie shop, and for every occasion, from her birthday to Valentine's Day, Alexi received some frothy bit of underwear. She smiled, glad that her things were respectable.

She hadn't realized that she was trembling with excitement until she tried to put her stockings on. She paused, inhaling a long breath. She was frightened. Rex was new to her, completely new. He was overwhelmingly male, yet there was that wonderful streak of honesty to him. She was excited, maybe dangerously so. But it was nice, too. The feeling was as wonderful as a fresh sea breeze, and it touched all of her. It was wonderful, and she felt that if it was dangerous, too, she really had no choice. She couldn't resist. He was as compelling as the relentless pull of the tide.

Alexi slipped into a pair of high-heeled sandals, dumped her things from her large purse into a smaller, beaded evening bag and hurried downstairs, afraid to sit and ponder her feelings too long. She glanced at her watch; it was barely seven. She was pleased that she had gotten ready so quickly.

Rex was in the kitchen, leaning against the counter, sipping his wine and watching the kittens as they tumbled over each other. He smiled when Alexi walked in, and his eyes fell over her with the same provocative warmth once again. He lifted his wineglass to her. "Stunning."

"Thank you."

He picked up a second glass of wine and handed it to her. She murmured a thank-you, then sipped at it far too quickly. Rex watched her, amused.

"Did you name them?"

She picked up one of the little silver bundles. "I went with Silver and Blacky—so far." She gazed at Rex and admitted. "I, uh, wasn't sure about their sexes, so I wanted to be careful."

Rex chuckled. "You've got one of each. Silver here is a—" he paused, picking up the kitten "—a girl. Blacky must be the male."

Alexi nodded, set her wineglass down and retrieved both kittens. She went to the back door with them and set them both outside. They tried to come in; she wouldn't let them.

"Cruel!" Rex said.

"Hmph!" Alexi retorted. "You didn't get me a litter box for them," she reminded him.

"How could I have been so remiss! We can stop by the store on our way to the restaurant."

Alexi picked up her wine again, swirling the pale liquid as she said, "I thought you hid out a lot, Mr. Fame and Fortune."

He winced. "That sounded like a low blow. I probably should be hiding out with *you*. But we're going to a Chinese restaurant just north of Jacksonville where every table is secluded."

"You didn't recognize me when you first saw me," Alexi reminded him. "And people just point at me, anyway. They don't want my autograph."

"People don't usually recognize me, either. And not everyone is a mystery fan. The only reason I 'hide out' here is that there are a few nuts out there."

"Excuse me," Alexi teased. She bit her lip then, wishing that she hadn't spoken. She remembered him telling her that someone had actually shot his horse. No wonder he liked solitude.

But he didn't seem bothered by her words. He came closer to her and touched his glass to hers. "This time you're excused," he promised solemnly. He didn't move away from her. His eyes were on hers, dark and deep. Again she was aware of the delicious scent of him. For the longest time, she thought he was going to kiss her, and she didn't think she would protest. She wouldn't have the mind left to do so.

But he didn't. He turned around suddenly, going to the door. He started to call the kittens, but they were right there, tumbling over each other to get back into the house.

"They have to be locked in the cellar," Alexi said. She wrinkled her nose. "I don't want to have to search the whole house for what they might have needed to do."

"Sorry, guys," Rex told the playful pair. "You're being jailed for the evening."

"Well, where's Samson?" Alexi challenged.

"Probably lolled out on the leather sofa," Rex admitted. "I forgot to tell him when he was a puppy that he was a dog." With that, he led her out.

His car was a sporty little Maserati. He asked Alexi if she minded the top down, and she assured him that she loved the air. They didn't speak much on the thirty-minute drive to the restaurant; the wind did feel good, and Alexi found herself content to lean her head back on the fine leather upholstery and close her eyes. He had a good stereo system, and the music and air seemed to blanket her in a shroud of comfort and lethargy.

"We're here—if you're awake," Rex told her when he parked.

"I'm awake—just a mess," she replied, fumbling in her bag for her comb. Rex came around to open the passenger door; when she stepped out, he took her hand, then smoothed back all the straying gold strands. Alexi didn't move; she just let him do that, wondering how such a simple service could feel so intimate and sensual.

"Ready?" he asked huskily.

She was ready... for almost anything.

The restaurant was beautiful. The lobby was dusky and intimate with ornately carved and very heavy chairs. A hostess in black silk trousers greeted Rex like an old friend, and Alexi experienced a moment's jealousy, wondering how often he came here—and with whom.

They were led down a little hallway. It was very intimate; silk screens and paneling divided each little room. The music was soft. When they reached their room, Alexi saw that the tables were low; she was to remove her shoes, and she and Rex would sit on cushions on the floor. The table was round, and they were seated very close to each other. Rex asked her if he could order the wine, and she said sweetly that since he knew the place so well, he should certainly do so.

Their hostess left them. Rex reached for her fingers and played with them idly in the small space between them.

"Jealous?" he asked.

"Why should I be?"

"I see . . . just naturally catty."

Alexi pulled her fingers back. "You forget, Mr. Morrow, I was in the most uncomfortable position of getting to hear all about your sex life."

"You didn't hear all about it. But if you want the finer details, I can always give them to you."

Their hostess bringing in the wine saved Alexi from having to reply. Once she had left again, Alexi turned her attention to the menu. Rex suggested the house specialty, which included samplings of their honey-garlic chicken and beef, and another platter with their mu-shu pork Cantonese and their spicy grilled fish.

Alexi closed the menu. "You know the place, Mr. Morrow."

He lifted her wineglass and handed it to her. "I wonder if you'll mellow out with age."

The way he said it, she had to laugh. She sipped the wine and found it delicious. And suddenly the whole evening seemed wonderful. The muted light, the soft Oriental music, the plush cushion beneath her...the man beside her. She felt as if one sip of the wine had given her senses greater power; she could hear more keenly, see more clearly and inhale and feel his scent sweep into her. She could have swirled around very easily, laid her head in his lap, closed her eyes—and luxuriated in the feel of it all.

"Who knows you're in Gene's house?" he asked.

"What?" Alexi shook her head to clear it. Rex was serious and intent; his eyes were brooding.

"Who knows you're here?"

She shrugged. "Gene. My agent. My family."

"Anyone else?"

"No—no, I don't think so. I wanted—I wanted to be alone for a while." Alexi hesitated, wondering. "Why?"

He shrugged. "Oh, I don't know. I was just curious, I suppose."

Alexi studied him. "You're lying to me. Why?"

He shrugged again, looking toward the doorway. Alexi followed his gaze and saw that their pretty hostess was returning again with another woman and half a dozen small chafing dishes.

The woman opened the dishes to describe the food, then closed them again to maintain the heat. Rex thanked them both, but when they had gone, he still seemed to hesitate.

"Rex!"

"What?"

"Why? Why did you ask me that?"

He didn't answer her. Alexi saw that he was still frowning as he stared at the thin screen that separated their little room from the hallway.

"Rex . . . ?"

He didn't look at her, but he pressed his finger to her lips and indicated the screen. He silently began to rise.

Alexi thought he had lost his mind. But then she saw it; the shadow of a figure standing in the hallway. There was something secretive about the shadow—someone had been listening to them.

Alexi didn't know that she was gasping until Rex swore softly at her, then bounded over the table like a talented linebacker and raced toward the door.

But the shadow, too, had obviously heard her gasp.

It straightened and disappeared just seconds before Rex went racing out after it.

7

Rex didn't return. Confused, Alexi waited for several moments, then rose and hurried out to the hall. There was no sign of any shadow man, nor of Rex. As Alexi stood in the hallway, a group of slightly inebriated businessmen made an appearance from a room farther down the corridor. It was a narrow hallway, and Alexi stepped inside again to allow them to pass.

A short, stout man named Harold was telling a tall, lean, bald man he called Bert that now was the time to dump his electrical stock. And while he was at it, Bert should dump his wife, too.

They passed Alexi, and Harold caught sight of her.

"Oh, Nelly, I am in heaven!" Harold slurred out. He had small eyes, which lit up to look like pennies. "Are you th' dessert, darlin'?" He braced himself in the slender doorway, leering in at her.

"No, I'm not the dessert," Alexi told him. He reminded her of her uncle Bob. Mild mannered by day—a lecher after one beer too many.

"You sure look like dessert."

"Go home," Alexi said. She couldn't help adding, "And Bert—I wouldn't dump your wife if I were you."

"You know Gertrude, huh?" Harold swung on into the room, staring at her incredulously. "Honey, you are cute. Come to think of it, I'm sure I know you. Don't we know her, Harry? Hey—aren't you from that massage parlor downtown?''

"No! I'm not from any massage parlor! Bert, go home and sleep it off."

"I'm in heaven!" Bert claimed. He winked. "We did, honey. We met before." He turned around to nudge one of the other men in the ribs. "She remembers me! She gave me the best little, er, massage I ever did have. You here with a loser, honey? You come on now, and Harry and Bert will make it worth your while."

He clamped sweaty, sausagelike little fingers around her wrist. Alexi sighed. So much for her Helen of Troy fame. He thought that she was a, er, massage artist.

"Bert, I'm not—"

She broke off. A pair of heavy hands had taken hold of Bert. He was lifted off his feet and set down in the hallway. Rex was there, rigid and scowling angrily.

"Hey, bud, I was just—"

Harold broke in nervously. "Bert, let's get home, huh?"

Rex crossed his arms over his chest. "Bert, I do highly suggest you leave—now."

Bert wasn't about to be put off. He straightened his coat and looked around the wall of Rex's chest. "Honey, you wanna stay here with this animal?"

"Now!" The command sounded like a bark; Rex took a lethally charged step toward Bert.

"Rex!" Alexi protested.

"Gentlemen, gentlemen! Have we a problem? How may I help you?" The pretty hostess, anxious and distressed, came running down the hallway, speaking softly.

"Rex!" one of the other men said. "Hey, you're Rex Morrow, aren't you? I've seen your picture on the book covers! Hey, I hate to bother you, but could I have an autograph? My wife would be so thrilled. She buys all your books. In hardcover. And we both read them, every word."

Bert stepped back as if he had been slapped. "You're him?" He gaped. Alexi thought that at any second he would stutter and say "Gaw-ly," just like Gomer Pyle.

"Gentlemen?" the hostess asked anxiously. She glanced at Rex pleadingly. Alexi saw him relax, and then he laughed. "I'm sorry. I haven't paper or a pen—"

They were quickly supplied. Rex scrawled out his name several times. When he had finished and the men started walking away, Bert paused long enough to look at Alexi longingly.

"So you're with him tonight, huh?" He gazed back at Rex. "She's expensive, but she's worth every penny."

"What?" Rex murmured.

"Good night, Bert," Alexi said sweetly.

Bert followed the others. Alexi turned on Rex. "That wasn't necessary."

"They asked me—"

"Manhandling that poor drunken sot wasn't necessary."

He was silent for a long moment, walking around to sink back into his seat at the table. Once there, he crossed his arms over his chest to stare at her. "So you enjoyed teasing that drunken sot, huh?"

"No—but I can take care of myself."

"Great. Next time four men are descending upon you, remind me that you can take care of yourself."

"You would've gotten into a fight if your ego wasn't so colossal that you were more determined to sign your name."

He stared at her a moment longer and then reached for one of the chafing dishes. Alexi didn't sit again, and he didn't pay her any attention. He dished out fried rice and then crisp, succulent little pieces of honey-garlic beef. The smell reminded Alexi that she was starving, and she wasn't sure whether she was still angry or embarrassed—or even a bit awed, since she had been taken for a prostitute and the whole explosive moment had been defused by his lousy signature.

At last his gaze fell on her again, and as it flickered over her length, the corners of his lips twitched with amusement. "So you're expensive, huh?"

"Maybe I should have gotten the old dear to take me home," Alexi said, sitting at last.

"Dear child, he was after one thing."

"Mmm. And what are you after?"

He grinned. "Several things." Then he sobered again, mechanically moving chafing dishes around to fill Alexi's plate. "I couldn't find him."

"Him who?"

"Him who was spying on us."

"Oh." Alexi shrugged. She was beginning to think that either Rex or she was crazy—or perhaps they were both imagining things. He was a mystery writer. Maybe—after a certain amount of time—that type of work played havoc with the brain. So there had been someone in the hallway. So what? Probably a hundred people walked down the hallway during the day.

"Rex—" She paused as she discovered that the honey-garlic beef was really delicious. "This is wonderful."

"Thank you."

"Rex, I don't think it's anything to worry about. Maybe it was another fan—"

"Yeah. And that was a fan running downstairs at Gene's the minute the lights went," he said.

Alexi set her fork down. Rex was eating with the chopsticks; she had decided not to make a fool out of herself with the effort. And now, on top of everything else, she was trembling.

"I thought you didn't believe me," she murmured.

"I never said that."

"You implied—"

"I implied nothing. You might have been reading me wrong."

She shook her head. "No. You didn't believe me. But I think you do now. Why? What changed your mind?"

"Nothing. Really. All right—I am worried about you. Nothing has happened out on the peninsula in all the time that I've been there, and you show up and it's a three-ring circus. Footsteps on the road, footsteps in the house, snakes, etcetera. And it's not as if the girl next door or Mary Poppins moved in. You're Alexi Jordan."

"Not Mary Poppins," Alexi agreed sardonically.

"I didn't say you were Jezebel—just not Mary Poppins. Alexi, do you have any enemies?"

She lowered her head over her chicken and shook her head. Did she? No, not real enemies. She had never stepped over anyone to get anywhere. The only enemy she could possibly have was—

"Alexi, what about your ex? Was he mad enough at you to come here and try to scare you? Make you a little crazy?"

John? She shook her head again. She trembled. John could be violent—but she couldn't see him being stealthy. When he had decided to accost her, he hadn't played any games. He had come straight to the apartment—and straight to the point.

"I—I don't think so."

Rex sighed softly. "Well, maybe we are imagining things, huh?"

She nodded woodenly.

"You're not eating."

"Oh. It's wonderful. It really is, Rex. I'm sorry."

Alexi was startled when he touched her very gently. With his knuckle he raised her chin. For the longest time his dark eyes gazed into hers; for the longest time he seemed to question what he saw there and to muse tenderly upon her.

Then he moved, lowering his face toward hers. His lips touched hers. She knew her mouth was sweet with the taste of plum wine and honey. His lips hovered just above hers, tasting them.

She felt his hand caressing her cheek. Then she felt the movement of his tongue within her mouth, hot and supple and sensual. She trembled, neither protesting the movement nor joining it, but feeling the rise of excitement inside of her, a longing, a sexual tension that knotted in the pit of her belly and seemed to flare throughout her.

His hand still at her nape, he moved back. His dark eyes surveyed hers again. She didn't know what he sought or what he saw.

Or what he felt. Perhaps he was thinking that it was all a loss. That she didn't even know how to return a kiss decently.

Her mouth went dry. She drew her eyes from his to look down at her hands. A tiny glass of plum wine sat before her; aware that he was watching her, she drank it quickly, not sure of what to say or do.

"Maybe you should leave the peninsula," he said.

She shook her head.

"Footsteps in the dark. Maybe something frightening is happening."

"I—I don't want to leave."

"Mmm. But you won't protest if I sleep on your sofa again, huh?"

Alexi stiffened. "You're being obnoxious again. I won't ever let you sleep on my sofa again. I promise."

"Damned right. If I sleep there again, Alexi, it won't be on the sofa."

She raised her head, staring at him, a brow arched challengingly. She was still trembling, but she hoped that he didn't know it. Why not? She was certainly of legal age, and she wanted him. She ached for him. His lightest touch had been magic.

Why not? Because she trembled too easily, because she was very afraid that she couldn't go through with it, that she would make an absolute fool of herself. She hadn't even been able to return his kiss.

She smiled, sweetly, seductively. Fever was alive in her veins, racing rampantly through her blood. "You're right, Mr. Morrow. If you ever sleep in my house again, it will be in my bed."

Startled, he drew back, a slow, entirely wicked smile curling the corner of his mouth.

"Do you mean that, Ms. Jordan?"

"I do."

"Then let's go."

He was up abruptly, a strong, bronzed hand reaching out to help her rise. Panic surged inside her; she stared at his hand for several seconds, completely at a loss.

Then she placed her own hand within it. His fingers curled around hers and she was standing beside him. For the longest time they looked at each other, standing together in that rice paper-screened section of the Chinese restaurant. She could hear his heart, and she could see his eyes, and she could see the hunger there, and the longing.

He wanted her. Badly.

And she wanted him.

He didn't say anything else. He turned, his fingers still wound around hers, leading her toward the hall. At the entryway he offered the hostess his credit card. Alexi escaped him to study a display of swords encased in a glass cabinet. She pressed her palm against her breast and felt her own heart surging. She must have been mad. He had teased her, but he'd never pressed her. And she had just all but whistled out an invitation to make love....

He caught her hand again. He smiled when she darted a quick, scared look his way. He wound his fingers around hers again as he led her out into the parking lot and to his car.

It was a beautiful night. Stars abounded in the heavens. Alexi sat stiffly in the Maserati, staring straight ahead. Rex talked casually as he gunned the motor. He pointed out a few of the constellations in the heavens. "Not a bit of fog tonight," he murmured.

"Not a trace of it," Alexi agreed.

Oh, he was so casual! So comfortable. But then, he was good at this, Alexi reminded herself, while she was only playing at it. She didn't really know the first thing about having a casual affair. She was deathly afraid that when he touched her she was going to scream.

No. She would not. It was all in her mind. She liked him so much, and she ached for him, feeling that sense of sexual arousal when he merely whispered her name. Like a coil inside of her, winding, sweet and heightened, yearning, when he was near. If she could not lie down beside him, she would never know what it was to make love again.

"Where?"

"Pardon?" She had to glance his way. And with a whole new sense of panic she realized that they were just about on the road leading out to the peninsula.

"Your place or mine?"

"Er...er..."

"Mine," he decided softly.

"Fine. Except—"

"Except what?"

"Isn't Emily there?"

Against the shadow and glow of the lights, she saw him shake his head ruefully. "Emily has gone home. She usually only works for me two days a week. She stayed longer this week because of you, but now she's gone home. The whole place is ours."

"Oh."

They were on the road out to their houses. Alexi closed her eyes and wondered what it had been like more than a century before. When Pierre had taken his Eugenia here, a bride, alone. Surely it had been completely barren then. It must have seemed as if the world were theirs, as if they owned paradise. The pines would have been the same, and the palms. The moon, rising clear and beautiful against the sky, must have been the same, too. And the stars... diamonds glittering against a panoply of black velvet.

The Maserati stopped. They were in front of the Brandywine house. Rex was smiling at her gently and was twisted slightly toward her. His fingers played idly in her hair.

"I'll walk you to your door."

"What?" She swallowed.

"You're all talk and no action, kid. You didn't mean it. Come on, I'll walk you to your door."

Startled, Alexi crossed her arms over her chest and sat grimly. Rex opened his door and came around for her. He opened her door. Alexi didn't move; she stared straight ahead.

He had just offered her an out. She couldn't take it. It was her chance to run, offered in tenderness.

"You're the one who is all talk, Mr. Morrow," Alexi murmured.

She heard him inhale sharply. "Last chance, Ms. Jordan. I'm a pretty nice guy, nine times out of ten. But if you don't get out of this car right now, I won't answer for the consequences."

Alexi didn't move. "Promises, promises, Morrow."

Her door slammed sharply. A second later, his did the same after he sank back into the bucket seat beside her. She felt his eyes on her, but she couldn't turn.

"Well, you know you're committed now, huh, Alexi?" She felt the anger that edged his words. "Is that what you want? Or is that what you need? 'Push the guy so far that there is no backing down'? Make sure it's what you want, Alexi. I'll be damned if I understand you. Make sure."

"Drive, would you, Rex?"

He shook his head. She felt herself pulled into his arms, pulled hard. His mouth came down hard on hers. Her lips parted; she felt the demand of his, forceful, hungry and entirely persuasive.

And it was good. Deliciously, wonderfully good. He tasted of the honeyed chicken and the plum wine and, beyond that, completely, tantalizingly male. This time she could respond. She trembled when his tongue thrust into the crevices of her mouth, filling her, arousing her. She grew bold and she herself explored, running the tip of her tongue along his lower lip and then his upper lip, against his teeth, against his tongue, in a sleek, sensual persuasion of her own. It was really wonderful. The scent of him filled her, as male as the taste of him, unique. Her fingertips played against the hair at his nape, over the strong structure of his cheek, to the fascinating breadth of his shoulders. And all the while she felt his kiss. Against her lip, against her throat, against the beat of her pulse there. She felt his fingers, feather-light, against her flesh; his knuckles, stroking her shoulder, drawing a line lightly over her collarbone. She nearly cried, the kiss alone was so very good....

She had never known this type of arousal. Aching in all parts of her, longing to touch and be touched...everywhere. He had her in his arms, on his lap. She was barely aware of moving, of being moved. The sense of being drugged with the pleasure of it was an encompassing one, overpowering

all else, giving her the wonderful feel of perfect fantasy. This
was it, the way of dreams. The need and the desire, the
feeling that she would simply die if she could not have him.
All of him.

It remained with her, all the magic, while he held her.
While his lips touched hers again and again. Even when his
eyes met hers, as dark and mysterious as the night, as probing, as curious, and still as seductive. She felt the palm of his
hand flat against her breast; she felt his fingers curl around
its weight, and his thumb as he sought her nipple through
the knit of her dress and the lace of her bra. She buried her
face against his neck, warmed by the intimacy, unable to
meet his eyes yet instinctively grazing her teeth against his
throat in response. It was a dream; it was magic. She was
alive and explosive and soaring with desire and relief.

But then she felt his hand again. Against her stocking. A
touch that made her shiver, a touch that wound the core of
her tightly, tightly. She wanted him. She wanted his touch,
an intimate touch, so badly. But even as his fingers roamed
along her nyloned thigh, she felt the overwhelming panic
begin to seize her.

She couldn't move at first.

She just felt his hand . . . his fingers. Higher, higher along
her thigh. Fingers rimming the elastic of her panties. Light
against her flesh again—bare flesh—as he slowly, seductively drew the nylons from her. She couldn't move. She
could only feel the panic welling, growing, sweeping through
her. . . .

For God's sake, they were still in the car, she registered
dimly. They were still merely playing.

Playing very, very intimately. The darkness seemed to
surround her.

She stiffened and drew away from him abruptly.

"Alexi!"

He caught her hands. She stared into his eyes. At that very moment, she wanted the earth to open up and swallow her. She groaned.

"Alexi, shh—"

She couldn't understand that he meant to soothe her; she knew only that she had led him where he had gone and that she had then pulled away from him.

She tore at the door handle and wrenched it open. She was so awkward, caught upon his lap in the small bucket seat.

"Alexi!"

Sobbing, she stumbled over him. Her shoes were lost; her nylons were a tangle. She yanked them off and set out upon the sand, running. The night was dark, with only the moon and the stars to guide her, but it didn't matter; she didn't know where she was running to, only that she had to escape.

Pine and sand were beneath her feet. Bare feet. The beach was out there, through a trail of pines that both sheltered and mysteriously darkened. Ahead, she could hear the waves, so soft and gentle here. Waves of the mighty Atlantic.

She reached the beach, the sand soft and cool now beneath her feet. She looked up and saw the stars and the crescent of the moon, and she inhaled raggedly, desperately.

She gasped, startled, as arms swept around her. Rex's arms.

"Oh, don't!" she pleaded. She couldn't look at him. He turned her around anyway, pulling her to his chest, running his fingers down the length of her hair.

"Please, don't. I'm so sorry. I—" she said brokenly.

"Alexi, stop. Listen to me. Stop."

She tried; she couldn't. She felt as if she sobbed raggedly for the longest time, yet she couldn't pull away from him; he held her firm. Then she tried again to tell him how embarrassed she was and how sorry, and he comforted her again. At last she inhaled a long, ragged breath and exhaled it and stood still.

Rex pulled off his shoes and socks and took her elbow. "Let's sit in the surf. And you can tell me about it."

"No!"

"Yes. I deserve that much."

"No, no, just forget about me, please. Believe that I didn't mean to do what I did—"

"Come on, Alexi."

She had little choice. Before she knew it she was sitting in the surf beside him and the waves were rippling over their feet and he was as unconcerned about his dress trousers as she was about the hem of her knit. He didn't make her talk at first; he just held her against him, her head against his chest, his arms around her waist, his chin resting upon the top of her hair.

"John Vinto?" he asked.

She shuddered.

"What in God's name did he do to you?" Rex exploded.

She didn't want to start crying again—and she knew he wasn't going to let her go. When she started to talk, she discovered that she could do it almost impersonally, as if it had happened to someone else, as if it were history, long gone.

"I, uh, I knew a lot of what he was doing. Granted, it took me a while. The spouse is always the last to know it all. And I was so desperate to make my marriage work, you know. I had more or less run away from a great home to make it on my own. My parents hadn't wanted me to marry John. Gene didn't even approve of him. It was simply so hard to admit I'd made a mistake...."

Her voice trailed away for a moment, and then she shrugged. "I became ill during a makeup session one day and came home. John was in bed with another of his models. I think it was then that I realized he probably fell a little bit in love with every woman he photographed. It hurt, though. A lot. I didn't make any threats or accusations or anything. I just turned away. I tried to call for a cab. By then the girl was running out of the house only half-dressed, and John was slamming down the receiver. He said that we had to talk. I said there was nothing to talk about; nothing would change my mind. I wanted a divorce. He became irate. He kept telling me that I didn't want a divorce. I tried to call a cab again, and he told me that I couldn't live without him, I couldn't survive without him, that I wanted him—and that he'd prove it to me." She stopped speaking, staring out at the ocean, wincing. It seemed so horrible even to say aloud. So humiliating. So degrading.

Rex didn't say anything. He tightened his arms around her. She wasn't even aware that she was speaking again.

"It was an awful fight. I realized what he meant, and I threw the phone at him and ran. He caught me and dragged me through half the house. He kept telling me that I was still his wife." She lowered her head. "And, of course, I was his wife, and just the night before, I'd loved him. I just can't describe the terror of being powerless. Of having no control over being forced..."

"My God," Rex whispered. Like quicksilver, he moved his fingers gently over her cheek. "To think that I accosted you like that on your first night at the house. Alexi, I'm so sorry. So, so sorry." He was silent for a moment. She felt his kiss, tender and light, over her brow. She felt his arms around her, and she wasn't afraid; she felt secure.

"You kept working with him!" Rex said incredulously. "You should have taken the bastard to court."

She shook her head. "Do you know how hard it is to prove spousal assault? I would probably have lost—and the publicity would have marked me for the rest of my life." She sighed softly. "John didn't want the divorce. I did threaten to take him to court. That was the only reason he agreed to the divorce—no-fault and quick. I agreed to finish out the Helen of Troy campaign as long as he swore never to touch me or come near me again.''

''Alexi, Alexi...''

She felt the soft brush of his kiss again; she felt the strength of his arms. The night was cool with the breeze, but the water was warm as it washed over her feet.

''I'll kill him!'' Rex swore suddenly, savagely. He was tense, as taut as piano wire. ''I swear, I'll damned well kill him!''

Alexi twisted, startled by the vehemence, by the passion, by the caring in his tone. He was her willing champion, a fury in the night. Touched, she stroked his cheek, somewhat amazed that he could show such fierce concern.

He caught her fingers and kissed them, and she met the dark fires of his eyes. She inhaled sharply, feeling everything within her quicken. She wanted him so badly! So very badly. And she was so frightened that she would pull away again. He wouldn't want her. He was fierce against brutality and injustice, but he could not want her again. A neurotic who teased.

But he was smiling, and smiling so gently, while the starfire blazed in the depths of his night-dark eyes. He kissed her fingers again, reverently, then dropped them, and to her amazement he was up beside her, struggling out of his jacket and vest and then his shirt as she stared up at him, incredulous of his strange, abrupt behavior.

''Ever been skinny-dipping?'' he demanded.

She flushed, staring at the ocean while he stripped. ''Rex, you saw what just happened!''

His trousers landed in her lap, then his briefs. In the darkness she saw the bright flash of his muscled buttocks as he raced past her, splashing seawater all over her knit.

In seconds he had swum out into the surf. ''Come on!''

''Didn't you ever watch *Jaws*?'' she retorted.

"I promise you—no great white is in water this hot!"

"How about a small shark?"

"Minutely possible, but highly implausible. Come on! I dare you. I double-dare you."

"Rex . . ."

"Alexi! Come on! The least you owe me is a bit of good ogling."

She bit her lower lip, then recklessly stood. What else could happen? He knew the truth now. Her worst nightmare had already happened. Rex knew that she was basically asexual. And that she couldn't really help it—and why.

He'd sworn he'd kill John. She trembled suddenly, remembering his vehemence. It had just been a turn of phrase, she told herself. Rex didn't even know John.

"Come on!" Rex called to her.

She hesitated only a second longer. She pulled her knit over her shoulders, then hastened out of her lacy undergarments. Even in the darkness, she could see the rich grin that slashed across Rex's features where his head bobbed along with the waves.

This was crazy. It was so dark. But she plunged into the water anyway. It was cool with her whole body immersed. Alexi had never been skinny-dipping. It felt divine. She dived and swam, shivering as she broke the surface again.

She looked around. She couldn't see Rex anymore. His head wasn't above the water.

Then she felt him. Below her. Far below her. He tugged on her foot, and she gasped, laughing as her face almost slipped beneath the waves. But he didn't pull her down.

He explored her.

She felt his hands all along her legs. Felt his touch as he cradled her buttocks, felt his mouth grazing her belly, felt his kiss against her thighs. . . .

She gasped, alive, electric, kinetic against the warmth of the Atlantic and the sheen of the moon. He had to breathe;

surely the man had to breathe. He couldn't stay down forever. . . .

But he could stay down a long time. A long, long time. Long enough to part her legs. Long enough to dive between them. To touch, to stroke, to glide . . .

He broke the surface, pulling her against him. She could barely stand against the sand and the water, the coil of sweetness was so tight within her.

"I'm going to drown," she warned him.

"No," he told her.

She barely knew the feel of his chest; she discovered it then: thick, dark hair a rich wet mat upon it. He let her touch him, then he swept his arms around her, and his kiss on her lips was demanding and thirsting and merciless, sweeping her away. She couldn't breathe; she couldn't protest. He broke from her, lifting her, and his mouth encircled her breast, drawing it in. She arched back, gasping, moaning.

"Rex . . ." she pleaded. "You know . . . I can't."

He slid her wet, sleek length against his own so that their bodies rubbed together provocatively. He waited until their eyes met, and he smiled triumphantly. "Oh, but you can."

He lifted her again, carrying her against the waves until they had just reached the shore. He laid her there and quickly stretched atop her, burrowing his weight between her thighs, kissing her hastily again, stealing breath and strength and protest from her. Kissing her so quickly, again and again. Her lips, her throat, her breast, her belly, her thighs, the very core of her, deeply, so deeply . . .

"Alexi."

He was above her, his eyes on her.

"Watch," he whispered. "You can. We can."

He touched her so erotically. And she watched. And she gasped again, crying out with the sheer pleasure of it, and he slowly, completely, insolently, possessively...electrically sank his body deep within hers.

8

"Me and thee and a jug of wine."

There was the most wonderful, laconic smile on his face. He was still stark naked and not a bit bothered by it. Flat on his back, Rex lifted his hands to the heavens and sighed with contentment.

Alexi had no choice but to smile, too, curling on her side to watch him. The moon was high overhead and the stars were shimmering over the sand and the water, and she had never imagined that night could be so beautiful. She leaned on an elbow and drew a tender line down the length of Rex's cheek.

"We haven't any wine," she reminded him.

"Ah, true. Me and thee, then. In Eden. This is heaven." He drew her on top of him, lulled and sated to an exquisite point where he could pause now and savor and appreciate each little nuance of her, of the things that passed between them. He could feel the sand, gritty against his back, cool, fascinating. He could feel the sand she brought with her, those tiny pebbles against the endless silken smoothness of her flesh. She leaned against his chest, slightly flushed. Her eyes were as brilliant as gems, more wondrous than all the stars in the heavens; her beautiful lips were curled into the most awkward little smile. Her hair was still soaked, a tangled mane swept clean from her flesh now, yet it showed off the elegant lines of her delicate, exquisite features. He leaned on his elbows, laughing as she went off balance and then pouncing on her as she lay on her back in the sand, touching her cheek because he had to and studying the length of her in the moonlight because he had to do that, too.

"Helen of Troy," he murmured softly, "the face that beyond a doubt launched a thousand ships. Face and form..." Softly, tenderly, with an awed fascination, Rex explored her length with his fingertips as well as with his eyes. Breasts this lovely had never graced the pages of a fold-out magazine, he thought, then corrected himself. Well, all right, maybe they had once in a long while, but not often. Long, lean torso, slim waist, the most feminine flare of hips and buttocks...

Even her kneecaps were glorious.

"Sweetheart." He grinned at her. And then he groaned softly in mock agony. "Had they seen her body, too, they could have launched a million ships."

"Rex, stop!" Alexi protested, but he had her laughing and she couldn't help it. She laughed until his head dipped over her and his face brushed her nipple. Then he took it into his mouth, sliding his teeth, and then his tongue, gently around it. She felt a sharp sizzle of desire strike her anew just from that action, and her breath caught as she threaded her fingers through the deadly-dark wings of his hair, trying to draw him to her.

His eyes, darker than the sea at night, far darker than the midnight sky above them, met hers.

"I'm not, you know," she murmured. "I'm not anything like a real Helen of Troy at all. I'm..."

Quite ordinary. Those were the words she was looking for. She never had a chance to find them.

"No, you're not Helen of Troy. And you're not fantasy."

Rex smiled as he leisurely stroked his fingertip over her lower lip. She was really so beautiful that night. And maybe it was part fantasy. They were on the beach, and there was nothing on the horizon, nothing at all. They might have been the last man and woman on earth, or the very first. The breeze was gentle and balmy and the water was warm and the earth seemed to cradle them and blanket them in some welcoming, tender embrace. And she really didn't look like the Helen of Troy image at all; she was all natural. All...divinely natural, from wet hair and face to her gloriously naked body. Her eyes, her expression, the beauty in her features...were all innocence. The curve of her body was wanton and lush. The combination was nothing less than magical.

Rex dipped his head to kiss her mouth. He raised himself just a breath away from her.

"No, you're not Helen. You're Alexi Jordan, and I—"

He broke off abruptly.

And I love you very much.

Those had been the words he had been about to say, he realized. They stunned him; they shocked him. He'd known he'd wanted her. Any male over the age of twelve who lived and breathed would have wanted her. He'd known that he could enjoy her company, that she could be fun and feisty and proud and temperamental, and even soft at times.

He just hadn't known that he was falling in love with her. Nor was it a particularly bright thing to have done. She was Helen of Troy, right? A woman who would be returning to a certain world. A woman who probably needed that world, had to have a certain amount of adoration in her life. She'd stay awhile, and then she'd go, and then he'd...

He'd spend the rest of his life missing her.

"Rex?"

Something in her tone was very soft and vulnerable. He'd forgotten. She'd come to him after a bad finale to a bad marriage, and she was as delicate as the fine marble she so resembled. He had to fall out of love with her. But not now. Not tonight.

"Alexi Jordan," he whispered, "is far more beautiful than Helen of Troy could have ever been."

"Flatterer," she said accusingly.

"Mmm-hmm," he agreed. His one leg lay cast over her. The prickly hairs of his chest tickled the soft flesh of her breasts mercilessly. He casually cupped her cheek and murmured huskily, "Think you want to go again?"

His were bedroom eyes if she'd ever seen them, and this dusky velvet patch of earth and water was the most erotic bedroom she had ever known. She smiled, wondering at the infinite tenderness in the man. He'd known exactly what to say, and when. And he'd known exactly what to do, and when. She'd never known a man more the epitome of the male, and she'd never begun to imagine that such a man could show so much sensitivity.

"Think you can?" he asked.

She gazed into his eyes and stroked her fingers over his cheek, savoring the shaven flesh. "Piece of cake," she told him, and she set both palms against his face, bringing him down to her. She reached for his mouth first with the tip of her tongue, rimming his lips with that delicate touch before she molded her mouth to his. She felt the great rush of his breath and the fascinating hardening of his body, muscles tensing and stretching and tautening with his growing sexual excitement.

Earth, wind... and fire. It was Eden.

She felt his touch against her, her breasts, her hips, the curve of her buttocks, the soft flesh of her inner thigh. His kiss seared her, and when his lips left her flesh, the breeze came to kiss it afresh. He whispered words that meant nothing and everything, and she knew that she whispered in return, like a breath of the sea, like the cry of the waves. Each cry, each whisper, was fuel to the fire, and each fire was a lapping flame creating sensation anew, a heightened tension. She dared anything. She touched him intimately; she exulted in the swell and pulse of him. She soared to the heat and thunder of his rhythm, and she felt the tiny little piece of death that blacked out the world with the wondrous force of the climax that he brought to her upon the beach just as the very first touch of dawn burst upon it to bathe their Eden in beauteous magenta.

Floating as if she were indeed adrift upon the waves, Alexi returned slowly to the earth beneath her, feeling again the fine grit of the sand and the coolness of the ocean at her feet. His arms went around her, and she rested on them. Only then did she shiver, watching the sky as the first tiny arc of the sun peeked out over the horizon like a shy young maiden.

"It's morning," Rex murmured.

"It certainly is," Alexi agreed. She shifted up onto her elbows. Rex stood and walked into the water, hunching down to splash water against his face, then standing again to stare out at the rising sun.

Alexi smiled, biting her lower lip. The sun was beautiful—but not nearly so magnificent as the man who stood before it, a tall, strong silhouette against that golden arc. She liked the whole of him very much, she decided, from the breadth of his shoulders to the muscles of his buttocks and thighs. She wondered if there was any more wonderful way to meet a lover than to come to him in this Eden, as he termed it.

He turned back to her. At her expression, he arched a brow.

"I'm deciding," she told him.

"Oh?"

"Mmm." She hesitated just a moment longer. "Can't decide. I like the frontside as much as the backside," she told him at last.

His dark brow arched higher. "Saucy wench, aren't you?"

"I tell it like it is."

He laughed and reached a hand down to her. She took it and stood and slid her arms around his neck and enjoyed kissing him in the light bath of sunlight. She loved feeling their naked, sandy flesh brush together.

He loved the feel of her breasts and hips against him, the feel of his sex against hers....

No, no, no, no, no, he thought. He could fairly well guarantee the privacy of his Eden by night, but not by daylight. God alone knew when the meter reader might decide to show up.

He broke away from her, found her dress and slipped it quickly over her head, then hurriedly searched for his trousers.

"All that talk and time to get my clothes off!" Alexi complained. "Now you're shoving me back into them!"

"I'm the jealous type," he told her, stumbling into his briefs. Alexi, still searching for her panties but comfortably clad in her dress, had to laugh as she watched him. He cast her an indignant glare that offered a definite threat once he was capable of standing straight.

Alexi held out a hand in a defensive gesture but kept laughing. "Don't be offended. I was watching you before, and you were just wonderful. Primal man—Atlas in the flesh. You really were just beautiful against the rising sun."

"Thanks," Rex muttered. He glanced up at her as he zippered his fly; then he started to laugh.

"What?" Alexi demanded.

"Green hair."

"What?"

"You have a lump of seaweed there. Left side—ah, you've got it."

She stared at him reproachfully, then started to smile. He stretched out his hand again and said, "I could stay here forever. But I'm afraid we might have some company."

Alexi nodded happily, curling her fingers around his. "Breakfast, Mr. Morrow? My place?"

"Sounds good. Let's pick up Samson first, though, huh? Emily went home yesterday, so he's been locked up all night."

Alexi nodded, lacing her fingers through his. She smiled as they started walking barefoot over the carpet of pine that led to the beach. "My purse and shoes are in the car. It's morning and you can't hear a thing but the breeze and the seabirds. I really do love it here."

Rex shot her a quick glance. Alexi, staring at the sky, didn't notice the penetrating quality of his gaze.

"Do you?" he said.

"Hmm?"

"No city lights."

"Well, everyone likes the city now and then. But, Rex—" She paused, looking at him with a very slight but honest, open smile. "This is like Eden. Don't you imagine that Pierre Brandywine must have thought the very thing when he first built the house for Eugenia?"

"You're a romantic," he told her.

"So are you," she said challengingly.

Was he? he wondered. Surely not.

They had reached his house. Samson came bounding out when Rex whistled. Rex asked her to hang on a minute while he got some clothes. "I'm really into sand when we're playing in it," he told her with a grimace, "and salt and all the rest. But I think I need a shower now, huh?"

"And where are you taking that shower?"

"With you."

"Presumptuous," she said with a sigh. But when they started out again, she had to stop. It was broad daylight now, with the bright, bright morning sun climbing higher in the sky. She stood in front of him, and she only hesitated for the fraction of a second. "Thank you, Rex. Thank you so very much. I—"

She hesitated again. Only the fraction of a second again, but the wheels of her heart and mind spun.

I love you.

The words almost spilled from her. Were they such easy words, then? she taunted herself. No, a heartbeat told her that they were not. She did love him. His smile, his dark eyes, the way he had looked, primitive and exciting and male, in the broad arc of the brimming sun. But that wasn't it. She loved him because he had been there. Hostile at first. Audacious at best. But he had been there for her in every sense of the words, sensitive, caring. Gentle and tender.

But he was good at that, she reminded herself. He was an accomplished lover. A good man, a practiced lover. Be his friend! she warned herself. Don't expect much; it will hurt too much if you let your feelings get out of hand.

Too late; her feelings were out of hand. She just had to take care not to let it show.

"You're very special," she finished quickly, feeling the probing of his ebony eyes. She smiled and stood on her toes to kiss him quickly. "Very special."

"Hey, I'm an obliging fellow," he said lightly. "Come on—the kittens must need an outing as badly as Samson."

"And the cellar will need a cleaning," Alexi moaned.

Rex didn't argue the point. When they reached the Brandywine house, Alexi retrieved her things from the car while Rex opened the house. By the time she reached the door, she practically tripped over the kittens to enter. Rex had let them up first thing, it seemed. Alexi quickly scooped the pair of them into her arms.

"Hi, sweeties. Did you think that you had been deserted? I'm sorry!"

Samson came running out of the kitchen and slid down the hallway, barking enthusiastically. The kittens squirmed in Alexi's arms, and she set them down to bat away at Samson. Samson tried to make a hasty retreat, but it was too late. The kittens tumbled after him.

"You asked for it this time, Samson!" Alexi laughed.

She started off for the kitchen herself, smiling as she inhaled the aroma of the coffee. Rex had gotten it going quickly.

She liked the way he looked in the kitchen, too. She paused in the doorway, watching as he moved from the cupboards to the refrigerator, barefoot and bare chested— and wearing his dress trousers.

Alexi went swiftly to the refrigerator herself and took out a carton of eggs and some cheese and bacon. Rex let her start the bacon and eggs, and he poured them each a mug of coffee.

"I'm probably the better cook," he warned her.

"Good. You can prove it tomorrow," she told him. Then she quickly lowered her head, letting her drying hair hide her features. What was she doing? She'd just come to the mature acceptance that he was a free agent, and here she was, assuming they'd be together for breakfast tomorrow.

"I will," he promised her smugly.

She breathed a little more easily and asked him to hand her the grater for the cheese. He did, then told her that she was only cooking so that he would have to go down to the cellar to see what kind of mess the kittens had made.

She watched him when he started down the stairs. She thought about the burnt brown hue of his shoulders and the weathered tan of his features and knew the color had come from endless hours in the sun he loved so much. Then she realized that she was daydreaming and about to burn something, so she turned her attention back to the stove. But as she did so she frowned, noting that the tea and sugar canisters were out of place, and she could have sworn that she had left the kitchen spotless the night before.

Alexi grated cheese over the eggs, then shook her head. Something about the kitchen didn't feel right. She couldn't explain it—after all, Rex had entered the kitchen before she had; maybe he had moved things.

She scooped the eggs off the frying pan and onto plates and quickly turned several pieces of bacon that were starting to burn. She should have started the bacon first, she told herself reproachfully. Rex probably was the better cook.

She heard a slight noise behind her and turned around. Rex had come up the stairway from the cellar and was watching her; on his lips was a curiously tender smile that brought a tug to her heart. He swung away from the doorframe, sauntered over to her, took her into his arms and met her eyes with his smile intact.

"Your hair looks like hell."

"I'm ever so sorry. I've just come from the most incredible night of my life."

"Thank you, ma'am."

She laughed and grew breathless and he started to kiss her, but they both smelled the bacon starting to burn. Alexi quickly retrieved it and popped bread into the toaster while Rex poured juice and more coffee.

While they ate, Alexi told him some of the things she wanted to do with the place. Rex listened and asked questions, and she grew more and more excited, trying to describe what she envisioned in the end. "I love this house. I always have. There's something about knowing that it belonged to my great-great-great-grandparents that just fascinates me."

"It is nice," Rex agreed. He caught her fingers across the table. "Were you going to start today, though?"

"I was."

"Is that negotiable?"

"Very."

They'd eaten every scrap of food. Alexi decided that being in love created enormous appetites. They'd barely picked up the dishes before they were both calmly and breathlessly discussing the need for a shower, and then they were in the shower—together, of course. Rex couldn't begin to make up his mind whether he preferred making love to her on the beach or against the steamy spray of the shower or in the bed she had chosen for her own with the fresh-smelling sheets and the sweet scent of shampoo and cologne dusting her flesh.

It didn't matter, he was certain. They were both drugged with it, and in the end it was about noon when they fell asleep, exhausted and content, and nearly dark again when he awoke.

Alexi was still sleeping. Her hair, dry and fragrant now, lay in tousled waves upon his shoulders and hers. He brought a lock of it to his lips, then silently held his breath while he admired the way it fell over her breasts as she slept.

He crawled from the bed, stared out at the dusk, then pulled on his clean pair of jeans and started down the stairs. He rummaged in the refrigerator and found some frozen steaks. He set them on the counter, shoved a few potatoes in the oven and made a fresh pot of coffee. That completed, he decided to grab some paper and make a family chart so that he could determine just which one of his characters was actually the murderer of all the others.

Alexi awoke first with the most marvelous sense of peace and warmth and contentment and security. Naturally, she reached out to touch him. Then her eyes flew open and she was not quite so warm and content, for she realized that he was gone.

She bolted out of bed and rushed to the window and saw that it was already dark, and ruefully admitted that maybe she hadn't slept all that much after all, since she had been up all night and all morning. Her heart began to beat, a little painfully, as she hoped that Rex had not left her. She wasn't afraid tonight; she just wanted to be with him.

She slipped quickly into a terry robe, ran her brush through her hair with a lick and a promise and started for the stairway. At the top landing she paused, gripping the banister and breathing with a sigh of relief and pleasure. He was still there. She could hear him. He was talking to someone, but who—?

She frowned, instinctively clutching her robe to her throat and silently coming down the stairs. She could hear him clearly. But who on earth was he talking to? His voice was rising and falling, rising and falling.

He was in the parlor. Alexi crossed the downstairs hallway quickly to go there, and then she paused, amused but determined not to laugh until he saw her.

Rex, scratching his head, paper and pencil in hand, was pacing from one side of the room to the other.

"No, no, no, no, no. That leaves just the butler. And the butler can't do it. I mean, the damn butler just can't do it!"

"Oooh, but he can! He can! Give the poor man a break!" Alexi cried.

Startled, Rex swung around to her. First he wore a very severe expression; then he swore softly at her—and then he laughed. "Caught in the act, huh?"

"Do you always talk to yourself?"

"You talk to paintings."

"Okay, okay—we're even," she promised. She stepped into the room and curled up on the steam-cleaned sofa in perfect comfort. She hugged her knees and asked him wistfully, "Tell me about it. Why can't the butler do it? Maybe I can help."

Rex looked at her doubtfully for a moment, then shrugged, smiled and joined her. He explained that having the butler do it would really be a cliché—unless it could be entirely justified. Of course, he might *want* it to be a cliché, if the book was to be a spoof. This wasn't going to be a spoof, though, so he had to be very careful that people didn't laugh at what was not intended to be funny.

Alexi listened while he went through his plot. To her amazement, his people quickly became as real to her as they were to him, and she could tell him why a certain character would or wouldn't behave in a certain way. She was excited to see that Rex was listening to her, and she was really pleased when he snapped his fingers, kissed her, picked up his paper and pencil and started back to work.

"You've got something?" she asked.

"I've got something.". He paused, looking up at her. "The potatoes are already baking. The steaks are on the counter. Put them in and toss up a salad, and I promise I'll be ready to come and eat when you're ready."

Alexi smiled and nodded. She gave him a kiss on the top of the head, but she wasn't sure that he noticed. She asked if he didn't need to get the information down on his computer, but he absently assured her he was just writing notes and would transfer his work in the morning. Still smiling, Alexi went out to heat up the broiler for the steaks.

Samson and the kittens were in the kitchen. The big shepherd was stretched out on the floor; the little puffballs were audaciously curled right beneath his powerful jaws. Alexi shook her head and started to work again.

She put together a salad, then paused, perplexed, as she went through the cabinets again. She'd left them so organized. She'd spent yesterday really knowing what she had done with everything. It just didn't seem right that so many things had been moved.

When she went down to the cellar to find another bottle of wine, she had the same feeling. She didn't know what exactly was out of place, only that it was. The kittens had been down there, she reminded herself. And Rex had been down there, too—to let the kittens out, then to clean up after them. But she couldn't imagine the strange little chills running down her spine being caused by Rex's having been there. It was stupid—or perhaps it was instinct or a sixth sense. She was certain that someone else had been there.

She had just slipped the steaks into the oven when a pair of strong brown arms encircled her waist.

"What's the matter?" he asked her.

"Rex! Did you finish with your notes already?"

"I did...thanks to that wonderfully conniving little mind of yours. What an asset—beyond the obvious, of course."

"Do I know you, sir?" Alexi retorted.

"If you don't now, honey, you're going to," he replied in a wonderful imitation of Cary Grant, swinging her around in his arms. But his smile faded to a frown as he met her eyes.

"What's wrong?" he asked.

"Nothing! Really."

"No. Something is wrong."

"You can read me that well, huh?" Alexi murmured, a little uneasily, her lashes sweeping over her eyes. She smiled at him, telling him he'd better get out of the way so she could turn the steaks. He obliged, but when she brought the broiling pan out and put the meat on the plates, he pressed the point.

Alexi picked up the platter with the two potatoes and the salad bowl and set them at the table. She handed Rex the bottle of wine to open and a pair of chilled glasses, then sat down.

Rex arched a brow in silence, opened the wine and poured it, then sat across from her. "Well?"

"Well, you never believe me," she murmured.

His mouth tightened. "I have never not believed you, Alexi. But what are you talking about now?"

She sighed and sprinkled too much salt on her steak. "I don't know. This time it really does sound silly. Rex, don't you dare laugh at me. I have a feeling that someone else has been in the house."

He chewed a piece of meat, his eyes on her. "Why?"

"Things have—moved."

"Like what?"

"The sugar and tea canisters."

He glanced across the kitchen. "Maybe I moved them when I was fixing the coffee."

She nodded. "Maybe." She shrugged. "I know, I know—I'm being ridiculous."

"Maybe not." His fingers curled around hers on the table. Her heart seemed to stop when she gazed into his eyes. He wasn't laughing at her—he wasn't even smiling. In fact, the glitter of suspicion in his eyes was far more frightening than amusing.

"Alexi, you're forgetting that I was with you in the restaurant. Someone was very definitely spying on us."

She swallowed and nodded.

He looked around the kitchen. "It's just that...why would anyone want to come in here and move things around?"

"An antique buff?"

"Was anything taken?"

"No...I don't think so."

Rex was silent for a minute. She felt his fingers moving lightly, pensively over hers.

"Alexi—would your ex-husband be jealous or spiteful enough to want to follow you?"

She inhaled sharply and stared down at her plate. She remembered holding her breath on her first day in Fernandina Beach, thinking that she had seen his handsome blond head in a crowd.

Cruel? Yes—that could be said of John. Opportunistic, callous, ruthless—determined. But this...this stealth? This senselessness?

She shook her head. "I don't think so, Rex. I really don't."

His voice seemed tight and very low. "After what you've told me about the man, Alexi..."

"I know, Rex, I know," she murmured uneasily. She met his eyes at last. She'd never felt so vulnerable, and she knew his temper, too, but she was entirely unprepared for the heat of the emotion that burned so deeply into her.

"Rex...I... John was certainly no gentleman, but the only time he really hurt me, he'd been drinking and he was in a fit. A lot of it was ego; I rejected him. It never occurred to John that his behavior was unacceptable. He wanted to hurt me for the fact that I could walk away."

"He did hurt you. Badly."

"But not like—this." Her steak was cold. She'd lost her appetite anyway. In fact, a tremendous pall seemed to be falling upon a day that had been the most magical in her life. She smiled, trying not to shiver. "I probably am imagining things."

"Well," he murmured, sitting back, and his obsidian lashes hid his immediate thoughts. When he looked at her again he, too, was smiling. His fingers covered hers once again. "No one can be around now, huh? Samson would sound an alarm as loud as a siren."

Of course. She had forgotten Samson. No one could be anywhere near them. It was a nice thought. Very relieving.

"You haven't eaten a thing," Rex reminded her. He poured more wine into her glass.

Alexi sipped it and grimaced. "I'm really not very hungry." She stood and smiled again, determined to recapture the laughter that they had shared. "I know exactly what to do with it!"

"Oh?"

"Samson? Come here, you great dog, you!"

Barking excitedly and wagging his tail a mile a minute, Samson came bounding toward her, the kittens not far behind. Alexi gave the kittens tiny pieces of the meat and the rest to Samson.

"You have a friend for life," Rex assured her.

She laughed and picked up the rest of the dishes. She and Rex decided to take a short walk, but when they had gone only a few steps, Alexi gave him a playful pinch, commenting on the fit of his jeans. He laughed and cast her over his shoulder, commenting on the lack of fit of her attire and on everything that was beneath.

They laughed all the way into the house, up the stairs and into the bedroom, and there the laughter faded to urgent whispers of passion and need.

And Alexi did forget about being nervous. This night, like the one before it, was magic.

9

One week later, the carpenters were just finishing up with Alexi's first project, the window seat in the kitchen.

Alexi, in a blue flowered sundress, stood by the butcher-block table, admiring the work and her own design. Her hair was drawn back in a ponytail, and she was wearing very little makeup. Joe's boy had brought out several pizzas, and Alexi had passed out wine coolers. Rex, coming in from the parlor, surveyed the little area of the house and admitted she had quite a talent for design. The window seat was perfect for the house; the upholstery and drapes were in a colonial pattern, and the seat added something to the entire atmosphere and warmth of the kitchen. It hadn't been there in the past, of course, but it looked like something that could have been.

Enthused, Alexi swung around to demand, "Well?"

"It is wonderful and perfect," he told her, slipping an arm around her. With a satisfied sigh, she leaned against him. Skip Henderson, the elder of the two Henderson carpenters, chewed a piece of onion-and-pepperoni pizza, swallowed and told Alexi, "It's a wonderful design. It's great. I might try something like it in my own place."

"Yeah?" Alexi asked him.

He was a nice-looking man with muscled shoulders—like Rex's, bare in the heat—and a toothsome grin. He offered Alexi a grave nod then, though, but grinned again when he looked over the top of her head to Rex to say, "Smart, too, huh?"

"As a whip," Rex agreed pleasantly.

Alexi kicked him.

"Hey! What was that for?"

"I'd kick Skip, too, except that I don't know him that well," Alexi retorted. "There was that nice assumption that blondes only come in 'dumb'!"

Rex wrapped his arms around her and drew her tightly against him, laughing. "I've never dared make any assumptions about you, Alexi."

"You'd be welcome to kick me if you wanted to get to know me a little better, too," offered Terry, Skip's partner and younger brother.

"No deal," Rex warned him with a mock growl. Alexi flushed slightly. She liked the note of jealousy in his voice as much as she liked the ease of the teasing repartee. Were she and Rex really becoming a couple? The thought was so pleasant that it was frightening. They'd been a couple, of course. Very much a couple. They'd barely been apart since the night on the beach. She couldn't count the times that they had made love, and that part of it was very thrilling and exciting . . . but there seemed to be so much more. She liked times like these almost as much. She loved the way that she could set about a project and, if she wanted his opinion, ask for it. He would take the time to answer her—unless he was behind a closed door, and then she knew that he needed his concentration. But they'd been together—living together— all these days, and they didn't seem to encroach upon each other's space. Sometimes she was so afraid that she held her breath a bit. Then she was wondering when he would decide that Eden had been fun for a spell but a woman as more than a lover was like a brick around his neck. He wasn't a cruel or cold man—he was the opposite in every way. But Alexi knew how the scars of the past could eat into a soul.

The longer she and Rex stayed together, the more domestic she came to feel.

Would he run from domesticity if it became too confining?

"Finish your pizza," Skip told his brother. "I think we're overstaying our welcome here."

Alexi laughed. "Don't be silly. You're welcome as long as you want to stay. I'm going to run down to the cellar, though, and feed the creatures. I'll be right back. You all sit and enjoy yourselves."

She spun out of Rex's arms, thinking that it was nice, too, that their neighbors—Rex's friends and acquaintances from the mainland—all appeared to think it natural and romantic that the two of them were together.

Only Emily disapproved. Well, she didn't disapprove, but she seemed unhappy. Rex had told Alexi once that Emily didn't dislike her—Emily thought that she was simply too nice a girl for him. Alexi was amused—and touched. Few people would assume that she was too nice for anyone. She had made the front pages of too many gossip magazines.

The phone started to ring as soon as she reached the bottom step. She could hear Rex, Skip and Terry discussing the chances of the Tampa Bay Buccaneers in the coming season.

"Rex! Get that, will you?" She needed an answering machine for the house, she decided. Rex seldom thought to answer a phone just because it was ringing.

"Rex!"

The phone kept ringing. Alexi dropped the fifty-pound bag of Samson's dog food with an oath. Samson barked at her; his tail thumped the floor, and he stared at her with huge, reproachful eyes.

She patted him on the head. "I'll be right back, big guy. I promise."

She almost stepped on a kitten as she started up. "I'll be back—I promise," she said again.

Skip and Terry were at the table. Skip pointed toward the hallway. Alexi nodded her thanks and hurried toward the parlor.

Rex was saying something. He looked up and noticed that Alexi had come into the room. "Hold on, will you? She's right here." He covered the mouthpiece and handed the phone to Alexi. "Your agent."

"Oh."

Alexi took the phone and greeted George Beattie with affection. George was great; five-three, stout, a very proper British chap with a heart of gold. Alexi didn't think that she'd have made it through the past year without him.

Rex knew he probably should have left the room, but he didn't. Alexi didn't really say much of anything; she listened mainly. She glanced at him, a little apologetically, and asked for a piece of paper and a pencil. She thanked him with a glance when he supplied them.

"September first... I don't know, George. I still don't know." She paused to listen. "I'll let you know by next week. Is that enough time?"

Rex knew he must have agreed. Alexi thanked him, asked after his wife and kids, told him to take care and hung up. She fingered the paper, then noted him standing there, watching her, his arms crossed over his chest.

"They want you back?" he asked.

There was no emotion in his tone. Alexi shrugged. "Oh, it was an offer from one of the clothing manufacturers. A new campaign."

Rex took the paper from her and looked at the dates—and the sums. "That's the money involved?"

She nodded.

"Who is the photographer on the shoot? Not Vinto."

"No, no. Once the Helen of Troy finished, George knew to make sure that such a thing couldn't happen again."

"Well," he breathed softly. "You'd be a fool not to take it, wouldn't you?"

He handed the paper back, smiled stiffly and walked back to the kitchen. Alexi watched the set of his shoulders and felt as if her heart sank a little.

He didn't care. She was falling into domestic bliss, and he was definitely finding it all to be a brief affair—cut short conveniently by her work schedule.

She'd known; she had only herself to blame. He'd never made any promises, and she wasn't really entitled to any complaints. No man could have given her more.

She stood there, watching his broad back as he disappeared through the door to the kitchen. What was the matter with her? They were hardly strangers. All she had to do was waltz right after him and demand to know what he had meant by that. She could be frank. She could take her chances. Gene had always said that you were a loser from the beginning if you didn't even try.

She trembled suddenly, thinking how much it meant to her. This little bit of time here—these hours they had shared in his "Eden"—they meant so much to her. They were everything she had always wanted, everything she had always searched for. She'd had to defy her family at first—she'd been young. But she'd always been looking for this... this very special relationship. This quiet, far from the crowds. This life... with Rex.

She couldn't go in and accost him emotionally. Not when he and Skip and Terry were discussing football. They would all stare at her as if she had lost her senses.

Alexi exhaled a little sigh and sank back onto the sofa. She remembered that she hadn't finished feeding the animals, but decided that she didn't really have the energy to do

so. Maybe if she stayed away from the kitchen for a minute, Skip and Terry would go home.

As she sat there, her chin in her hands, the phone started
to ring again. Alexi idly reached over to answer it. "Hello?"

She waited, not alarmed at first.

"Hello?" she said more impatiently.

She could hear breathing in the background. Harsh and
heavy.

"Hello, dammit! Say something."

She was just about to hang up when a voice said something at last.

"Hello, Alexi."

She was startled by the power that voice still held over her.
She had seen him almost daily for almost a year after it had
all happened, and she had dragged up a facade of cool and
cordial indifference—and she'd even managed to believe it
herself. But now time had passed, and she was hearing his
voice. It touched her spine and raked along it—and she was
afraid.

"Alexi?"

She almost hung up. But it seemed smarter to talk, to find
out what he wanted.

"John. What do you want? How did you find me?"

"Oh, you were easy to find, sweets. And I just want to
talk to you."

"Why?"

"Don't sound so hostile, babe."

"I am hostile."

"Alexi, come on! Think of the good times."

"I'm sorry. I can't remember any."

"I've got to see you."

"I don't ever want to see you again."

"Alexi—"

"Where are you, John?"

"Close, babe, real close."

How close? she wondered. She felt the tremors rake along her spine again. Her tongue and throat felt dry; her palms were damp.

"Well, John, forget it. I—"

She was startled when the receiver was wrenched from her hand. She gasped slightly and looked up to see that Rex was back. She hadn't heard him come into the room. Nor had he ever looked at her quite like that. His eyes were burning coals. His features were taut and strained, and he seemed a very hard man at that moment, striking, but cold as ice.

"What do you want, Vinto?"

"Who the hell are you?"

Even Alexi heard John's reply. She bit her lip, listening to the harsh tone of Rex's answer. He told John exactly who he was and exactly where he could be found. And then he told John to leave Alexi alone—or else.

Then he slammed down the receiver.

Alexi sat motionless for several long moments. She felt drained, and found that curious, for Rex seemed to be a mass of tension and knots, fists clenching and unclenching at his sides as he watched her.

"I didn't tread on any toes, did I?" he said.

"What?" She looked up at him at last.

"Did you want to see him?"

"No! Of course not. You know that! I—I'd like to feel that I could have handled it myself, but—"

"Sorry."

He turned around again and was gone. Miserable, Alexi continued to sit there. She got up at last and followed Rex across the hall.

Skip and Terry had gone. Rex was sitting there by himself at the butcher-block table, staring at the window seat that had so recently given them both such pleasure.

Alexi came and sat down next to him. He glanced her way. A brief smile touched his lips and then was gone. He squeezed her fingers and rose. "I'm going out for a few hours." He started for the kitchen door.

Alexi rose, too. "Rex?"

"It's all right," he assured her. "I'm just going out for a few hours."

The kitchen door swung. She heard Rex's footsteps on the stairway, going up. Then, seconds later, she heard them coming down again. He hesitated, as if he was going to walk straight to the front door but then decided not to.

He came back into the kitchen. He'd donned a striped tailored shirt and moccasins and was busy tucking the shirt into his jeans. He came around behind Alexi. With his fingers he lightly stroked her upper arms.

"I'll be back," he promised her.

There was so much she wanted to say. She didn't seem able to say any of it. She nodded, and he kissed the top of her head.

"Alexi, I . . ."

"What?"

"I, uh, I'll try not to be gone too long."

She looked up at him curiously. He smiled and kissed her distractedly on the forehead again. A moment later, the kitchen door was swinging in his wake, but then he caught it again to say, "Come on out and lock the door."

Samson started barking. He raced up from the cellar stairs and brushed past Alexi and jumped on Rex.

"Get down, you monster."

"He doesn't want to be left behind," Alexi murmured.

"All right, all right, you can come for a ride," Rex told the dog impatiently. "Alexi, make sure you lock the door."

"I will, dammit, Rex. I know how to do it now."

He didn't answer her. Alexi heard him yell at Samson to get into the car; then she heard the Maserati rev. She locked the door and leaned against it and felt like crying.

She muttered fervently to herself about the absurdity of such a thing and went back into the kitchen. She threw away the pizza boxes and the empty beer bottles and swore softly as she washed down the table and the counters. She curled up on her new window seat, but she couldn't seem to take any pleasure in it. Then she heard a mewling and remembered that she still hadn't fed any of the animals—his or hers.

"Okay, my loves. I'm coming." Alexi uncurled herself and started down the cellar stairs. The kittens played around her feet. "Samson went out without any dinner. Serves him right, don't you think? Men. They're all alike, and they deserve what they get, huh?"

Alexi glanced through the shelves of food. "Chicken, tuna or liver, guys?"

She shrugged and decided on cans of chicken. She picked up the bowls to wash them in the big, ancient sink and bit her lip against the temptation to cry again.

Rex had been in such a hurry to get out, to get away from her. He'd been counting the damn days, she thought spitefully. He wanted her to go back to work.

And then he'd grabbed the phone away from her. He hadn't thought her capable of dealing with John. But then, really, just what did he think of her, and what could she really expect? They'd met because she'd broken in—because she hadn't been able to get that stupid old key to work. Then she'd heard the footsteps of someone chasing her in the sand. And she'd been convinced that someone was in the house that night the lights had gone out. And then again, when they'd come back after their night out on the beach, she'd been so sure...

He thought she was neurotic, surely. He'd run out tonight because he just had to have a break from a neurotic woman who was perhaps becoming just a little bit too much like a clinging vine.

Alexi ruefully turned the water off, thinking that the kittens would surely have the cleanest bowls in the state. Then she paused, startled, her heart soaring with hope as she thought she heard the door open and close.

She dropped the bowls into the sink and hurried back to the bottom of the stairs. ''Rex?''

She didn't hear anything, but she could have sworn that the front door had opened. Alexi started up the stairs and entered the kitchen. There was no one there. She hurried out into the hallway and saw that it was growing dark. The stairs to the second floor and the landing above them loomed before her like a giant, empty cavern, waiting to swallow her whole.

''You are neurotic!'' she charged herself aloud. In a businesslike manner she turned on the hallway light, and she felt better. She moved on into the parlor and turned on the globe lamp behind the Victorian sofa.

''A little light shed on the matter,'' she murmured. Then she paused uneasily again, shivering. It felt as if someone was near. She couldn't really describe why—it just felt that way.

John.

Ice seemed to course through her veins. He had said that he was near, hadn't he? Had he been here all along, stalking her? Running after her on the sand the second night she was there, somehow slipping into the house once she had run into Rex, escaping when she had screamed ...

No. It just couldn't be John. What could he want with her?

He said that he wanted to talk to her....

The shadow in the Chinese restaurant, watching them through the screen ... could that have been John?

Who else? She gave herself a shake, then stood very still. She hadn't heard a thing. She was just nervous because Rex was gone and she was so accustomed to being with him now.

Alexi cut across the hall. She meant to go into the kitchen, but paused and walked into the ballroom instead. She turned on the lights and walked down to stand beneath the portraits of Pierre and Eugenia.

"You were really so beautiful!" she told them both softly. And she smiled, wondering if they had ever loved each other on the beach, watching as the sun came up in an arc of beauty. Had they laughed in the waves, played in the surf?

They had been great lovers, she knew, according to family legend and some documented fact. Eugenia's father had been a rich Baltimore merchant, but she had defied him to marry Pierre Brandywine, a Southern sea captain. They had eloped and run away to Jamaica to honeymoon, even as the conflicts between the states had simmered and exploded. In 1859, Pierre had brought Eugenia to the Brandywine house on the peninsula and carried her over the threshold of his creation.

Alexi studied her great-great-great-grandfather's handsome features and deep blue eyes. He seemed to be looking at her with grave concentration. Alexi smiled. "I don't believe you haunt this place, Pierre. And truly, if you did, you would surely never hurt me! Flesh and blood and all that, Pierre!"

She looked over at the picture of Eugenia. She loved that picture. She must have been such a sweet and gentle woman, so lovely, so fragile—and so very strong. She had been here alone with one maid and an infant through much of the war.

"I suppose I can deal with a night's solitude," Alexi told the portraits dryly. She turned around, squaring her shoulders, and left the ballroom. The poor kittens. She really had to forget her problems and her fears and feed the little things.

To her annoyance, she paused in the kitchen again. Now she could have sworn that she had heard a board creak on the staircase in the hallway. She hesitated a long moment, swearing silently that she was a fool; then she rushed back out to the hallway again. There was no one there.

She went into the kitchen and didn't hesitate for a second. She went straight to the cellar doorway, threw it open and started down the stairs.

She was about five steps from the cellar floor when the room was suddenly pitched into total darkness.

And even as she stood there, fear rushing upon her as cold and icy as a winter's storm, she heard a sound on the steps behind her. A definite sound. She wasn't imagining things, nor was it a ghostly tread.

Someone was in the room with her.

She turned, a scream upon her lips, determined to defend herself. But she never had a chance. Something crashed against her nape, hard and sure. Stars appeared before her momentarily in the darkness; then she pitched forward, falling the last few steps to land upon the cold stone floor below.

Rex kept the gas pedal close to the floor. He was going way too fast in the Maserati, he knew, but tonight it felt good. He'd felt so hot in the house, so hot and tense, and had been winding tighter and tighter, until he felt he might explode.

What the hell was the matter with him? He'd known she didn't really belong on the peninsula. He'd known she'd come to the place looking for a safe harbor, a place to lick her wounds, a place to stand up on her own two feet. He'd helped her to do that. Yeah. He'd helped her. And it was nothing to feel bitter about; he was glad.

He had to be. He loved her.

He just hadn't realized, not really, that she would be leaving. That she came from another world. A busy world of schedules, of ten-hour days. Hell, she had the face that could launch a thousand ships, right? She enjoyed her work, all right—she'd run from John Vinto, not the work. She was beautiful; the world had a right to her.

"Wrong, Samson, wrong," Rex sighed.

Samson, his nose out the window, barked.

He didn't want to share her. Ever again. Maybe that was selfish. He wanted her forever and forever. On the peninsula with him. With her hair down and barefoot and no makeup and—hell, yes!—barefoot and pregnant and together with him in their little Eden. He hadn't thought that he'd ever want to marry again. To take that chance, make that commitment. But nothing from the past mattered. It was all unimportant. Because he loved Alexi.

She didn't intend to stay. He'd known that. He'd known it, but it was a painful blow. . . .

And that was nowhere near the worst of it, Rex reminded himself. He glanced at the road sign and saw that he was south of Jacksonville; and he'd been gone about thirty minutes. He was making good time.

John Vinto.

He scowled thinking of the name. His fingers tightened fiercely around the steering wheel, and the world was covered in a sudden shade of red. He'd like to take his hands and wind them around the guy's neck and squeeze and squeeze. . . .

"You won't touch her again, Vinto—I swear it!" he muttered aloud. Samson turned around, panting and whining, trying to get his big haunches into the little bucket seat. He licked Rex's hand.

"I sound like a lunatic, huh?" Rex asked the dog. He inhaled and exhaled slowly, reminded himself that he'd never met the guy; he'd never even seen him, except on the covers of the gossip rags. Still, the guy had problems. Anyone who behaved the way he had with Alexi had problems. Were those problems severe enough for him to be playing a game of nerves with her now?

He glanced at the sign he was passing. St. Augustine was just ahead. Rex drove on by the main road, heading south. At last he came to the turnoff he wanted and slowed considerably, watching for the small lettering that would warn him he was coming closer and closer to the Pines.

He pulled beneath an arcade. A handsomely uniformed young man came to take the car, greeting Rex by name. Rex returned the salute, asking how Mr. Brandywine had been doing.

"Spry as an old fox, if you ask me!" the valet told Rex. "You just watch, Mr. Morrow—he'll outlive the lot of us!"

Rex laughed and asked the valet if he'd mind giving Samson a run, then entered the elegant lobby of the Pines home. It didn't appear in the least like a nursing home—more like a very elegant hotel. Rex went to the front desk and asked for Gene, and the pretty young receptionist called his room. A moment later she told him that Mr. Brandywine was delighted to hear that he was there. "Go on up, Mr. Morrow. You know the way."

Gene's place was on the eighteenth floor. He had one of the most glorious views of the beaches and the Atlantic that Rex had ever seen. The balcony was a site of contemporary beauty, with a built-in wet bar and steel mesh chairs. Rex found Gene there.

"Rex! Glad to see you, boy. Didn't know you were coming!"

Rex embraced Gene Brandywine. He was a head taller and pounds heavier than the slim, elderly man, but Gene would have expected no less. With real pleasure he patted Rex on the back, then stood away, looking him over.

"I've missed you, Rex." He winked, taking a seat after he'd made them both a Scotch and water. "But I've been hoping that you've still been keeping an eye on that ornery great-granddaughter of mine."

Rex lowered his head, sipping quietly at his drink. "Uh...yeah, I've been keeping an eye on her."

"A good eye, I take it?"

Something about his tone of voice caused Rex to raise his head. Gene hadn't lost a hair on his old head, Rex thought affectionately. It was whiter than snow, but it was all there. And his face was crinkled like used tissue at Christmas, but he was still one hell of a good-looking old man, with his sharp, bright, all-seeing, all-knowing blue eyes.

"Why, you old coot!" Rex charged him. "Seems to me you planned it that way, didn't you?"

Gene waved a hand in the air. "Planned? Now, how can any man do that, boy? You tell me. I kind of hoped that the two of you might hit it off. You didn't know what a good woman was anymore, Morrow. And she needed real bad to know that there was still some strength and character...and tenderness...in the world. You're going to marry her, I take it?"

Rex choked on his Scotch, coughing to clear his throat as Gene patted him on the back.

"Gene...we've only known each other a few weeks."

"Don't take much, boy. Why, I knew my Molly just a day before I knew she was the one and only woman in the world for me. We Brandywines are like that. We know real quick where the heart lies."

Rex straightened, twirling his glass idly in his hands. "Gene, I'm out here because I'm kind of worried about her. A couple of strange things have happened."

"Strange?"

"Nothing serious. Alexi has thought that she's heard footsteps now and then. And we were watched one night at a restaurant. Then tonight..."

"Tonight what? Don't do this to me, Rex. Spit it all out, boy!"

"John Vinto called her. He said he wanted to see her."

"And?"

"And I snatched the phone out of her hand. I talked to him myself. I said that he should leave her alone, and that if he didn't he'd have to deal with me."

Gene didn't say anything for a long time. He studied the ice floating in his glass. "Good!" he said at last.

Rex watched him, perplexed. "Gene?"

"Yeah?"

"Do you think that this guy could be really dangerous?"

Gene inhaled and exhaled slowly. "I don't know. I wanted her down here badly when this stuff first hit. I don't know exactly what happened—" He paused, giving Rex a shrewd assessment. "Her mother didn't even know, but I'm willing to bet you're in on more than we were. Still, I know Alexi pretty good. She's always been kind of my favorite—an old man's prerogative. I know he hurt her. I know he scared her, and I was glad in a way that she stood up to him to finish off that campaign. But I never did like Vinto. Smart, handsome, slick—and cruel. There's not a hell of a lot that I would put past the man."

Rex looked down at his hands. His knuckles were taut and white. He forced himself to loosen his grip on the glass. He stood and set it down on an elegant little coffee table. "I'm going to get back to her, Gene."

"You do that, Rex. I think you should."

"When are you coming out for a visit?"

"Soon. Real soon. I was trying to give Alexi a chance to finish something she wanted to get done."

"The window seat in the kitchen," Rex said. "The carpenters were there today. It's all finished up."

"Then I'll be by soon," Gene promised. He shook Rex's hand. "Thanks for coming out. And thanks for being there. I love that girl. I'd be the cavalier for her myself, but I'm just a bit old for the job." He shook his head. "Strange things, huh? You make sure that you stay right with her."

Rex nodded. He hesitated at the doorway. "Gene, you don't think there's any other reason that strange things could be happening out there, do you?"

"What do you mean by that?"

Rex considered, then shrugged. "I don't know. I've been there years myself—and I've never had anything happen before."

"Pierre isn't haunting the place, if that's what you mean," Gene assured him. Rex thought his eyes looked a little rheumy as he reminisced. "Eugenia always said he was the most gallant gentleman she ever did know. She outlived him for fifty years, and never did look at another man. No, Pierre Brandywine just isn't the type to be haunting his own great-great-great-granddaughter."

Rex smiled. "I didn't really think that Pierre could be haunting the house. I was just wondering..."

"There's nothing strange about that house. I lived there for years and years!" Gene insisted.

"I was thinking about Pierre's 'treasure.'"

"Confederate bills. Worthless."

"Yeah, I suppose you're right." Rex offered Gene his hand. They shook, old friends.

"See you soon."

"It's a promise," Gene agreed. Rex stepped out. "It's a good thing I know you're living with her!" Gene called to Rex. "This is an old heart, you know! Not real good with surprises."

Rex paused, then smiled slowly and waved.

Downstairs he picked up his car, thanked the valet, whistled for Samson—and, as he headed back northward, felt ten times lighter in spirit. So Gene had planned it all, that old fox.

Whatever "it" was. All Rex knew was that he wasn't going to give it all up quite so easily. Not only that, but she needed him, and he sure as hell intended to be there for her.

He drove even faster going back. It should have taken at least two hours, but he made it in less than an hour and a half, whistling as he drove onto the peninsula and approached the house.

His whistle faded on the breeze as he pulled in front of the Brandywine house. Samson panted and whined unhappily. Rex stared, freezing as a whisper of fear snaked its way down his spine.

The house was in total darkness.

_____ Interlude _____

He wasn't even supposed to be there.

As a lieutenant general in the cavalry, Pierre served under Jeb Stuart. But, returning from his leave of absence, he'd been assigned to Longstreet's division, under Lee. They'd been heading up farther north—toward Harrisburg—but one of the bigwigs had seen in the paper that there were shoes to be had in Gettysburg, and before long the Yanks were coming in from one side and the rebs were pouring in from the other. The first day had gone okay—if one could consider thousands of bodies okay—as a stalemate. Even the second day. But here it was July 3, and the Old Man—Lee—was saying that they were desperate, and desperate times called for some bold and desperate actions.

Pierre, unmounted, was commanding a small force under a temperamental young general called Picket. A. P. Hill was complaining loudly; Longstreet—with more respect for Lee—was taking the situation quietly.

It was suicide. Pierre knew it before they ever started the charge down into the enemy lines. Pure, raw suicide.

But he was an officer and a Southern gentleman. Hell, Jeb had said time and time again that they were the last of the cavaliers.

And so, when the charge was sounded, Pierre raised his sword high. The powder was already thick and black; enemy cannon fire cut them down where they stood, where they moved, and still they pressed onward. He smelled the smoke. He smelled the charred flesh and heard the screams of his fellows, along with the deadly pulse of the drums and the sweet music of the piper.

He could no longer see where he was going. The air was black around him. It burned when he inhaled.

"Onward, boys! Onward! There's been no retreat called!" he ordered.

He led them—to their deaths. His eyes filled with tears that had nothing to do with the black powder. He knew he was going to die.

Fernandina Beach, Florida

Eugenia screamed.

Mary, startled from her task of stirring the boiling lye for soap, dropped her huge wooden spoon and streaked out to the lawn, where Eugenia had been hanging fresh-washed sheets beneath the summer sun. She was doubled over then, hands clasped to her belly, in some ungodly pain.

"Miz Eugenia!" Mary put her arms around her mistress, desperately anxious. Maybe it was the baby, coming long before its time. And here they were, so far from anywhere, when they would need help.

"Miz Eugenia, let me get you to the porch. Water, I'll fetch some water, ma'am, and be right back—"

Eugenia straightened. She stared out toward the ocean, seeing nothing. She shook her head. "I'm all right, Mary."

"The baby—"

"The baby is fine."

"Then—"

"He's dead, Mary."

"Miz Eugenia—"

Eugenia shook off Mary's touch. "He's dead, Mary, I tell you."

"Come to the porch, ma'am. That sun's gettin' to you, girl!"

Eugenia shook her head again. "Watch Gene for me, please."

"But where—?"

Eugenia did not look back. She walked to the trail of pines where she had last seen her love when he had come to her. She came to the shore of the beach he had so loved. Where he had first brought her. Where they had first made love upon the sand and he had teased her so fiercely about her Northern inhibitions. She remembered his face when he had laughed, and she remembered the sapphire-blue intensity and beauty of his eyes when he had risen above her in passion.

She sank to the sand and wept.

Grapeshot.

It caught him in the gut, and it was not clean, nor neat, nor merciful.

He opened his eyes, and he could see a Yank surgeon looking down at him, and he knew from the man's eyes and he knew because he'd been living with it night and day for years that death had come for him and there was no denying it.

"Water, General?"

Pierre nodded. It didn't seem necessary to tell the Yank that he was a Lieutenant General. Not much of anything seemed necessary now.

"I'm dying," he said flatly.

The young Yankee surgeon looked at him unhappily. He knew when you could lie to a man and when you couldn't.

"Yes, sir."

Pierre closed his eyes. They must have given him some morphine. The Yanks still had the stuff. He didn't see powder anymore, and he didn't see black. The world was in fog, but it was a beautiful fog. A swirling place of mist and splendor.

He could see Eugenia. He could see the long trail that led from the beach along the pines.

She was running to him. He could see the fine and fragile lines of her beautiful face, and he could see her lips, curled in a smile of welcome. He lifted his hand to wave, and he ran....

She was coming closer and closer to him. Soon he would reach out and touch the silk of her skin. He would wrap his arms around her and feel her woman's warmth as she kissed him....

"General."

Eugenia vanished into the mist. Pain slashed through his consciousness.

He opened his eyes. The surgeon was gone. He had moved on to those who had a chance to live, Pierre knew. A young bugler stood before him. "Sir, is there any—?"

Pierre could barely see; blood clouded his vision. He reached out to grab the boy's hand.

"I need paper. Please."

"Sir, I don't know that I can—"

"Please. Please."

The boy brought paper and a stub of lead. Pierre nearly screamed aloud when he tried to sit. Then the pain eased. His life was ebbing away.

Eugenia, my love, my life,
I cannot be with you, but I will always be with you. Love, for the children, do not forget the gold that is buried in the house. Use it to raise them well, love. And teach them that ours was once a glorious cause of

dreamers, if an ill-fated and doomed one, too. Ever yours, Eugenia, in life and in death.

Pierre

He fell back. "Take this for me, boy, will you? Please. See that it gets to Eugenia Brandywine, Brandywine House, Fernandina Beach, Florida. Will you do it for me, boy?"

"Yes, sir!" The young boy saluted promptly.

Pierre fell back and closed his eyes. He prayed for the dream to come again. For the mist to come.

And it did. He saw her. He saw her smile. He saw her on the beach, and he saw her running to him. Running, running, running...

Three days later, an officer was sent out from Jacksonville to tell Eugenia Brandywine of her husband's death on the field of valor. The words meant nothing to her. Her expression was blank as she listened; her tears were gone. She had already cried until her heart was dry. She had already buried her love tenderly beneath the sands of time. When his body reached her, weeks later, it was nothing more than a formality to inter him in the cemetery on the mainland.

Pierre's second child, a girl, was born in October. By then the South was already strangling, dying a death as slow and painful and merciless as Pierre's. Eugenia's father sent for her, and with two small mouths to feed and little spirit for life, she decided to return home. Her mother would love her children and care for them when she had so little heart left for life.

One more time she went to the beach. One more time she allowed herself to smile wistfully and lose herself in memory and in dreams. She would always remember him as he had been that day. Her dashing, handsome, beautiful cavalier. Her ever-gallant lover.

She would never come back. She knew it. But she would tell the children about their inheritance. And they would come here. And then their children's children could come. And they could savor the sea breeze and the warmth of the water by night and the crystal beauty of the stars. In a better time, a better world.

Eugenia left in January of 1863. By the time the war ended and the young bugler—a certain Robert W. Matheson—reached Fernandina Beach in November of 1865, there was no one there except a testy maid who assured him that the lady of the house—Mrs. P. T. Brandywine—had gone north long ago and would never return.

"Well, can you see that she gets this, then? It's very important. It's from her husband. He entrusted it to me when he died."

"Yes, young man. Yes. Now, go along with you."

Sergeant Matheson, his quest complete, went on. The maid—hired by Eugenia's father and very aware that he didn't want his daughter reminded of the death—tossed the note into the cupboard, where it lay unopened for decade upon decade upon decade.

10

Rex ran up to the house, Samson barking at his heels. "Alexi!" he called, but all that greeted him was silence. In rising panic he shouted her name again, trying the door only to discover that it was locked. He dug for his own key, carefully twisted it in the lock and shoved the door open. Samson kept barking excitedly. His tail thumped the floor in such a way that Rex knew damn well there were no strangers around now. Rex was certain that if there had been a stranger about the place, Samson would be tearing after him—or her.

"Alexi!" He switched on the hall light. There was no sign of anything being wrong. Nothing seemed to be out of place. "Alexi!" He pushed open the door to the parlor and switched on the light. She wasn't there. He hurried on to the library, the ballroom, the powder room, and then up the stairs. "Alexi!" She wasn't in any of the bedrooms, he discovered as he swept through the place, turning on every light he passed.

He should never have left her. Something was wrong; he could feel it.

Maybe nothing was wrong. Nothing at all. Maybe she had just decided that it was time to call it quits with the small-town stuff, with the spooky old creepy house and the eccentric horror writer who seemed to come with it. Maybe she felt that Vinto was a threat and that she needed far more protection than she could ever find here.

Maybe, maybe—damn!

She hadn't gone anywhere. Not on purpose. She would have left him a note... something. She wouldn't have left him to run through the house like a madman, tearing out his hair.

He stormed down the stairs and burst into the kitchen. She wasn't there. Rex pulled out a chair and sank into it, debating his next movement. The police. He had to call the police. He never should have left her. Never. Or—oh, God, he groaned inwardly. At the very least, he should have left Samson with her. He'd blown the whole thing, all the way around. He'd gone out and gotten her a pair of kittens— kittens!—when he should have come back around with a Doberman. Or a pit bull. Yeah...with Vinto, it would have to be a pit bull.

"Where the hell is she?" he whispered aloud, desperately.

Samson, at his feet, thumped his tail against the floor and whined. Rex gazed absently at his dog and patted him on the head. Samson barked again loudly.

Rex jumped up.

"Where is she, boy? Where's Alexi?"

Samson started barking wildly again. Rex decided he was an idiot to be talking to the dog that way. Samson was a good old dog—but he wasn't exactly Lassie.

But then Samson barked again and ran over to the cellar door, whining. He came back and jumped on Rex, practically knocking him over. Then he ran back to the cellar door.

"And I said that you weren't Lassie!" Rex muttered. The cellar. Of course.

But he felt as if his heart were in his throat. He hadn't believed her. Not when she had told him that someone had chased her from the car. Not when she had been convinced that someone had been in the house. He had barely given

her the benefit of the doubt when she had been certain that
the snakes had been brought in.

And it was highly likely that John Vinto knew that she
was terrified of snakes.

He had left her tonight.

And now he knew that she was in the cellar. But the cellar was pitch-dark, and he was in mortal terror of how he
would find her.

"Alexi!" he screamed, and ripped open the door and
nearly tumbled down the steps. Samson went racing down
as Rex fumbled for the light switch.

The room was flooded with bright illumination.

And Rex found Alexi at last.

She was at the foot of the stairs, on her back, her elbow
cast over her eyes, almost as if she were sleeping, one of her
knees slightly bent over the other. The kittens, like little
sentinels, sat on either side of her, meowing away now that
he was there.

"Alexi!" This time, he whispered in fear. Then he found
motion and ran down the steps to drop by her side. She was
so white. Pasty white. How long had she been lying there?
Swallowing frantically, he reached for her wrist, forcing
himself to be calm. She had a pulse. A strong pulse.

"Oh, God," he breathed. "Oh, God. Thank you."

What had happened? He glanced quickly up the stairs,
wondering if she had tripped and fallen. That didn't seem
right. Why would she turn off every light in the house to
come down to the cellar?

"Alexi . . . ?" He touched her carefully, trying to ascer-
tain whether she had broken any bones. She moaned softly,
and he paused, inhaling sharply. She blinked and stared up
at him in a daze, groaning as the light hit her eyes.

"Rex?"

"Alexi . . . stay still. I think I should call for an ambulance—"

"No! No!" Alexi sat up a little shakily, gripping her head between her hands and groaning again.

"Alexi!"

"I'm all right, really I am. I think." She stretched out her arms and legs and tried to smile at him, proving that nothing was broken. But he didn't like her color, and he was worried about a head injury that had left her unconscious.

She gasped suddenly, her eyes going very wide as she stared at him. "Did you see him, Rex?"

"Who?"

"Someone was here. Really, Rex, I swear it."

"Alexi, maybe you just fell—"

"I didn't! I heard someone in the house after you left. I kept trying to assume that I was imagining things, too. But there was someone here, Rex. Behind me on the stairs. I came down to feed the kittens, and when I tried to turn . . . I was struck on the head."

"You're . . . sure?"

"Damn you, Rex!" She tried to stand, to swear down at him. But the effort was too dizzying, and before she could get any further, she felt herself falling.

She didn't fall. He caught her and lifted her into his arms.

"I'm . . . all right," she tried to tell him.

"No, you're not," he told her bluntly, starting up the stairs. She laced her fingers around his neck as he carried her and studied his face as he emitted a soft oath at Samson to get out of his way so that he wouldn't trip.

"There's no one here now?" she asked.

"There's definitely no one here now. But I am going to call the police."

A silence fell for a moment as he reached the top of the stairs and closed the cellar door behind him. Alexi, cradled in his arms, kept staring at the contours of his face. She reached up to brush his cheek lightly with her knuckles.

"Were you angry, Rex? Or did you just need to escape?"

"I was angry," he told her. He carried her on through the kitchen and out to the parlor, laying her down carefully on the sofa. He told her to hold still, and ran his fingers over her skull, wincing when he found the lump at her nape.

"Police first, then the hospital."

"Rex—"

He ignored her and picked up the phone. Alexi closed her eyes for a moment. Maybe he was right. She still felt the most awful pain throbbing in her head.

But, curiously, she felt like smiling. He had come back— all somber and gruff and very worried—but back nonetheless. And he hadn't been running away from her—he had left because he had been angry, and for him, walking away had probably been the best way to deal with it.

He set the phone down and came back to her.

"With me?" she asked him.

"What?"

"Were you angry with me?"

He frowned, as if he wasn't at all sure what she was talking about. "I'm going to get a cold cloth for your temple. That might make you feel a little better." He started out of the room.

"Rex!"

"What!"

"Where did you go?"

He held in the doorway and arched a dark brow, smiling slowly as he looked at her. "I beg your pardon?"

She flushed and repeated herself softly.

He hesitated, still smiling. "Inquisitive, aren't you?"

"Not usually."

"Well, that rather remains to be seen, doesn't it?" he asked her huskily. Then he said, "I went out to see Gene."

"Gene?" She sat up abruptly, then moaned and slid down again. "Gene? He's my great-grandparent."

"Yeah, but he's my very good friend. I saw him every day, you know. I lived here. You were off in New York."

There was a strange sound to his voice as he said that; Alexi didn't have time to ponder it, because he went on to say, "I'm sorry. Maybe I had no right. I went out to ask him if he thought John Vinto could be behind all these strange occurrences."

Alexi watched him, then offered up a soft smile that Rex knew was not for him.

"How is he?" she asked.

"Gene?"

"Of course Gene."

"He's fine. He'll be out soon. He wanted to give you time to surprise him."

She was still smiling when he left the room. By the time he came back with a cloth for her head, they could hear the sound of a siren as the sheriff's car headed for the house. Alexi closed her eyes as Rex placed the cold cloth on her head.

"Mark's here," he told her, listening as the sound came closer and closer.

"Mark?"

"Mark Eliot. A friend of mine."

He saw the deep smile that touched her lips. "You have a lot of friends around here, Mr. Morrow—an awful lot of friends for a recluse."

"It's a friendly place," he said lightly. He squeezed her hand and went on to answer the door.

Mark Eliot was a tall man with sandy-blond hair and a drooping mustache. Rex shook hands with him at the door and was glad to see that Mark seemed to be taking it all very seriously—not with the humor he had shown when Rex had suggested that the snakes might have been set loose in the house purposely.

"Was anything taken?" Mark asked as they came into the parlor.

"Not that we know of," Rex said. He frowned as they came in, noting that Alexi had chosen to sit up. She still seemed very pale.

"Alexi, Mark Eliot, with the sheriff's office. Mark, Alexi—"

"Alexi Jordan." Mark took her hand. He didn't let it go. "Anything, ma'am. Anything at all that we can do for you, you just let us know."

"Mark—we're trying to report a break and enter and assault."

"Oh, yeah. Yeah."

He sat down beside Alexi. Rex crossed his arms over his chest and leaned back against the wall and watched and waited. Mark did manage to get through the proper routine of questions. He even scribbled notes on a piece of paper, and when he was done, Rex had to admit that even tripping over his own tongue, Mark was all right at his job.

"There is no sign of forced entry. Nothing was taken. Rex, when you came back, the house was still locked tight as a drum. Miss Jordan..." He hesitated.

"I didn't imagine a knock to my own head," Alexi said indignantly.

"Well, no..." Mark murmured. He looked to Rex for assistance. Rex didn't intend to give him any.

"You did fall down the stairs," Mark said.

"After I was struck," Alexi insisted quietly.

"Well, then..." He stood up, smiling down at her. "I can call out the print boys. May I use the phone?"

"Of course. Please."

Mark Eliot called his office. Rex offered to make coffee. In very little time, the fingerprint experts were out and the house was dusted. Alexi insisted on coming into the kitchen with the men. While the house was dusted, Mark excitedly told Rex about the book he was working on, and Rex gave him a few suggestions. Alexi put in a few, too, and was somewhat surprised when they both paid attention to her.

It was late when the men from the sheriff's department left. Alexi started picking up the coffee cups that littered the kitchen. Rex caught her hand.

"Come on."

"Where?"

"Hospital."

"Rex, I'm fine—" she protested.

"You're not."

"I don't—"

"You will."

She set her jaw stubbornly. "Rex, dammit—"

"Alexi, dammit."

"I'm not going anywhere. It's been hours now, and I feel just fine."

Rex leaned back and thought about it for a minute. Independent. She was accustomed to being independent. She really didn't like to be told what to do. Women were like that these days—independent—and they meant it. If he forced her hand, it could stand against him.

But she really needed to go to a hospital. Just as a precautionary measure. She'd be mad at him, but...

"Rex...?"

Alexi didn't like the way he was looking at her as he came toward her. "Rex!" She screamed out her protest when he scooped her up into his arms. "Rex, damn you, I said—"

"Yeah, yeah, yeah. I heard you."

"You can't do this!"

"Apparently I can."

He stopped by the kitchen table to slip his pinky around the strap of her purse. He hurried through the house, yelling at Samson to get back when the shepherd tried to follow him. Alexi struggled against him, but he didn't give her much leverage. A moment later he deposited her in the car and locked the door. He slid into the driver's seat and revved the car into motion before she could think about hopping out.

She didn't say anything to him. She stared straight ahead, rubbing her wrist where he had gripped it.

Rex put the car into gear and glanced her way. "Alexi, your face is pale gray!"

She didn't say anything. She just kept staring ahead, watching as they left the peninsula behind and sped on to the highway.

"Gray, mind you—ashen."

She cast him a rebellious stare, her blue eyes sizzling.

"Sickly, ash gray."

She sighed and sank into the seat. "You could have at least let me get my toothbrush!"

Rex laughed and turned his attention back to the road. She would, he felt sure, forgive him for this one.

"Maybe they'll say that you're fine and that you can go right home."

She smiled at that. But when they reached the hospital, the doctor determined that she did have a minor concussion and that she should stay at least overnight for observation. Alexi cast Rex a definitely malignant stare, but he ignored her—and promised to run down to the gift shop and buy her a toothbrush.

He had no intention of leaving her. From the coffee shop, Rex called Gene and very carefully chose the words to tell him what had happened. Gene was in good health, but Rex was wary, never forgetting that the man was in his nineties and didn't need any shocks in his life.

Rex told Gene that he was wondering if there wasn't a way to get her out of the house. Gene shrewdly warned him that if the danger was directed at Alexi, it wouldn't help to get her out of the house.

Rex asked him harshly, "Then you think that it is John Vinto?"

"I didn't say that," Gene protested. He paused a moment. "I don't know what to think."

"Just for the weekend, then," Rex murmured.

"What? What, boy? Speak up there. I can't hear you!"

"Oh. I said just for the weekend. I've got the sloop in berth in town. Maybe we'll take her out for a sail. Just to have a few days without anything else happening. I'll leave Samson at the house to guard it, and Emily can come over to feed him and the kittens."

Gene was very silent. Rex barely noticed, he was so busy taking flight with his plans in his imagination.

"I'll be there to see you off," Gene said. "We'll have lunch."

"I haven't even mentioned it to Alexi yet," Rex cautioned Gene.

"You'll figure something out," Gene said. "I'm a man of boundless faith."

Rex stayed at Alexi's side, watching her as she slept, and as the night passed he felt as if more and more of her stole into his soul. It seemed to him that she remained too pale, and yet there was an ethereal quality about her that was beautiful. He was afraid to touch; she was so very fine. Small and fine boned and delicate to look at—golden, like exquisite porcelain or china. But she wasn't really so delicate, he knew. Despite the battles she had waged and lost in life, she was still fighting, a golden girl, a glittering, shimmering beauty.

He was in love, he realized as he watched the swell of her chest while she breathed. He folded his hands prayer-fashion and tapped his fingers against his chin and wondered how it had happened. He could remember loving Shelley.

Vaguely. It had been a different feeling. They had been growing apart, and he hadn't even known it. She'd whispered at night that she had loved him, too.

And then she had been gone.

Alexi was different. Very different. She didn't bother with the lies. She'd never whispered that she loved him, and he'd been careful to guard his own heart. All good things came to an end. He was a fool if he thought that she would stay. Hers was perhaps the face of the century. He couldn't make her stay. He couldn't make her love him.

But, he decided grimly, he could make her get on his boat for a few days. A little time for dreams and the imagination, time enough to savor all the could-have-beens.

When dawn came he stroked a length of her hair and smoothed the golden tendril over her shoulder. A smile curved her lips. He leaned over to kiss her lightly, then stood and tiptoed out of the room, telling the nurse he'd be back soon.

He drove quickly back to the Brandywine house. Samson nearly attacked him. Rex patted the dog absently and hurried upstairs to the bedroom. He found his duffel bag in the closet and hastily chose a few things for himself, then paused, wondering what Alexi would want for a few days on a boat.

Underwear, of course. He looked through her drawers, then paused again, fascinated by the beautiful collection of slips and panties and bras. Then he smiled—and chose his favorites.

Another few minutes and he had found a few short sets, a bathing suit, sneakers, shirts and jeans. Samson barked when he tried to leave the house. Rex paused, knowing that he was seeing Samson's hungry look.

"Okay, boy. Come on. I'll feed you."

He had just finished feeding Samson and the kittens when he heard the phone ringing. He reached the parlor to answer it—only to hear a breath, then have it go dead.

He swore at the empty line. When it began to ring again, Rex almost chose not to answer it. But when he picked it up that time, Emily's concerned voice came over the phone.

"Oh, Rex! I've been calling and calling. I tried all night. Is everything all right?"

"Emily! Good, good." He'd needed to talk to her to see that the animals were fed, he remembered. He told her quickly what had happened—and he admitted that he suspected Alexi's ex-husband. Emily was very upset but thought that Rex was right—getting away for a few days might be best for the both of them.

"Samson will be in the house, Emily. I don't think anyone would dare try anything with him around. Think you'd mind coming by to feed him and the kittens? If you're in the least nervous, I'm sure that Mark Eliot will come out with you."

Emily told him that she wasn't nervous at all when Samson was around and promised to come and feed the dog and the kittens and let them out for exercise and their daily "constitutionals." Rex thanked her, then hurried on out, anxious to return before Alexi could awaken.

Alexi wasn't at all fond of the idea. "Leave? Rex, I don't think that's a good idea at all." A frown puckered her brow. "It's like giving up."

"It's not giving up. It's taking a breather."

"Or," Alexi murmured skeptically, "it's like a rest home for a neurotic."

Rex swore impatiently and walked over to the window, shoving his hands in his pockets. He spun around to her. "Alexi, I believe you—I believe you a thousand times over.

I don't think you're a neurotic—I think you were married to a very dangerous man. I need the break if you don't."

"A break from what? We live in Eden, remember."

Rex decided to change his tactics. "I'm asking you to do it, Alexi. Just for me."

"What?"

"You're going back soon, right? Summer ends. Beach bunnies go back to their Northern retreats. Helen has to go launch a few more ships. Let's do it for us."

Alexi looked down quickly, allowing a fall of her hair to shield her face. She braced herself, then looked up again.

"Sure. Why not? A last fling, more or less."

They stood there staring at each other for a long moment. Rex wondered how they could be planning any kind of a "fling" when hostility seemed to be raking the air about them with bolts of electric tension.

A crisp-coated doctor stuck his head in to smile and tell Alexi that her release papers were all ready. She was chagrined to be forced to leave in a wheelchair, and Rex tightened his lips with a certain grim satisfaction—someone else had told her what to do that time.

Rex drove his Maserati up to the door to collect her downstairs. She exhaled with a great deal of pleasure when she was out of the wheelchair. Rex turned the car out of the drive, noting that it was going to be a beautiful—but deadly hot—day. There wasn't a sign of a cloud.

"Where are we going now?"

"To the club at the dock."

"What if I were to tell you that I get seasick?"

"I wouldn't believe you."

She hesitated, looking down at her hands. "I really don't think that this is such a good idea, Rex. I mean, I was even thinking that I should go home ... and that you should go to your own house."

He had never known that words could cut so deeply. The wheel jerked in his hands, and it took everything within him to straighten out the car and keep his eyes on the road ahead.

"I kind of thought you liked me around," he said.

She remained silent.

"I can't leave you alone right now, Alexi. You could be dead next time."

"I can't keep sleeping with you because I'm afraid to be alone in my own house, either."

This time he did drive the car off the road. The gearshift made a horrible grinding sound as the engine died, and Rex wound his fingers around the steering wheel like steel.

"What?" he demanded in a breath of fury unlike anything she had ever heard.

"I—I—"

She didn't mean it. Not that way, of course. But the words were out and she didn't really know how to undo them. She was, at that moment, more afraid of Rex than of any mysterious entity in her house. His temper was afire, while the way he stared at her was ice; he looked as if he hated her.

"For one thing, Ms. Jordan, you haven't the God-given sense to be afraid!"

"You know I didn't mean it that way!" Alexi cried desperately.

He didn't look at her again. He shoved the car back in gear in such a manner that she wondered about the Maserati's life span, and then her own. He took to the road in a flash. She sat back, biting her lower lip so that she wouldn't cry out. She wanted it—she wanted a "last fling." But something bitter inside her—maybe common sense—warned her that she was becoming too involved—falling too deeply in love. She was spending too much time fantasizing about a forever-and-ever kind of love. It would be a good idea to end it all now, and maybe that was just what she was going to get. Rex wasn't mad—he was lethally furious. When she glanced his way, his face might have been carved in stone: eyes black as pitch; mouth grim.

Alexi gripped the leather seat, wondering if he wouldn't just head back for the peninsula. She shivered, remembering the feeling of being stalked yesterday. Yes! Yes, she did have the sense to be afraid. But she couldn't keep running away. She had come here to get away from New York and John and all her fears there. She couldn't run from here, too.

But she wasn't suicidal, either. She had to be intelligent about it all. A good security system could be installed. And she could get a wonderful big shepherd like Samson to go along with the kittens. But no other shepherd would be Samson....

Just as no other man would be his master.

But Rex Morrow didn't want to be tied down. He'd been burned once, and he was determined not to trust again. She should understand. She'd been hurt.

But he'd taught her that the world could be beautiful, too. He'd taught her to love and to laugh....

Couldn't she teach him the same things?

The car jerked violently. She didn't even know where they were. Her heart beat violently. Did he still intend for them to go away? She cleared her throat.

"Er, where are we?"

"The marina," he said curtly. "If you would deign to come into the dining room, someone wants to meet you."

He got out of the car, slamming the door. Ignoring her, he started toward a building with a painted sign that boasted of the yacht club's famous Florida lobster thermidor.

Alexi followed him slowly. She felt so numb. What had she done? The best thing in her life, and she was letting it all slip through her fingers. Losing it all, because she didn't know how to hang on.

She got out of the car and followed Rex. He had waited for her at the restaurant door and was holding it open for her.

Curious, she stepped inside. The place was bright, pretty and air-conditioned but open to the sun, with wall-length plate-glass windows on all sides. The tables were made out of varnished woods and heavy ropes, and the scent of fine seafood was unmistakable. A hostess in navy shorts and a red-white-and-blue sailor top was just coming toward them when Rex waved toward the back of the restaurant.

Alexi followed his gaze, then gave a glad little cry as she saw Gene standing there, waiting for them to join him.

She hugged him fiercely, receiving his tight hug in return. He talked in fragments, and she did, too. Then she smiled brilliantly, kissed his cheek and told him she was very glad to see him.

Rex came to the table, and they were all seated. Alexi realized after a moment that Gene was studying her as surreptitiously as she was studying him. He lifted her chin with his thumb and forefinger, openly looking her over with a thorough scrutiny.

"Still pale," he commented.

"I'm fine! The doctor let me go."

"Hmmf. Well, it's good you're going out to sea for a few days. Sea air has always been the best thing in the world."

Alexi stared at him blankly, wondering just what Rex had told him. It wasn't that she wasn't old enough to indulge in an affair; it was just that it seemed very strange to be quite so open with him.

The waitress came. Alexi quickly ordered some wine and the lobster thermidor. She sipped her wine after it was poured, not daring to look at Rex at all and nervously aware that Gene was still watching her, a good deal of humor in his deep and wonderful blue eyes now.

After a few moments, Alexi realized that Gene and Rex were going on almost as if she wasn't there. They were discussing different security systems for the place, the possibility of a big dog—all the things she had been thinking about herself.

"Hey, I'm here, you know," she reminded them. They both stared at her. She wished for a moment that she could tell Rex to go jump in a lake, that she could take care of herself. But she couldn't really do that—not then. Although Gene had turned the Brandywine place over to her to reconstruct and refurbish as she saw fit, the property belonged to him, not her.

She sipped more wine, then smiled, a little spitefully, and sat back. "Well, I am here, but please, don't let me bother you. You two just go right ahead without me."

They glanced at her again, arched their brows at each other, then thanked the waitress as she delivered their lunches. Then Rex went on to tell Gene that he thought maybe Alexi needed to have some sort of peace warrant sworn out against John Vinto.

Alexi decided to ignore them then. Her lobster was delicious, and the wine was dry and good.

Toward the end of the meal, Rex excused himself to get the check. Alexi looked down at her plate, unable to think of a thing to say to Gene. She felt a blush rising to her cheeks; she knew he was watching her.

"You're not surprised that we're together," she said.

"I'm overjoyed."

"Oh?" Alexi stared straight at him, but she quickly lowered her lashes again. Gene, it seemed, had amassed all the wisdom of the ages. She had always felt that he was incredibly wise. That his gnarled and leathered face and fantastic eyes held all the wisdom of the ages. He could read her mind—and he could read her heart.

"Let me just say this. I like you both very much."

"But, Gene!" Alexi protested softly, loving him. "Liking us both doesn't make us right for each other!"

"Haven't you been?"

She didn't answer him, and he went on. "I've lived a long time, Alexi. A long, long time. I remember the turn of the century; I remember Teddy Roosevelt and the Roughriders, and I even remember what clothes were being worn when World War I broke out. I've known thousands of people, Alexi. Thousands. And out of that, only a handful could I really call friends, could I really admire. I learned to know people from the soul, Alexi. Appearances mean little; even words can mean little. What's in a man's heart and what's in his soul, those are the important things. Rex—he just doesn't like crowds. But then, well, I'm not so fond of fuss and confusion myself."

"He has an awful temper," Alexi supplied. "And he has a way of being horrendously overbearing."

"Does he now?"

"Yes."

"Well, you have a way with you yourself, Alexi. You can't listen to good sense if you've got your mind set. Oh, here comes Rex now."

Alexi glanced up. Rex, so dark and arresting that even in his jeans and polo shirt he was drawing fascinated glances, was coming back toward them, a thoughtful expression knit into his features. He scowled, though, as he saw Alexi's eyes on him. She felt a little chill run down her spine. He was still ready to kill. She might have added to Gene that he didn't seem to be a bit forgiving. But then, of course, maybe she deserved his anger for what she had said. Even for a male ego that wasn't particularly fragile, that might have been a low blow.

I just want you to love me! she thought, watching him. Love me forever, believe in me, trust in me . . .

A pretty brunette in very short captain's shorts suddenly jumped up from a table, barring Rex's way. She had one of his books in her hands—a hardcover text. Rex paused, gave her a devastating smile and signed the book.

Alexi looked down at her plate again. She wasn't the jealous type. Things like that would never bother her—normally. But she couldn't help wondering what Rex was thinking as he looked at the young woman. Was she someone that he would want to call once Alexi had returned to New York?

"Before I forget," Gene was saying, "I thought you might enjoy this."

"Pardon? I'm sorry."

Alexi returned her attention to Gene. He was handing her a small, very old and fragile-looking book that had been carefully and tenderly wrapped in a plastic sheath.

"What is it?"

"Eugenia Brandywine's diary. She left it to me—I was always such a pesky kid. Interested in war and life before Mr. Edison came along with his electric lights. I thought you might enjoy it. She made entries after the war, but an awful lot is about Pierre, meeting him, running away with him. Very . . . romantic."

"Oh, Gene!"

Alexi stared down at the little book. She would enjoy it; she would treasure it, just as she treasured the old house and the very special history Gene had always given her. She looked up at him again. "I can't take this. It's a family treasure—"

"Alexi, you are my family." He patted her hand. "Eugenia's family. Keep the book. Take good care of it."

"I will!" Alexi promised. She leaned over to kiss his cheek. "Thank you so much."

He smiled at her, covering the softness of her hand again with the weathered calluses of his own. "No, Alexi, thank *you.''* He stood then, abruptly, an amazingly handsome man of immense dignity. "I've got to go."

"Go?" Alexi echoed hollowly.

"Good heavens, yes. I have a chess match with Charles Holloway in less than half an hour, and I'll be damned if I'll let that youngster catch me napping."

"Youngster?"

"A mere eighty-eight," Gene told her. "Kiss me again, Alexi. It's an old man's last great pleasure."

She kissed his cheek. By then, Rex had finished with his fan and reached the table. He shook hands with Gene.

"Have a good sail, now," Gene said.

A streak of stubbornness flashed through Alexi. If Rex had been over at the other table, planning his future dates, then he should already be asking one of them out on the boat.

"I don't think I'm going, Gene." They both stared at her. She certainly had their attention. She smiled serenely. "Maybe I'll scout some nearby kennels for a good German shepherd."

"Alexi, you know that you are making me insane," Rex said softly.

"Really? Then I'm quite sorry."

"Alexi, you're going on the boat."

"Rex, I am not."

He looked as if he wanted to explode. At the moment, it was nice. He couldn't possibly make a move against her. They were in a public restaurant, and Gene was standing right beside him.

Rex looked at Gene. "What the hell am I supposed to do?"

Gene shook his head. "Women. They're very independent these days."

"Yes, but is a man supposed to let one get herself killed?"

"That's up to the man, I suppose," Gene mused.

Alexi, who had been watching the interplay between them, suddenly gasped. Rex caught her arm and dragged her out of the chair and threw her over his shoulder.

"You can't do this!" Alexi wailed. "We're in a public restaurant! Gene...?"

The world was tilting on her. Rex was walking quickly past tables and waitresses and startled customers.

"Have a good time, Alexi!" Gene called.

"Rex, damn you, you can't—"

"Alexi, most obviously," he promised her, "I can."

And, most obviously, he could. They were already out in the bright sunlight again, and Rex was hurrying down the dock toward a beautiful red-white-and-black sloop with the name *Tatiana* scripted in bold black letters across her bow.

11

Alexi was dizzy. He was walking so quickly that her chin banged against his back and the ground waved beneath her feet. She spat out his name, then swore soundly. But he didn't seem to hear a thing—he didn't even seem to notice that she was ineffectually struggling to rise against his sure motion. "Rex—"

He swung sharply—and made a little leap that seemed to Alexi like a split-second death plunge on a roller coaster.

"Rex!"

They were on the boat. He still didn't stop. Alexi had a blurred vision of a chart desk and a radio and a neat little galley with pine cabinets. They quickly passed a dining booth and a plaid-covered bunk and a little door marked Head. Then Rex barged through a slatted door and dumped her down on something soft. For such a tiny cabin, it was a big bed, built right into the shape of the boat and full of little brown throw pillows to go with the very masculine brown-and-beige quilt that covered the bed.

"This is absurd," she told him, curling her feet beneath her and trying to rise to a dignified position. She got high enough to crack her head on the storage shelves that stretched over the bed.

"Small space," he warned her. "And you're absurd. Yes, no, yes, no—dammit, use some common sense and don't act like a school kid."

"Me?"

"You!"

"You have the nerve to say something like that to me when you're acting like a Neanderthal?"

"It's better than behaving like a jealous child."

"What?"

"This one all started because I gave out a lousy autograph."

"Oh, you know, Morrow, you really do overestimate your charms. I just don't want to be here."

He touched her face with his palm. "Don't worry, sweetie. There's nothing to be afraid of out here. You won't need to sleep with me. You can have the cabin all to yourself."

"I—"

Her rejoinder froze on her lips because—despite his bitter denunciation—he was slipping his shirt over his head. Still staring at her in a cold fury, he kicked off his shoes, then started to slide out of his jeans.

"What—what are you doing?" Alexi gasped out, pained.

"Oh, don't get excited," he tossed back irritably. Naked except for his briefs, he turned from her, bronzed and supple and so pleasantly muscled. He opened a drawer, pulled out a pair of worn denim cutoffs and climbed into them, smiling at her sudden speechlessness. "Eat your heart out, Ms. Jordan," he told her. And then he was gone, slamming the slatted door in his wake.

Alexi, numb, stared after him for several seconds. A moment later, she heard the rev of a motor and felt movement.

The cabin was lined with little windows. Alexi bolted to the left to look out and saw that the dock was fast slipping away from them.

"Why, that . . . SOB!" she muttered. They were passing the channel markers to the right and left and heading for the open sea. She was off with him for the duration—with or without her agreement.

She threw a pillow across the room in a sudden spate of raw fury. He couldn't do this. He really couldn't—she had said no. But he was doing it anyway. He deserved to be boiled in oil. Someone needed to tell him quickly that this was the modern world. That he couldn't do things like this.

It wouldn't matter, she decided grudgingly. Rex would do what he wanted to do anyway.

After a moment, Alexi realized that the hum of the motor had stopped. She could hear footsteps above her.

And she could hear Rex swearing.

She smiled after a moment, realizing that he had turned off the motor to catch the wind with the sails. And he was having a few problems. She kicked off her shoes and lay back on the bunk, smiling. He'd planned on her giving him a hand with the sails, she realized. And now, of course, he was presuming that she wouldn't move a muscle on his behalf.

"Right on, Mr. Morrow," she murmured.

But then her smile faded, because she was remembering how cute he had looked, stripping out of his jeans to don his cutoffs—then indignantly denying her suppositions about him. Maybe "cute" wasn't the right word. Not for Rex. He was too deadly dark, too striking, too mature, too dynamic.

No... at that moment, "cute" had been exactly the right word.

Maybe she *had* been acting like a schoolgirl, and, at the end, maybe she had balked and refused the trip because of pure and simple jealousy. No—there was definitely nothing pure and simple about it. Painful and complex. She didn't know where she stood with him. And she was afraid to make any attempt to find out.

Something dropped with a bang. She could clearly hear Rex muttering out a few choice swear words.

Alexi sat up and smiled slowly and wistfully. They were far from shore; they were together, and alone with the elements. Maybe she wouldn't exactly offer a white flag, but...

Alexi hopped off the bed and hurried through the door. The boat pitched to the right, and she had to grab the wall to keep from falling. "I hope I don't get seasick," she muttered to herself. She steadied herself and hurried down the hallway, past the head, past the neat-as-a-pin little dining room and living room and on through the galley to the short flight of ladder steps that led to the topside deck.

"Watch it!" Rex snapped, annoyed, as her head appeared.

Standing on the top step of the little ladder, she ducked as the boom of the mainsail went sweeping past her. "Grab the damn thing. Help out here!" Rex called to her.

He was at the tiller, leaning left, trying to control the wayward sail at the same time.

"What do you want me to do?"

"Trim the sail."

"What?"

"The sail!"

"I don't know what you're talking about."

He paused. The wind ripped around them, pulling his hair from his forehead, then casting it back down again. "Come on, Alexi—"

"I don't know what you're talking about. I've never been out on a sailboat in my life."

"You were born a rich kid!"

"And I play tennis and golf, and I've even been on a polo field or two, but I've never been on a sailboat!"

Rex stared at her for a long moment. "Damn!" he murmured. Then he ordered curtly, "Come over here."

She shook her head. "I don't know how to steer, either."

"Just keep both your hands on her and don't move!" he bellowed. "Alexi—"

There was something so dangerous about the way he growled her name that she decided to comply. She slid next to him on the hollowed-out seat and set her hands on the long tiller. "Don't move it!" he warned her.

He jumped up, leaving her to watch as he nimbly maneuvered around the boat. Barefoot, in cutoffs, he seemed every inch the bronzed seaman. He quickly brought the sail under control. Red-white-and-black canvas filled with wind. Alexi had to admit that it was beautiful. She lifted a hand to shield her eyes from the sun and stared out at the horizon. It seemed endless. If she looked to her right, though, she could see the coast, not so very far away.

Rex jumped down beside her. He slipped his brown hands over hers. "Thank you," he said curtly.

"Aye, aye, sir!" she said mockingly. She stood, glad she'd left her sandals below so that she could present a facsimile of coordination when she climbed forward, holding on to the mainmast, to look out at the day. With her fingers tightly clenched around the mast, she closed her eyes and inhaled and decided that the air was wonderful. The wind, alive and brisk, felt so good against her face. If only she weren't at such odds with the captain at the moment.

She decided that for the time being, no action was her best action. She went back below, and for almost an hour she immersed herself in Eugenia's diary. She was amazed to discover that Eugenia's plight could actually make her forget her own.

But she hadn't really forgotten. She set the book down pensively. She would finish it later, maybe that night. Rex hadn't tried to talk to her. Alexi realized ruefully that she was more concerned with her own life than Eugenia's.

Alexi went back topside. She pretended to ignore Rex and sat on the fiberglass decking and leaned her head against the mast. The sun beat down upon her while the breeze, salty and fresh, swept around her. Talk to me, Rex, she thought. She closed her eyes and enjoyed the warmth.

She must have dozed there, for when she opened her eyes again, the sails were down and the boat was still except for a slight rocking motion. Twisting around, she could see that the anchor had been thrown and that they were just about twenty or thirty feet off a little tree-shrouded island.

Rex was sitting at the bow, a can of beer in his hand, wearing mirrored sunglasses, his skin and hair wet from an apparent dive into the sea.

Alexi stood and stretched and hopped down to the scooped-out tiller area and then down to the ladder. She was sure he heard her, but he didn't turn. She went on into the galley and opened the pint-sized refrigerator to find a can of beer. She smiled, popped the top and crawled up the ladder again.

Perching just a few feet behind Rex, she watched his back. He turned around, arching a brow to her, but she couldn't begin to read his thoughts in the reflections of herself mirrored in his sunglasses.

She smiled sweetly and raised her beer can to him. "Cheers."

"Cheers." Solemnly he lifted his own.

He looked out to sea again, then stood and took a long swallow of the beer. Alexi set her can down and rose, too, slowly coming up behind him. She pressed her lips against the flesh at his nape, then followed along his spine...slowly. She slipped her arms around his waist and grazed her teeth against his shoulders. He tasted of salt and sun and everything wonderfully male.

"I thought you were angry," he said gruffly.

"I am. Furious." She got up on tiptoe to catch his earlobe between her teeth.

"Alexi—"

"You had no right to drag me out here. None at all."

"I had every right! You don't use your common sense. You're a little fool. You need protection now, and I'm it."

"I am not a fool!" She nipped his shoulder lightly, then laved the spot with her tongue.

"Alexi—"

"Will you please shut up?"

"Alexi—" He tried to turn and take her into his arms. Alexi pushed away from him, smiling.

She reached for the hem of her shirt and pulled it over her head, then neatly shimmied out of her shorts. "Want to go skinny-dipping?" she asked him, casually slipping from her bra and panties. She offered him one sweet smile, then posed for a fraction of a second and dived into the sea.

She swam with long, clean strokes toward the island, then paused, panting slightly and treading water as she looked back toward the *Tatiana*. Rex was nowhere in sight.

She gasped, nearly slipping beneath the surface, when she felt a tug upon her foot. Then he was with her, sliding up from beneath the surface, his body—all of it—rubbing against hers. Next to the chill of the sea, he was vibrant warmth, his arms coming around her, his legs twining with hers, his desire hot and potent and arousingly full against her thighs. She saw his eyes then for a moment, dark and glittering with the reflections of the sun. Then she saw them no more. His mouth came to hers, sealing them together in a deep, erotic kiss that sent them sinking far below, into the depths. So wonderfully hot ... his tongue raked her mouth with that fire while his fingers moved over her in the exotic world of the sea. She would die ... in seconds she would smother. But his touch in the watery world was already a taste of heaven.

Rex gave a powerful kick, sending them both shooting back toward the surface, still entwined. As they broke the surface, Alexi cast her head back, gasping for breath and laughing. She had barely inhaled when his lips were there again, against hers. He alternately rimmed her lips with his tongues, then whispered things to her. She and Rex did not sink, for he held her tight against him, treading water. She swallowed, weak and dizzied, as he moved his hands in concord with the warning of his whispers, teasing her breasts, working along her lower abdomen, stroking her thighs, taunting her implicitly.

"Oh . . ." she whispered.

"Alexi."

She leaned her head against him, closing her eyes, unable to reason against the sensations. She would sink again. Sink forever in the swirling realm of bliss where she floundered now.

"We've got to get back to the boat."

"Yes."

"Alexi."

"Yes."

"*Now*," he laughed, "or I won't have the strength left to do us justice."

"Oh!" Lost in the sensations of his loving, she realized that he had been doing all this while keeping them both afloat. "Oh!" she repeated, slightly embarrassed. She kicked away from him, hard, and began to swim. He caught her at the rope ladder by the motor at the back of the *Tatiana*. He raised her to the deck, then curled his leg around the ladder himself for balance. Alexi tried to rise. He stopped her, caught her foot and stroked the arch while he kissed her ankle.

"Rex!"

"What?" Tenderly he moved his mouth up along her calf.

"The sun is out and shining. We're in broad daylight. There's nothing to shield us—"

"And there isn't another boat around for miles," he assured her. Her kneecap received his ministrations next.

She thought that she had died. Where he did not touch her, the breeze moved erotically over her wet body. And there, in pagan splendor beneath the captivating rays of the sun, he made very thorough love to her. He treated the length of each leg with the same exotic care as he did the juncture between them, with incredible, exotic savoir faire—so sweetly that she was nearly numbed, consumed again by tiny explosions of delight. She could scarcely move... but then agility came to her and she reached for him, eager—desperate—to love him as he had loved her.

He came up beside her; they stood, damp and sleek, their fingers entwined. And she pulled him close to her and kissed him, consuming his lips again and again, savoring just that touch to the fullest, like a fine delicacy. She brushed her breasts against his chest as she tiptoed up to him, then slid against him, tasting the salt on his shoulder, all that lingered on his chest, falling to her knees and returning each subtle nuance. She moved on to his feet, his ankles... then up the length of his legs to the pulse of him. He whispered frantically—urges, cries. She obeyed them all and gloried sweetly in her power, in the absolute intimacy. She had never loved like this; she knew that she never would again.

They sank together upon the deck at last in an inferno of mutual desires and hungers, with a need deeper than any words they could ever whisper. To Alexi the earth seemed to tremble, to shake, to explode in a blinding brilliance. The sun was the brilliance, she knew, riding high above her, very real in the sky. But it seemed to live inside her, too, a life-giving warmth, given to her... by him.

Rex turned to her at last, stroking her breast, then her cheek, a curious twist to his lips.

"Am I supposed to apologize now for dragging you out here against your will?"

"An apology would be nice."

"All right!" he said, pressing her down on the deck. "I'm sorry I dragged you. Now you can apologize."

"I beg your pardon? *I* was the abused party. But not only did I take incarceration in stride, I went way beyond the call of duty."

"That you did," Rex admitted with a broad smile. Then his smiled faded and he sat up, wrapping his arms around his legs.

"Rex—"

"Why did you say that to me, Alexi!"

"What?" she asked, at a loss.

"That bit about sleeping with me because you were afraid." He twisted around to stare at her, harsh and accusing.

"You knew it wasn't true!" she cried. Please, please, she thought. Don't ruin this. This is ideal. This is the type of day that one remembers for a lifetime.

He shook his head. "No, I didn't," he said lightly. "Tell me what is and isn't true, Alexi."

"I don't know what you're talking about."

He touched her lower lip with the tip of his thumb, studying her face. "Tell me what you've felt—what you've wanted."

"I have told you," she gasped out, herself turning. She didn't want him to see her eyes. To read any of the secrets within them. Love made one so vulnerable. She wished she were dressed.

She shivered. "Rex, do you have robes aboard this boat? It's getting so chilly—"

He pulled her into the curve of his arm. "I'll keep you warm," he promised her.

"I told you," she murmured, her eyes downcast, "that you were very special."

"The Easter Bunny is special," he told her.

"I have been with you every time because I wanted desperately to be with you. Is that what you want?"

"No." He lifted her chin to force her eyes to his, holding her close against his chest. "I want more, Alexi."

Her heart seemed to thunder and stop, then race again and soar. Her lips were dry, and she moistened them with her tongue, "I hear that you're the one with a girl in every port."

"A gross exaggeration. And reasonable." He smiled ruefully. Smiled at her, deep into her soul, and she instinctively stroked his face, musing again about how she loved it. Dark and macabre... To think that she had once thought he must be that way, when he smiled at her now so openly, so ruefully, so tenderly.

"I've been scared. I've been running. And I'm still very, very scared."

"Of me?" she whispered.

He nodded. "Alexi?"

"Yes?"

"Do you have to go back? Do you have to do that commercial or whatever it is?"

"Er, no."

He hesitated. He gave her a crooked smile, dark lashes covering his eyes. He released her and stood, hands on hips, beautifully naked, staring out to the sea.

"That wasn't the right question," he said at last. "Do you want to go back?"

She had thought that she was safe; his back was to her. But he spun around swiftly, and she felt that she was seared through by the probing intensity of his eyes, by the demand within them. She felt herself blush—all of her, from head to toe—and she felt painfully, terrifyingly bare and vulnerable.

"I don't know."

It wasn't the right answer, she knew. Or she had hesitated too long. She saw the disappointment that darkened his eyes before he turned away. "Of course you want to go back," he muttered.

"Rex!" She jumped to her feet, coming to his back as she had earlier, pressing against him and groaning softly. "Rex! I'm frightened, too."

He remained tense. "You should be frightened. I keep telling you that."

She shook her head vehemently. "I don't mean that. I'm not talking about whatever is going on at the house."

"Then exactly what are you talking about?"

"You. Me." Alexi groped for an answer. "Rex, I'm afraid of you."

"Afraid of me!" The narrowing of his eyes, the glint within him, warned her that he had misunderstood.

"No, no—not that you would ever hurt me. Not that way. Let's face it. We've both been burned. In different ways, perhaps. I ran; you put up high walls around you and learned to play rough."

"I don't know—"

"Yes, you do," Alexi said softly, lowering her eyes. "I overheard you talking to Emily that morning, remember? You like the chase, Rex."

He made an impatient sound. "Alexi, dammit. So this whole thing *was* over the girl back in the restaurant—"

She shook her head furiously. "No! All right, I did feel a twinge of jealousy—"

"That was childish! I had to watch the pizza delivery boy practically trip over his tongue when he was near you!"

The way he said it, she had to laugh, her eyes meeting his. But then her laughter faded, as did the wry smile that had touched his lips. "Rex! Don't you see? It isn't like me to be like that. I enjoy you, I enjoy your success. I just..." Her voice trailed off.

He came closer and lifted her chin. "You just what?" His eyes probed hers deeply, searching. He was so close again. She wanted to lay her head against his chest and forget everything. He didn't intend to let her. "Alexi...?"

She shook her head. "I don't know. Maybe I want to believe in magic and forever and I'm just a little too world-weary to really take the chance."

His touch, his voice, grew tense. "You just said that you knew I would never hurt you."

"But you don't trust *me*, either!"

He released her, his eyes narrowing. "What are you talking about?"

"You're not honest with me. At least, if—if you care you're not."

"Meaning?"

"You said that I should go. That I should go back to New York. You made me feel as if what we had was nothing more than a brief affair between consenting adults. Either you want me to go—or you don't want me to go."

Rex laced his fingers around his knees and stared out at the water. Then he swung around to her, heatedly intense again. "All right. I don't want you to go. Is that going to change anything? I can't really do that, Alexi. If I ask you not to go—and you don't do it because of me—you'll resent me for it in the long run."

"But I don't know if I even want to go back!"

Rex inhaled and exhaled slowly. He touched her cheek softly. "You just said it, Alexi. You don't know. I can't hold you back—"

"You could come with me."

"If something can't be solved about all these things that keep happening," Rex said harshly, "you can bet I'll come along."

"What?"

"I said—"

Alexi didn't let him finish. She laughed and caught his cheeks between her hands and kissed him. "You'd do it? You'd really do it? You'd leave all your privacy behind and come with me?"

He caught her hands and held them tight between his. "I'd do it because I'm afraid for you," he told her sternly. "I haven't changed my mind. I like the peninsula. I like the peace, and I like the privacy."

She still smiled. "But you'd leave it for a while."

"Alexi—"

"You started this! You gave out the ultimatums."

He watched her, then slowly shook his head, drawing her to him, ruffling her hair, speaking very softly. "Ultimatums don't work, Alexi. That's what I'm saying. I can't force you to live my way; I couldn't promise to stay in New York. We're on dangerous ground, you know."

Alexi felt his fingers against her hair. She closed her eyes and inhaled the scent of him and felt the warmth of his body next to hers. "I thought you wanted me to leave. You'd have your whole peninsula back."

His arms tightened around her. "I've decided that I like you there."

"Sometimes I think you've decided that I'm insane."

"Why do you say that?"

"I know you think I imagined footsteps the night I ran into you on the sand, and I know you think I imagined noises in the house when we came in from the beach. I wonder if you even believe I was hit on the head yesterday—the police, I know, think I fell down the stairs and invented the intruder."

"You're wrong. I might have doubted you once, but I believe you now."

"Because you think that John is out to—to do something."

"Yes."

"I might not be a very good deal, you know," Alexi warned him. "I could very well be neurotic myself, and I seem to come with a half-crazy ex-husband."

"I'm not worried."

"Oh?"

"No. I'm a big boy. I can handle it."

"But do you *want* to handle it?"

"Yes."

"Rex?"

"Alexi?"

"I *think* I'm falling in love with you."

His arms tightened around her so much that for a moment she couldn't breathe. Then she discovered that she was falling in his arms to lie against the deck and he was over her, his eyes afire, a smile on his lips.

"Let's hear that again." His hold was fierce; his words were full of a harsh command. She twisted against the force of his arms.

"Rex, damn you—"

"Alexi, please!"

"I said..." She paused, watching the blaze in his eyes, watching that small smile that curved his lips. "You're just terrible!" she said accusingly. "Every time you want something, you just decide that if you sit on me—"

"Not every time," he protested. But he was straddled over her and she inhaled sharply, feeling all her senses begin to swim again beneath the dazzling command of his eyes and the easy feeling of him against her—his hands upon her, his chest, muscles rippling in the golden heat of the sun, his thighs tight around her own. "Alexi!" He lowered himself against her until his lips hovered just above hers.

"I'm falling in love with you, too, you know. And you're right. It's very, very frightening," he said.

"We're both afraid of the future," she whispered in return.

"Yes," he told her, kissing her lips.

"What do we do about it?" She opened her eyes to him, very wide, very blue, trusting and innocent. She curled her arms around his neck and pressed her body against his.

"Maybe we could take a chance," he murmured, moving slightly to the side to stroke the length of her. The sun was gloriously hot upon their bodies.

"Maybe," she murmured.

"Let the feelings grow."

"For now, at least."

He tensed, staring down at her. "Sure. For now," he murmured bitterly. He rose over her again, lifting his arms to the sky. "For now. We've got the sun and the sea and a warm Atlantic breeze. What else could we possibly want?"

"We could pretend," Alexi told him. She placed her fingers on his shoulders, then let them run over the rippling muscles of his chest. She drew them lower, so that he sucked in his breath as he watched their progress. "We could pretend that this is never going to end. That there is no future, no worry over it. We could spend these few days forgetting to argue or wonder what can and can't be. We could just talk about the water and the day and the night and the sun and the moon. And laugh and relax and—"

He caught her cheeks between his palms and tenderly massaged them with the callused tips of his thumbs. He cut off her speech with a slow, deep kiss, cradling her breasts, stroking the nipples to high peaks with his fingertips.

"Make love?" he suggested.

"It's a wonderful way to explore one's feelings," she offered solemnly.

He stretched out carefully atop her, distributing his weight along her legs, moving against her hard and erotically.

"A wonderful way to explore," he repeated. He caught her lower lip between his teeth, then kissed her deeply, exploring her mouth with a sweep of his tongue and the intimate recesses of her body with his fingers.

She gasped his name, amazed at the molten fire spreading throughout her, tantalized . . .

"Sweetheart," he murmured, staring into her eyes, "I do *think* that I love you." He thrust himself deep inside her, shuddering at the feeling of the velvet encasement of her love. She wrapped her limbs around him, and he whispered all the things about her that he loved.

The sun started to fall, but neither of them felt the chill as the warmth left the sky. Beautiful pinks and mauves stretched out over the horizon as twilight made a gentle descent.

Alexi saw stars streaking the heavens in a splendid outburst. She whispered to Rex that she had seen them bursting out all around her.

He laughed and told her that it was night. They rose lazily at last and made spaghetti and salad for dinner in the galley, then sat out beneath the stars. They talked about the sky and the sea, and he tried to tell her exactly where they were, pointing out the islands and the coast, which were alive at night with a glow of light.

They didn't challenge each other anymore. They had made an agreement. They were going to take a chance.

But Rex couldn't stop worrying. Eventually, they were going to have to go back. And nothing could ever be right between them—

Until he found out what was really going on at the Brandywine house.

12

By the time they came back in, three days later, Alexi had grown fairly adept with the *Tatiana*. The sails were furled when they approached the dock, though; the motor was softly humming to bring them in at a slow, safe speed.

Alexi—ready to jump onto the dock and tie the *Tatiana* up in its berth—started, openmouthed, when she saw that Gene was waiting for them farther down the dock.

"Alexi!" Rex yelled.

"What?"

"Now! Hop off and secure her."

She obeyed him mechanically. She slipped the little nooses over the brackets just as he had shown her. When he leaped off himself to check her work and tighten the ropes, Alexi pointed down the dock. "Gene's here. Did you plan this?"

His quick look assured her that he had not. "Run and see if there's a problem while I rinse her down," Rex said. Then he abruptly changed his mind. "No. Wait. Start making sure that the boat's all in order, and I'll go tell Gene we'll be with him as soon as we rinse her off."

Hurrying off, he didn't give Alexi much of a chance to protest. She muttered something under her breath, then paused, smiling. He was darker than ever now. Striding down the dock, barefoot and in cutoffs, he was agile and smooth and dark and sleek and muscled, and, being in love with him, Alexi had to take a moment to admire him and determine that he was a perfectly beautiful male. Then she muttered beneath her breath again and hopped back onto the *Tatiana* to crawl below. She thought she'd start in the galley, making sure that the pots and pans and dishes were secured.

Approaching Gene, Rex looked back to assure himself that Alexi wasn't trailing right behind him. She was gone from the deck; below, he hoped.

"Gene!" Rex caught the old man's hand, instantly worried about the way he was standing there in the heat. "How long have you been out here? What's wrong?"

"Not that long out here in the heat," Gene said. "I've been here all morning, though. Long enough for breakfast, Bloody Marys and lunch. I knew you planned on coming back in today, and I didn't want to miss you."

"What's up?"

"John Vinto is what," Gene said worriedly. He gazed at Rex keenly. "I'm glad you came up to me alone, Rex. Vinto has called her mother, her cousin, and me—three times. He insists he has to see Alexi. He's determined to make an appointment to talk to her." He looked down the dock and lowered his voice, even though Alexi was still nowhere in sight. "I think he's going to show up at the Brandywine house. He knows she's there."

"I think he's already shown up at the Brandywine house a few times," Rex muttered.

"Maybe. Maybe not. Amy—that's Alexi's mother—is certain she saw him nosing around Alexi's apartment in New York just last week."

"One can come and go easily these days," Rex insisted. "Jet transportation. And between here and New York there are flights just about every hour."

"I don't know," Gene said. "I just don't know. And since I don't know quite what happened between them, I didn't know how worried I should be."

"I'll be there with her," Rex said grimly. "And Samson will be there, too." He didn't want to say any more to Gene. He wasn't sure whether John Vinto was a dangerous man or had just been dangerous to Alexi because she hadn't been as physically strong as he.

He thought of how she had screamed that night in the car in front of the house and what a trauma it had been for her to tell him what had happened. John Vinto had hurt her in many ways. She had stood up to him after that—but then she had run away. Rex wasn't sure Alexi should see him again.

"I'm going to take her to my house," Rex said. "I'll leave her there with Samson, and I'll meet John Vinto, see just what it is he wants from her."

"Good," Gene said, indicating with a nod something slightly past Rex's shoulder. "She's on her way over to us."

"Alexi!" Gene stepped past Rex and threw his arms out for a big hug. Alexi returned the hug and kissed his cheek. She was in white shorts and a red-white-and-blue halter top, with her hair pulled up into a high ponytail. She had on very little makeup, and her cheeks were tinged from the sun. Rex thought that she seemed exceptionally appealing, fresh and young and innocent and stunning all at once.

And delicate, slim—and vulnerable.

He tensed, thinking again that he did love her, thinking of the things he'd said to her and the things that she'd whispered to him. He was falling in love—hard. Like a rock. And he could even begin to believe in a future for them.

He couldn't let her face Vinto again. Not without him there. Because if Vinto so much as touched her...

"Gene, what are you doing here?" Alexi asked him, smiling, and quickly added, "not that I'm not glad to see you, but it's so awfully hot out here!"

"I, uh—lunch! I knew you were coming in, and I thought I'd meet the two of you for lunch again."

Alexi cocked her head, watching him suspiciously. "What's up?"

"Nothing." Rex, safe behind Alexi's back, arched a brow as Gene flatly lied to her. "Well," Gene hedged, "I was just hoping that you weren't mad at me, after the way you left and all. I mean, Rex there was acting just like a caveman and I didn't do anything to help you."

"You both have atrocious manners, and neither of you seems to be aware that women did earn the vote," Alexi told him sternly. She was smiling, though, and Rex breathed a little sigh of relief. She had fallen for it. Rex knew Gene. He wasn't a bit sorry for letting Rex stride out with her over his shoulder. Gene had decided that the two of them were good for each other. When he made a decision, that was it. Good or bad, he never regretted it. "Can't go back," he always told Rex. "That leaves you with forward, boy. No other way to go."

"Why don't you two go ahead and have lunch?" Rex suggested. Alexi swung around, ready to insist that they all have lunch together. Rex caught her shoulders, dazzled by her smile, and shook his head regretfully. "Seriously. You're both dressed, and I'm a mess and I want to hose down the *Tatiana*."

"But, Rex—"

"Please, Alexi." He lowered his lips to whisper in her ear. "It's too hot for Gene to stand around out here. Go on in with him! I'll join you a little later."

"Oh!" she murmured quickly. She turned around and slipped her arm through Gene's. "Let's have lunch, then. How are their Bloody Marys?"

"Wonderful. Tall and cool and wonderful."

"Oh, Gene!" Alexi told him, full of bright-eyed enthusiasm. "I've been reading Eugenia's diary. Oh, it's so sad, the way she would wait for Pierre, wait and wait and watch the beach! It's been wonderful, Gene. I feel like I know her—and Pierre through her. She loved him so much!"

Rex waited until they had disappeared into the yacht club restaurant; then he hurried down to the pay phone by the ice and soda machines and put a quick call through to Mark Eliot. Mark came on the line and started a long dissertation about the latest mystery he had read. Rex tried to listen politely, but he had to cut Mark off.

"Mark, great, we'll get together soon and talk. Right now I need some help."

Mark told him he'd be happy to do anything he could. Rex explained that he wanted to know anything that Mark could find out about John Vinto. Was he in town? Had he been in town? Anything Mark could get.

Mark whistled. "That's a tall order, but I'll see what I can do. Where are you now?"

Mark told him he was at the public phone at the dock and that he'd be around there for at least a half an hour. "Then I'll be in the club, then back out at my house." Rex thought grimly that it made good sense to keep Alexi away from the Brandywine house until he'd had a chance to see Vinto. He thanked Mark for his help then and hung up.

He hurried back down the deck and got a hose to start rinsing down the *Tatiana*. He'd barely started, though, when he heard the public phone he'd used ringing down at the other end of the deck. He dropped the hose, ran toward it and answered it.

"Rex?" Mark said.

"That was quick."

"I didn't have to go that far. I checked the airlines. Your friend Vinto is around here somewhere. He flew into Jacksonville yesterday morning."

"I see," Rex murmured. "Thanks, Mark."

"I'm still checking on the rest of his activities."

"Thanks. I really appreciate it."

"I'll call you tonight, at your house."

"Great."

Rex hung up. Vinto was very near—he could feel it. And he didn't want the guy anywhere near Alexi. He was growing more certain that Vinto had been in the Brandywine house. Rex didn't know what the man's motives were, but he was sure Vinto had stalked her—had even struck her down.

And none of it was going to happen again.

He hurried down the dock and hastily finished rinsing down the boat. Then he went down into the cabin, changed into street clothes and joined Gene and Alexi in the restaurant.

He gave Alexi a kiss on the cheek and slid into the chair beside her, smiled broadly and asked them what they'd eaten.

Rex studied the menu quickly, noting that Alexi was watching him, then smiled at her and ordered.

He was acting very strange even for Rex, Alexi decided, and she couldn't quite put her finger on the problem. He was being very sweet and charming—he just seemed tense.

"So," Gene said to her, "it's all starting to look really good, huh, young lady?"

Alexi nodded eagerly. "I do love that house, Gene. And the window seat came out perfectly. Why don't you come out with us now and see it?" Alexi suggested.

"What?" Gene murmured uneasily.

"He can't!" Rex told Alexi quickly.

"Oh?" Alexi leaned back in her chair, crossing her arms over her chest. "Why can't he?"

"Chess championships," Rex supplied. Alexi gazed at him skeptically. He'd already drunk half of his Bloody Mary, and he was merely picking at his food. She looked over at Gene. "Do you really have chess championships today?"

"Oh, yes, yes."

"You're a liar. You're lying because Rex wants you to lie. What I want to know is why."

Rex made a sound of impatience. "He doesn't want to come out now, Alexi, all right?"

"No, it isn't all right—"

"Dammit!" He threw his napkin down on the table. "Do we have to make a major production out of everything?"

Alexi went dead still, staring at him in sudden fury. Gene cleared his throat, then looked at his watch. "Wow. I'm going to miss those chess championships if I don't go back. Now."

Alexi stood up. "We'll drive you—"

"No, no. I have a driver waiting," Gene assured her. He kissed her cheek, waved to them both and left. Alexi stared at Rex. He wasn't looking at her; he was glaring down at his plate. Ignoring her, he raised his hand to ask for the bill. They maintained a tense silence while he signed it. Walking out of the restaurant, Alexi jumped when he slipped a hand around her waist. She drew back from his touch and hurried ahead.

In the car, he bounced angrily into the seat beside her. As they drove along, neither of them spoke for at least ten minutes. Then Alexi burst out with a demand to know what was wrong with him.

"Nothing," he insisted, but he didn't look her way, and he didn't have another thing to say as they headed along the peninsula. She didn't know what to think or what to feel; she was simply baffled and hurt. Hadn't he said that he was falling in love, too? Hadn't they admitted the same fears and then agreed to let things blossom and grow as they naturally would?

Maybe she had closed the doors against him; maybe he had never really opened them as far as she had thought. For all that the days had been between them, they were as distant now as the sun and moon, and she couldn't begin to understand what had caused his fit of temper.

"Drop me at my house," she told him, and added softly, "then go home yourself. I think we need some time apart."

"You must be crazy!" he thundered out to her.

"No! I'm not crazy!" she retorted after several seconds of incredulous silence. "You're yelling at me, and I don't feel like being yelled at! Let me off—and go home!"

He cast her a murderous stare. The type that reminded her that she had once thought he might have a dark and wicked soul. "You were conked on the head not too long ago—being in that house by yourself. Have you forgotten that?"

She looked down at her hands, which were folded in her lap. "I—no. And I do have the good sense to be afraid of— to be afraid. Maybe it is John—and maybe it isn't. Maybe something else is going on—"

"Like what?"

"I don't know! It doesn't matter. I'll be all right; I'm not stupid. Samson is there, and you know as well as I do that no stranger could ever get past Samson."

"You'll come home with me."

"There you go again!"

"There I go again what?"

"Cracking the whip, laying down the law, whatever! Will you please quit telling me what to do? Now, Samson is in that house. And I appreciate that, Rex, I really do—"

"You can't borrow my dog, Alexi."

"Rex! What—"

They drove right past the Brandywine house and kept going. Alexi gritted her teeth. She really wanted to land a hard punch right to his jaw. "Rex, I swear, this time you really can't do this! I want to go to my house, and so help me, I will!"

He ignored her. The car jerked to a halt before his house. Alexi turned to her door, ready to storm out. Rex's hand fell upon her arm. She started to wrench it away from him.

"Alexi!"

He turned her to him. He caught her lips in a long, burning kiss. She tried to push away from him; she couldn't. And despite her anger, or perhaps because of her anger, the heat of him took flight and seared into her. When he drew away from her, she was breathless. Furious, but breathless . . .

"Marry me," he said.

"What?"

Rex wasn't at all sure what had made him say that. He wanted her; he wanted her forever. And he wanted to keep her here, far from the Brandywine house. But marriage . . .

He really didn't know where the words had come from, but once they were out, he knew it was what he wanted. It was exactly what he wanted. She was beautiful, she was sweet, she was fire, she was a tranquil pool where he found peace.

"Marry me."

"Rex—you're crazy."

He stepped from the car and came around to her side, jerking the door open. None too gently, he caught her hands and pulled her up and into his arms and kissed her slowly and heatedly, holding her tightly to him. He lifted his lips a bare half inch from hers.

"Marry me."

"You're a temperamental bastard," she whispered in return. "You think you're some he-man. You think you can tell me what to do all of the time. I still don't believe you trust me—"

"I want your property," he told her, smiling.

"I don't even own it."

"Close enough."

He picked her up and smiled at her as he started for the house. She curled her arms around his neck, but she still watched him skeptically. "Rex, I'm going home."

"Later."

"Rex—"

"Please, Alexi. Please. I want you.... I need you."

"You're hardly deprived at the moment," she murmured. "We've been off together alone—playing—for three days now."

His arms tightened around her. She felt the keen burning flames in his eyes, glitter against ebony. It was crazy; it was mad—but she felt the touch of his eyes and the heat of his arms, and it was something that came to her, that built in her, and it was as if they had been apart for days, for months, for years. She felt the rapidly spreading wings of desire take flight, deep inside her, at her very core.

As he opened the door and brought them into the house, she was caught by the flare in his eyes, and was held by it as he headed for the bedroom. The shades were drawn and it was dark and cool, and when he put her down she couldn't remember why it had been imperative that she leave; now leaving was the last thing on her mind. He set her down upon the spread, and she was still, watching in silent fascination as he quickly stripped. She shivered in a whirlwind of anticipation and sensation then as he lay down beside her and removed her clothing with the same careless, nearly desperate abandon with which he had shed his own. She melded quickly with him in that same fierce, desperate heat. The urgency remained with them.... In moments, the culmination of something so fiercely desired burst upon them, sweet and exciting and exhausting. Alexi curled up at his side.

"Marry me," he repeated softly after a moment.

Yes! she wanted to shout. But she didn't know whether or not it was right; she knew he feared the commitment, and the question had been so sudden. And she still couldn't begin to figure out what made him tick—she had no idea why he had been so angry at the restaurant or why he had been determined to keep her away from the Brandywine house.

"I do love you," she whispered.

He turned to her, fierce, protective and somehow frightening in the shadows. "I love you, Alexi." He said it slowly, as if professing the words without qualification was difficult. "I do. I love you."

He kissed her again, running his fingers sensually over her lower abdomen and curling his naked feet around hers. Instantly she felt little flaming licks of desire light along her spine. She pulled away from him and threw her legs over the side of the bed to sit up. She and Rex should rise, she thought.

Softly, throatily, he whispered her name. He rose on his knees behind her, and she felt his lips against her shoulders. He turned her in his arms...and she was lost. This time he was very, very slow, making love like an artist. They'd been so hurried before, but now he took his time. He touched her....

And touched her. Stroking the soles of her feet, finding a fascination with the curve of her hip, laving her breasts with endless kisses that each sent waves of sensation flooding through her. He said the words to her again and again.

"I love you...."

She didn't know quite what it was about those three simple words. When the climax exploded upon her that time, it was as if a nova had burst across the heavens.

Three little words—difficult for him to say, but whispered with a joyous sureness. Difficult for him to say, and so incredibly special because of that. She whispered them in return. Sweetly and slowly and savoringly, she whispered them against his flesh. Then she curled against him and slept.

Later, she vaguely heard the phone ring. She even knew, because the warmth was gone, that he had left her. But she was so very drained and tired. She just kept sleeping.

He hadn't meant to sleep. He'd planned on Alexi doing so, but he hadn't counted on winding up quite so exhausted himself. But certain things just had a way of leading to certain other things.

The phone woke him. At first he didn't even recognize the ringing sound. He swung his legs over the side of the bed and ran his fingers through his hair, dimly aware that the machine in his office would pick it up. He heard Mark Eliot's voice, though, and leaped to his feet, anxious to catch the bedroom extension before Mark could hang up.

"Mark!"

"Rex. You know the guy you're so worried about, this Vinto character?"

"Yeah, what have you got?"

"He's out there somewhere. On the peninsula. I got a make on a rental car—a blue Mazda—and Harry Reese just told me he saw a blue Mazda turn down the road for the peninsula about half an hour ago."

"I'll be damned," Rex murmured. "Mark—thanks a lot. I'm going to get over there now—before Alexi can find out anything about him being here."

"Oh," Mark said. "*Oh!* That's the John Vinto on the pictures of the magazines! The photographer. The ex-husband!"

"Yes!" Rex said. "I'm going to run, Mark. Thanks again. I'll talk to you soon."

He hung up and glanced over at Alexi. She murmured something, curling deeper into her pillow. Her hair was a spill of gold over his sheets; her form, half draped beneath covers and half bare, was both evocative and sweet. Emotions unlike anything he had ever known rose and swirled in a tumult inside him. Rex pulled the covers up around her and kissed her on the forehead.

He'd be damned if he'd let John Vinto anywhere near her again. Ever.

Rex dressed quickly in dark jeans and a pullover, grabbed a flashlight from his drawer and glanced at Alexi one more time. She was still sleeping. He hurried out of the house. Deciding not to take the car, he began a slow jog down the path. It was windy, he noticed, and the air had grown cool. Looking up at the sky as it grew dark with the coming of night, Rex noticed black patches against the gray. There was a storm brewing. A big one. He started running faster.

The porch and hallway lights had been left on at the Brandywine house; Emily had been taking care of the animals, and it seemed reasonable that she would leave lights on. Rex thought absently that he should have called Emily to tell her that he was back.

He saw the blue Mazda, sitting right before the path to the house. Then, right behind it, he noticed Emily's little red Toyota.

His heart began to beat too quickly. Emily. What if John Vinto *was* dangerous?

"Emily!" he called and charged up the path to the house. He swore, aware that he had forgotten his key. It didn't matter; the door was open. He pushed it inward.

"Emily! Samson! Vinto!" With a sense of déjà vu, Rex tore up the stairs. There was no one in any of the bedrooms. What really worried him the most was that Samson didn't answer his calls.

He searched the downstairs, absently noticing that the wall beneath Pierre's portrait had been torn apart. Something must have started to fall, he thought, and Emily had called in help. What the hell difference did it make now? Vinto might well be a psychopath, and he was missing, along with Emily, one massive shepherd and two kittens.

Where the hell could they be?

Rex tore out of the house and raced toward the beach, trying to search through the trees. He traveled all the way through the trail of pines until the waves of the Atlantic crashed before him. He turned back. They had to be the other way.

His gaze fell on his own house. The lights were all on upstairs.

A streak of lightning suddenly lit up the sky; a crack of thunder boomed immediately after. Through the pines, Rex saw a jagged flare of fire catch, sizzle... and fade.

And then the lights in both houses went out. "Alexi!" he screamed. The rain began to fall as he raced back toward his house. He threw open the front door. "Alexi! Alexi! Alexi!"

There was no answer but the sure and ceaseless patter of the rain. He'd known she was gone. She was somewhere within the darkened Brandywine house.

"Alexi!" He started to run.

* * *

The bed was still warm beside her when Alexi awoke. She smiled. He was up, but he had to be nearby.

It had grown dark. She reached over to switch on the bedside lamp. "Rex?"

He didn't answer her. Alexi crawled out of bed and scrambled into her clothing. "Rex!" she called, zipping up her shorts. She started down the stairs and headed for his office. He wasn't there, and some sixth sense told her that he was nowhere in the house. She noticed that his answering machine was blinking. Curious, she went over and pressed the playback button, hoping that a message might give her a clue to his whereabouts. Maybe Gene had called. Maybe Rex had gone to meet him at the house.

Rex seemed to have a dozen messages. She sat through six business calls, two friends saying "hi" and then a call from Mark Eliot—a call that made her start in surprise. Rex's answers had been recorded, along with Mark's information.

Listening to the exchange, Alexi felt a numbness of fear sweep over her. John was there, on the peninsula. Why? Had he been there all along, watching her, spying on her, stalking her?

She gasped aloud, suddenly more afraid of the sound of Rex's voice. *He meant to meet John.* And God only knew what he meant to do. "No, oh, no!" She hurried toward the door. She didn't know what to do; she was too frightened to really think. John was her problem, though. Rex shouldn't be dealing with him. And she was afraid to think about just how Rex might be dealing with the man.

She ran, barefoot, toward the Brandywine house. Against the darkness of night, it seemed ablaze.

She hadn't noticed the coming storm. She screamed out, startled and cringing, as a bolt of lightning lit up the sky.

Thunder cracked immediately, and then she saw a flash of fire. The fire sizzled out—and the world was pitched into an ebony darkness.

Rain started to fall against the earth in great, heavy plops.

Alexi swore softly and raced on toward the house. In a flash of lightning she saw an unfamiliar blue car and Emily's red Toyota. She kept going up the path. The front door was ajar; Alexi pushed it inward.

"Rex! Emily? Samson!" She swallowed, straining to see in the darkness. "John...?"

Alexi stumbled into the kitchen. She groped around the cabinets, reaching to the top to find a candle, then swore vociferously in her efforts to find matches. At last she came across a book of them and managed to light one with her chilled, dripping fingers. She cajoled the wick into catching, then raised the candle high. The kitchen seemed eerie in the darkness.

Something drifted over her bare foot. Alexi screamed and nearly dropped the candle, and for one instant she was convinced that her ancestral home was haunted—and that a ghost had wafted over her. Then she heard a soft, plaintive mewling.

"A kitten!" she whispered, stooping to find the little pile of fluff that had rubbed against her. She picked it up and smiled at the brilliant, scared eyes that met hers. "Silver. Where's your cohort? And where in heck is Samson? Hey, you're all wet...."

Alexi frowned and raised the candle higher. She gasped then, realizing that the back door was open. She stepped toward it and the porch beyond it, her frown deepening as she noticed a large, huddled form there. Her heart quickened with fear.

"Rex?"

She kept going. She wanted to scream, and she wanted to stop—and she could not. She set the kitten down in the kitchen and stepped out onto the back porch.

The huddled form was a body. She began to shake, terrified. She had to touch it.... Someone was hurt; someone needed help.

She went down on her knees, and her eyes widened. She saw a patch of blond hair.

"John!" She gasped. She touched his shoulder nervously. "John?" She pulled her hand away and began to shake in earnest. There was blood all over her hand.

"Oh, my God!" she breathed. She heard the front door slam. Then she heard footsteps racing through the house. A scream of terror rose to her throat.

Rex. Rex had come here, and Rex had killed John. It was her fault. John was dead. She'd hated him; she'd feared him—but, oh God, she'd never expected this....

She screamed as a figure burst out upon her.

"Alexi!"

It was Rex. He raced over to her and paused, staring at her, then at the body. He dropped to his knees beside the body and pressed a finger against John's throat. He looked at Alexi again.

"This is Vinto?" His voice had a harsh, strangling sound. Alexi gazed at him blankly. He *knew* this was John. *He had done this thing to him.*

"You...you..."

"We've got to get help out here right away," he muttered.

"Oh, Rex! Oh, God!"

"Alexi, you're going to have to tell the police everything that happened between you. Everything. From before."

"What?"

"I love you, Alexi. Whatever happens, I'll be by your side."

"What?" she repeated, amazed and ready to burst into tears. She'd fallen so in love with him. She should have known it was too good to be true. This morning they'd sailed a turquoise sea under a golden sun, and now they were sitting here, drenched and ashen, staring at each other over the body of a man....

"Samson!" he said suddenly. "I hear Samson."

She looked up. He was right. The shepherd was racing toward them, skidding across the kitchen floor so fast that he nearly flew into Rex's arms once he'd left the doorframe behind. He barked excitedly, jumping over John's body to crash into Alexi. She burst into tears, hugging the shepherd. It was too much. "Alexi—" Rex began.

"There you are!"

Rex turned to the doorframe and distractedly noticed Emily standing there in her trench coat. "Emily, thank God you're all right," he said. He reached out for Alexi. She winced, jerking from his touch. "Alexi, it's going to be all right!"

"Rex!" Emily said in a strangled voice. She'd seen the body, Rex thought.

"Emily—" He began to turn.

"Oh, my God!" Alexi shrieked. "Rex—*she's* got a gun."

But somehow that fact didn't quite penetrate Rex's mind. "Emily, what in God's name are you doing?" He started to walk toward her. She raised the barrel so it was even with his chest. "Stop where you are, Rex."

He knew from her tone that she meant it. "Emily—"

"Back up, Rex—now. I mean it. I—I'm sorry. I didn't want to hurt either of you. I've got to figure this out now. You'll all have to be found together. A love triangle. I don't know. Maybe you found the two of them together, Rex. Then shot yourself.''

Fingers were touching him. Reaching for his arm. It was Alexi. Numb, Rex encircled her with an arm, drawing her tightly to him.

"Why?" Alexi whispered. Emily looked at her and spoke as if she was trying to explain things to a half-witted child.

"Why, the treasure, child, of course. I finally found it. Today.''

"It's worthless, Emily!" Rex thundered. "It's worthless paper! It's not—"

"It's not paper at all, Rex Morrow!" Emily corrected him. She sniffed. "No one knew Pierre Brandywine—not even his beloved Eugenia! It was gold he left her. Gold bars! · A fortune. A real treasure. And it's been in this house all these years because some foolish little maid didn't bother to forward a letter." Emily smiled. "I found it, you see. I was cleaning up in the old kitchen before Gene had them put the new stuff in. I found Pierre's letter. Telling Eugenia he left her gold. Only Eugenia knew where it was hidden. I didn't. I had to search and search.''

Alexi's fingers were a vise around Rex's arm. He could feel her trembling, but she was determinedly standing there—buying time.

"You tried to scare me out, right, Emily?" she said shakily.

"I tried.''

Alexi kept stalling. In the terrible dark of the night, against the endless monotony of the rain, she was desperately stalling for time.

"You had no reason to ever be afraid of Samson. Samson was your best friend. You could search and search—and he wouldn't bark.''

"It was easy before you came," Emily agreed. "I went through the house at my leisure. I looked and looked and couldn't find it, but I knew that gold was here somewhere. I followed you when you first came. You ran right into Rex. I slipped into the house. I thought you might believe in ghosts. I had to knock you out the other night. And now this man found me. I had to shoot him. It's your fault—you just wouldn't leave. And Rex... I am so sorry. Really."

He was going to have to jump her, Rex decided. Throw himself against her to at least give Alexi a chance to run. Alexi's fingers tightened around his arm again. She was thinking the same thing!

"*Oh!*" Emily let out a startled little scream. The gun raised for a split second. "Oh, you damned dog!" Samson had nudged her with a cold nose. Maybe he wasn't her best friend after all.

"Get down!" Rex shouted to Alexi. She dived for the porch just as he threw himself at Emily and knocked her down, sending the gun skidding away along the old wood of the porch. Emily screamed then, striking out at Rex with her nails. "Stop!" Rex commanded her. Alexi was there then, drawing her belt from her shorts, then slipping it around Emily's wrists. Rex caught hold of it and tied it securely.

Lights suddenly appeared, blinding them at first. A car stopped; they could hear the doors slamming. "Alexi! Rex!" It was Gene.

"Rex? Miss Jordan?"

"We're here, in the back!" Rex called out. "Mark Eliot," he told Alexi. She smiled.

"If you can give that nice boy any bit of help, you do it," Alexi said.

"I will," Rex promised. He glanced over at John's body. "He might still make it."

"He's alive?" Alexi demanded.

"Just barely." He smiled at her ruefully. "I thought you had tried to kill him."

"And I thought *you* had!"

"He hurt you so badly."

"You once said that you *would* kill him," she reminded him.

Rex groaned. "Alexi! That was a term of speech!"

"Well..." she murmured.

Emily was swearing viciously, but by that time, Gene and Mark had reached the porch. They both stared at John and then at Emily. It seemed to Alexi that everyone was talking at once. Gene looked so white that she quickly put her arms around him, anxious to assure him that she was fine. Rex was trying to explain the situation to Mark Eliot. Mark took one look at John Vinto's body and hurried to the car, calling for an ambulance. Then he returned and checked the body. "There's still a pulse—just barely," he said grimly, staring at Emily.

"Come on, Mrs. Rider. Let's go to the car." Mark exchanged the belt around her wrists for handcuffs. By then they could hear the ambulance's siren. A moment later, two paramedics were carefully working on John Vinto. Alexi stared at her ex-husband's features. She was shivering, but her fear of him was completely gone. She prayed that he would live. Rex slipped his arms around her as they took John away. "I wonder what he did want," she murmured.

"I don't know," Rex said.

"Why on earth did she shoot him?" Gene murmured.

"He just happened to come upon her when she had discovered her stash of gold at last," Rex wearily told Gene.

"Gold!"

Rex smiled ruefully. "Pierre really did leave a 'treasure,' Gene. No Confederate bills. Gold. Could I have your flashlight for a minute, Mark?"

"Take this, Rex," Mark said. "I've got to take my prisoner on in. I'll need you all in the morning. Mr. Brandywine, now, you take care."

"Thank you, Mr. Eliot," Gene said. Rex and Alexi echoed his words, waving until he was gone.

Rex led the way, and they followed him to the ballroom. The bricks around the lower mantel under the portraits had been pulled out. An ancient, rusting trunk lay amid the rubble on the floor.

"It's your trunk," Rex told Gene.

Gene stepped forward, lowered himself to his knees and flipped the lid on the old trunk. Bars and bars of gold sparkled before them in the glare of the flashlight.

"I'll be darned," Gene said, flashing his head. "All these years..."

"He meant it to go to his heirs," Rex murmured. "You're his grandson, Gene."

Gene smiled at Rex a little wearily. "Poor man. He worried so much, and his wife and his children were a lot stronger than he gave them credit for." He flashed a quick smile at Alexi. "A lot stronger, girl."

Rex slipped his arms around her waist and pulled her back against him. "Very strong," he said softly. "What are you going to do with it all?" he asked Gene.

Gene scratched his head for a minute. "A museum. Yes, I think a museum. We'll put Eugenia's diary in it, and the clothes from up in the attic—Pierre's old sword and the like. He'd approve, don't you think?"

"That I do, sir. That I do," Rex agreed.

"Well, well," Gene murmured. "It's a bit too much excitement for me for one night. Pierre's treasure almost cost me something he would have prized far, far more." He touched Alexi's cheek. "I think I'll go on up to bed here. Do you mind, dear?"

"Gene! It's your house."

"Yes. But of course you'll have a chaperone now." He cleared his throat. "Rex Morrow—just what are your intentions regarding my great-granddaughter?"

Rex laughed. "The very best, sir."

"Well?"

"I intend to marry her. As soon as possible."

"He's only after your land!" Alexi warned Gene.

"Does she ever shut up?" Rex asked Gene.

Gene smiled wickedly. "Sure she does, boy. You've got the knack, I'm quite sure."

"Do I?" Rex said, smiling down at Alexi.

"Do you?" She slipped her arms around his neck, standing on tiptoe. He kissed her. He meant just to brush her lips, but there was just something about her....

The kiss went long and deep, very long and deep, until Gene cleared his throat. Rex broke from her. His eyes were glittering ebony as he challenged her, his voice gruff with tenderness, "Will you, Alexi? Will you marry me?"

She smiled. Rex knew that treasure had never lain in gold, nor in silver—nor in any other such tangible thing. Treasure was something that any man could find on earth, if he could trust in himself enough to reach for it.

"Yes, Rex. Yes!" Alexi told him.

He stared into her eyes, dazzled. "I love you, sweetheart."

"Well, then, if it's all settled, go ahead and kiss her again," Gene said. "But excuse me. I'm an old man."

"An old fox!" Rex whispered.

"I heard that!" Gene said.

Alexi and Rex laughed and waved good-night. They heard a door close above them.

"Well, my love?" Rex whispered.

"You heard him," Alexi murmured. "Go ahead. Kiss me again. Hmm . . . Morrow . . . Alexi Morrow."

"I'll come with you to New York."

"No, we'll live here."

"But you don't have to give up your career—"

"I really don't care."

"You don't have to give it up!"

"Don't tell me what to do!"

"I'm not! I'm trying—" He broke off suddenly, staring up at the picture of Pierre. He shook his head. "Maybe there is only one way to do it."

"To do what—" Alexi began.

She never finished. He had decided to kiss her again.

Epilogue

There he is, Alexi. Down on the beach.''

Alexi stared out through the long trail of pines to the beach, where Gene's call directed her. She rose, a smile curving her lips, her heart, as always, taking flight.

Rex was alighting from one of their new acquisitions, a silver raft. The waves of the beach pounded against his bare, muscled calves as he splashed through the water. From a distance, he was beautiful and perfect.

"Rex!"

Upon the porch of the old house, Alexi called his name. He couldn't hear her, of course. He was too far away. She was certain, though, that his eyes had met her own, and that the love they shared between them sang and soared likewise in his soul.

He had seen her. He waved. He started to run. To run down the sand path carpeted in pine and shadowed by those same branches. Sun and shadow, shadow and sun; she could see his face clearly no longer.

"Gene? Take the baby for a minute?"

"With the greatest pleasure."

Carefully—he was a very old man—Gene slipped his hands beneath the squirming body of his very first great-great-grandson. Alexi smiled at him briefly, then leaped down the steps, waving to Rex.

"I'll take him inside!" Gene called to Alexi. "It's getting a little bit hot out here. And don't you two worry—I can rock the boy to sleep just as well as the next person."

Alexi turned in time to give Gene an appreciative thumbs-up sign. Then she started to run, running to meet her husband, running to meet her man.

Run...run, run, run. Sunlight continued to glitter through the trees, golden as it fell upon her love. She felt the padding of her feet against the carpet of sand and pine, and the great rush of her breath. Closer. Closer. She could see the love he bore her, the need to touch.

Her breath, ragged, in and out, in and out. Down that long, long trail of sand and pine.

"Rex!"

"Alexi!"

Laughing, she flew the last few steps; those steps that brought her into his arms. He lifted her high; he swirled her beneath the sun. He stared into her eyes, his smile soft as he cherished her and the life they had created between them.

"The baby?"

"He's with Gene."

"They're okay?"

"They're perfect."

Rex smiled and laced his fingers through his wife's. They started to walk toward the beach again. At the shore, where the warm, gentle water just rushed over their bare feet, Rex slipped his arms around Alexi's waist.

Time had been good to them; life had been good to them.

For one, John Vinto had lived. Rex had been worried when Alexi had insisted on visiting him in the hospital, but in the end he had been glad. John had wanted to see her just to apologize; he had thought there might be some way to hang on to his marriage. He'd met a new girl, but somehow he'd needed Alexi's forgiveness before he could start out in a new life. Alexi had promised her forgiveness with all her heart—if he would promise to get some counseling.

It hadn't been easy for Rex, standing there. Vinto was a handsome man, beach tan and white blond, successful—and earnest. But trust had been the ingredient he needed to instill in his heart, and when he had seen Alexi's eyes fall on him again, he had known that she loved him. She didn't need to make any comparisons between men—she loved Rex, and that was that. He had sworn to himself in a silent vow that he would give her that same unqualified love all his life.

Gene had used the gold to open a small Confederate museum. It gave him a new passion in life—the hunt for artifacts. Alexi and Rex had grown fascinated with the search themselves, and the three of them frequently traveled throughout the States to various shows to see what else they could acquire.

They'd had a wonderful wedding. A big, wonderful wedding in the Brandywine house, with Alexi's folks and his folks and cousins and aunts and uncles—and Mark Eliot and the carpenters and Joe's boy and anyone else in the world they could think of to invite. Rex had insisted on Alexi tying up some loose ends with her Helen of Troy work, and then Alexi had insisted on staying home for a while. She had a new line of work in mind. That new line of work— Jarod Eugene Morrow—was just five weeks old, and the center of their existence.

"What are you thinking?" Alexi murmured to him.

He squeezed her more tightly. "That it's been so very good here. That I love you so much. That we're so very lucky. Pierre Brandywine picked a beautiful place. I wonder if he can see that—even though he lost his own life and his own dreams—his family is still here. Jarod is his great-great-great-grandson."

"Great, great, great, great—but who's counting," Alexi murmured. "I'm sure Pierre knows," she added softly.

"Yes, I like to think so."

"Yes," Alexi whispered. She smoothed her fingers gently over his hands. "It's been good."

He nuzzled his chin against her cheek. "What were you thinking?"

"Hmmmm...well, I was thinking that Gene really is so very good with the baby."

"Yes?"

"He took him inside, you know."

"Yes?"

"It's just like we're alone in our very own Eden again."

"Yes?"

She hesitated, a charming, slightly crooked smile curving into her features in such a way that he instantly felt the heat aroused tensely in his body. His pulse skipped a beat and then thundered, and he inhaled deeply. "Yes, Alexi?"

"Want to go skinny-dipping?"

"Yes!" He twisted her around and kissed her lips and smiled down into the beauty of her eyes. "I was hoping that you might ask."

Alexi laughed as he fumbled eagerly with the zipper of her halter dress. "This is skinny-dipping. We both disrobe by mutual consent."

"I'll dip you and you can dip me," Rex retorted. The dress came over her head and landed in the sand. A moment later they were both down to their birthday suits and racing out to the water.

Rex caught Alexi beneath the benign warmth of a radiant sun. Their smiles recalled the first time—and reminded them that there would always be forever.

His arms swept around her. "I love you, Alexi."

"And I love you," she returned. Heat and salt and sea and the endless breeze swirled around them as they kissed, becoming one.

The pines dipped and rustled.

Back at the house, Gene stood beneath the beautiful old paintings of his grandparents and frowned curiously.

He wasn't superstitious, and he sure as hell didn't believe in haunted houses. He could remember Eugenia as clear as day, even though she had been dead for years and years and years.

No, he was too old for ghost stories. But holding Jarod Eugene Morrow beneath the portraits, he could have almost sworn that a little twist of a smile came to Pierre's lips.

"More than a century later, Pierre. And the boy here— he'll grow up right here, Pierre. More than we might have dreamed, huh? More than we might have dreamed."

Gene winked at the picture.

And he was almost sure that the damned thing winked back.

*A Selection of Recent Titles by Heather Graham
from Severn House*

ALL IN THE FAMILY
FOR ALL HER LIFE
ONE WORE BLUE
STRANGERS IN PARADISE